As the daughter of an officer in the Royal Air Force, Sandra Wilson has travelled and lived in various parts of Europe. She now lives in Gloucestershire with her family, where all her spare time is spent writing.

THE CHALBOURNE SAPPHIRES

When Amy van Allen arrives from America to spend Christmas with her English friend Olivia at Chalbourne Park, the house is in mourning. Olivia's sister-in-law, Lady Chalbourne, has been killed. Then snow forces Amy to shelter at the home of Olivia's lover, Charles Pemberton, whom Amy likes. However, Jonathan, Lord Chalbourne, accuses Charles of seducing the late Lady Chalbourne and stealing a famous sapphire necklace. Amy dislikes Jonathan, and the two fall out, but she stays to help Olivia prove Charles' innocence. Only then Amy sees another side to her enigmatic host — a man with a dark and tragic secret.

SANDRA WILSON

THE CHALBOURNE SAPPHIRES

Complete and Unabridged

ULVERSCROFT
Leicester

First published in Great Britain in 2007 by
Robert Hale Limited
London

First Large Print Edition
published 2008
by arrangement with
Robert Hale Limited
London

British Library CIP Data

Wilson, Sandra, *1944* –
    The Chalbourne sapphires.—Large print ed.—
Ulverscroft large print series: general fiction
    1. Regency novels
    2. Large type books
    I. Title
    823.9'14 [F]

    ISBN 978–1–84782–141–6

Published by
F. A. Thorpe (Publishing)
Anstey, Leicestershire

Set by Words & Graphics Ltd.
Anstey, Leicestershire
Printed and bound in Great Britain by
T. J. International Ltd., Padstow, Cornwall

This book is printed on acid-free paper

1

The American sloop *Patuxent* slid smoothly over the calm waters of the Bristol Channel, nearly at the end of her twenty-nine day voyage from New York. The December weather had been so unusually mild that the passengers frequently strolled on the deck, the ladies discarding their heavy winter cloaks in favor of pelisses, their parasols making bright splashes of color in the sunlight. The atmosphere on board was light-hearted and cheerful, for many of the passengers were traveling to England to spend the Christmas season with friends and loved ones.

One passenger, however, felt no such light-heartedness as she stood on the starboard deck looking across to the English shore as it slipped swiftly past. She did not smile as she watched the countryside of wooded bays and hills, for of all the lands in the world, England was the very last one she should ever have contemplated visiting. The very last.

The breeze fluttered the green ribbons of her bonnet and she put up a gloved hand to push back a stray lock of her dark red hair, tucking it carefully into place again. She wore a green pelisse beneath which was a yellow lawn gown, her shoes were of the very latest patent leather which was becoming all the rage, and her whole appearance was elegant and fashionable. She was a very striking young woman, tall with deep blue eyes and a complexion which other women could only envy. Amy Magnolia van Allen was privileged, beautiful, and wealthy, the toast of Washington society, and considered by many to be *the* catch for some lucky man. But as she stood there her expression was withdrawn. 'Amy van Allen,' she whispered to herself, 'you should have listened to Winfield and stayed back home in Washington.'

For a brief moment she thought of the young man she had left behind. Winfield Kenney was a rising politician for whom great things were predicted, and he so desperately wanted to marry her, but she was undecided — maybe this separation would help her to come to a decision about her future . . .

The sails cracked overhead as the sloop caught a side wind, and Amy forgot Winfield. She glanced up at the billowing canvas and the American flag which streamed proudly from the mast. Again she was reminded that she was about to set foot on what she still regarded in her heart as enemy territory.

But it's 1817 now, she told herself sharply, and the war has been over for two years . . . But the past would not go away, she could not forget that the British had once stormed Washington, burned her home on North Capitol Street, and killed her brother at the battle of Bladensburg. She had been left the sole remaining member of an illustrious family which had been connected with Washington since that city's earliest days.

Yet here she was, sailing to England to stay with an aristocratic English family — and all because of a chance meeting in the oval drawing room of the White House. President Madison himself had insisted upon introducing an exceedingly reluctant Amy to a young Englishwoman named Olivia Chalbourne and that had been the beginning of it all. Livvy Chalbourne had proved to be a delightful companion and a very close friendship had sprung up immediately between the two, a friendship which had culminated now in an invitation for Amy to go to England. She was to be the guest of Livvy's brother, Lord Chalbourne, and in the new year she was to attend Livvy's wedding. Everyone back in Washington had advised Amy against accepting, but she had placed a higher value on friendship than upon grim memories of the past. But now the misgivings were impossible to ignore.

She looked at her trunks and baggage which were piled on the deck nearby. On the very top nestled the package of Christmas gifts she had brought with her. Choosing such things for people she did not know had been so very difficult — oh, Livvy herself had proved no problem, but Amy knew nothing at all of her brother, Jonathan Chalbourne, or his wife Alice. Amy sighed heavily, her gaze returning to the shore. Maybe she should have listened to Winfield after all . . .

The King's Head Inn, where Amy was to be met by someone from Chalbourne Park, was a large, many-windowed establishment built around a courtyard where a constant stream of mail coaches and stages arrived and departed with a great deal of noise and bustle. The sounds of wheels, hooves, dogs barking, horns blowing, men shouting, and children playing vied with the scratchy music of an old fiddle played by a blind man. There was a smell of hot meat pies from a pieman's tray and his bell rang loudly, jarring with the cacophany of other sounds which greeted Amy as she alighted from the hired chaise which had conveyed her from the ship.

Nervously she smoothed down her pelisse and adjusted her bonnet for what must have

4

been the hundredth time. She caught a glimpse of her reflection in a bow window and cast a critical eye over her appearance. Without a maid to attend her she had found the voyage very difficult, dropping pins, fumbling with countless hooks and eyes, and generally struggling to achieve a satisfactory effect for a lady of fashion. On the whole she congratulated herself for managing quite well under the circumstances, and she consoled herself with the thought that she had really had little choice in the matter. It was not at all the thing for a lady to travel alone, but when her maid had announced her intention of leaving to marry a parson on the very eve of the departure from New York, there had been very little Amy could do but accept the situation with as good a grace as she could muster. She consoled herself too that there would surely be maids in plenty at a house as grand as Chalbourne Park, and that would mean an end to sore fingers and aching arms.

As the landlord came out to greet her, she smoothed the pelisse for a last time. Yes, she looked well enough under the circumstances — certainly well enough to look the enemy in the eye at last. She bit her lip immediately, she really would *have* to stop thinking like that if she was to make any sort of success of this venture!

The landlord was hot-faced and obviously very busy, but he bowed politely to her. 'Good day, ma'am.'

'Good day, sir. My name is Miss van Allen. I understand I am to be met here.'

'Why — er — yes, ma'am,' he said, hesitating noticeably, 'Lord Chalbourne's landau comes each day at two o'clock. You — you have time to partake of my inn's excellent fare if you so desire.'

She noticed the unease in his tone. 'Is something wrong, sir?'

'Wrong? Why, no ma'am, nothing at all. We have a very fine table in a window if you would care . . . ?'

The smell of food wafting from a nearby doorway was delicious and Amy had only eaten a light breakfast on board the *Patuxent*, so she nodded. 'Thank you, sir, I think I will take some luncheon.'

He turned to beckon a maid who hovered nearby, and Amy could not mistake the uneasy glance which passed between the two. 'Rosie? Rosie, you show the lady to the window table and see that she's attended to.'

'Yes, sir.'

The maid bobbed a neat curtsey, her large white mob cap wobbling forward on her short fair curls. Her shoes tapped on the stone-flagged floor as she went into the inn, and her plain blue gown looked almost gray as she led Amy through a low, dark archway and into the dining room.

The walls of the long, bright room were decked with Christmas greenery and there were hams and flitches of smoked bacon hanging from the beamed ceiling. A table down one side of the room was laden with various joints of meat, some hot and some cold, and a man was engaged upon carving them to order. At the far end of the room was a large inglenook fireplace where a fire crackled and roared, the flames reflecting in the highly-polished copper pots and pans which stood around the hearth. A roasting jack rattled before the fire and a plump white dog sat next to it, watching each drop of hot fat as it hissed into the tray beneath. From time to time the dog sighed longingly in a way which was almost human.

The maid showed Amy to a sunny table by a window and took her order for beefsteak pie, beans and potatoes, with a glass of good red wine to sip with it. Amy sat back, glancing around. Most of the other diners were men, some talking together and others merely reading newspapers — *The Times* or the *Morning Chronicle* according to political persuasion. The only two ladies present apart from Amy were seated nearby busily eating roast chicken and discussing the merits of the latest ladies' journal. Occasionally, however, during the silences when those ladies were engaged upon the roast chicken, Amy caught drifts of male conversation, low murmurs of depressed markets, falling prices, lowered rents, and general recession since the ending of the wars with both America and France.

A stage coach was pulling noisily out of the courtyard, the horn echoing through the inn, and a chair scraped in the dining room as an army officer in a bright red uniform stood to leave. Amy stared at the uniform for a moment before looking quickly away. *You're here now, Amy van Allen, you're among the enemy now . . .*

'Excuse me, ma'am.' The maid was standing by the table, the hot plate held carefully with a cloth as she waited for Amy to sit back so that she could place the meal on the table. 'I hope as you enjoy it, ma'am, the very best beef went into it, I swear.'

Amy smiled faintly. 'Thank you, it looks very good.'

The pie was as excellent as it looked, and Amy ate heartily. She had almost finished when she glanced out of the window and saw the black landau drawn by a matched team of black horses pulling into the inn's yard. She surveyed it approvingly, for it was surely a

8

magnificent equipage. Its blinds were drawn down as a sign of mourning, however, and the coachman was garbed in black from head to toe. She sipped the cool red wine, wondering whose carriage it was.

A moment later someone coughed discreetly beside her. 'Miss van Allen?'

She looked up to see the landau's coachman standing by her table, his black hat in his hands so that its armozeen weepers trailed to the floor. He was a thin man with a sallow face and heavy eyebrows which almost met over the bridge of his nose, and his pale complexion was not helped by the unrelieved mourning.

'My name is Daniels, madam. I am Lord Chalbourne's head coachman and I've been sent to convey you to Chalbourne Park.'

A feeling of dread crept over her. Let it not be Livvy he wore mourning for . . .

He cleared his throat uncomfortably again at her continued silence. 'Madam, Miss Olivia has charged me to ask if you've brought mourning clothes with you.'

Amy exhaled slowly. It wasn't Livvy. Until then she had not realized that she had been holding her breath. 'Mourning? No — no, I haven't. There has been a bereavement at Chalbourne Park I take it?'

'I fear so, madam. Lady Chalbourne met

with a fatal riding accident six days ago, the very day after the Hunt Ball.'

Stunned, Amy stared at him. Now she understood the landlord's unease. Alice Chalbourne, Livvy's sister-in-law and Amy's hostess. for the coming weeks, was dead? 'Oh no, surely not . . . '

'The funeral is in two days' time, madam, which is why Miss Olivia was concerned that you should equip yourself with suitable attire before leaving Bristol. Her dressmaker, Madame Secherell, has already been informed and she will be honored to serve you in any way possible.'

'I see. Well — well, I haven't brought any black with me so you will have to convey me to this Madame Secherell,' Amy's mind was racing as she tried to gather her scattered thoughts. Alice Chalbourne's death would surely alter so many things. Would Lord Chalbourne even want a houseguest at such a time?

'Very well, madam, I will take you to her whenever you are ready. Er — your maid . . . ?'

Amy sighed inwardly, for she knew what his reaction to her reply would be as it was just not done for a lady to travel unchaperoned. 'I am without a maid.'

'Yes, madam.' He cleared his throat again.

10

Slowly she stood. 'We may leave now.' She took some coins from her reticule and placed them on the table. Whatever else she may have dreaded about this visit to Chalbourne Park, a funeral and family bereavement had not entered her darkest thoughts.

Her luggage had already been loaded onto the waiting landau, and out in the sunlight again she saw how the black lacquerwork was so highly polished that it reflected like a mirror. The Chalbourne coat-of-arms was emblazoned on the doors and the whole equipage attracted a great deal of admiring attention as the coachman handed Amy inside. He closed the door and she sank back against the oyster velvet upholstery, her face shadowy in the darkness as the light was excluded by the heavy blinds at the windows.

The gloom settled over her inwardly as well, weighing down the spirits which she had tried so to keep buoyant.

2

Madame Secherell was a busy little Frenchwoman with bright black eyes and almost white hair which was pinned back neatly beneath a lacy day cap. Her brown taffeta skirts rustled as she ushered Amy through the narrow crowded shop toward some heavy velvet curtains at the far end. These she held aside, beckoning Amy into the cozy sitting room beyond. 'Here we can be more comfortable, Mademoiselle van Allen. That poor Lady Chalbourne should die so suddenly is a terrible shock, non? And so young, *Dieu, mon Dieu.*' The dressmaker shook her head sorrowfully. 'You are a friend of the family, Miss van Allen?'

'I know only Miss Chalbourne.'

'Ah, the pretty Miss Olivia. So, the coachman has informed me that I am to find for you some mourning clothes, yes?'

'If you can at such short notice.'

'*If?* What is this *if?* Of course I can. *Monique? Vite! Vite!*'

A mousy girl in a gray woolen dress came scuttling in from the shop. '*Oui, madame?*'

'Bring the things we made for the Countess of St Victoire.'

The dressmaker sniffed disparagingly when the girl had gone. 'Always that girl runs everywhere, it does not look good when my ladies see so clumsy a creature *hurrying* all over the place!'

Amy felt instinctively sorry for poor Monique. 'Will — will the Countess of St Victoire not be wanting the clothes herself?'

Again there was a disparaging sniff. 'That one! No, mademoiselle, for she has left the country post haste because her debts caught up with her. She is the Earl of Bendon's sister, but she is definitely *not* a lady!'

'The Earl of Bendon?' The name sounded familiar to Amy.

'Yes — his estates are in Gloucestershire, as are Lord Chalbourne's. They are neighbors, yes?'

Then Amy remembered hearing Livvy mention the Earl from time to time. And his only daughter, Lady Christabel. Livvy and Christabel didn't like each other in the slightest, but that was all Amy could recall.

Monique brought the clothes. There were two gowns, one of bombazine stitched with tiny black beads and the other of radzimir trimmed with Brussels lace. For outdoor wear there was a black corduroy pelisse with smart

13

epaulettes and a tall military hat adorned with black tassels. Madame Secherell arranged everything proudly on the sofa and then stepped back to admire her work. 'Ah, such finery, *non?* It would have been wasted on one such as the Countess. Now then, Miss van Allen, I can tell without measuring you that these things will fit you to perfection, so all you need now are the accessories to go with them. Oh, and a good shawl — Miss Olivia has only lived at Chalbourne Park this one winter, but always when she sees me she grumbles about what a cold house it is.'

Amy had forgotten that until recently Livvy had lived with an aunt in London. The aunt's death had meant that Lord Chalbourne insisted his sister come to Gloucestershire, and no amount of protesting on Livvy's part had made the slightest difference.

Madame Secherell turned to the luckless Monique again. 'Monique, bring the accessories and that black chenille day dress in the end storeroom, the one with the drawstring bodice.'

'*Oui, madame.*'

'And Monique — walk, do *not* gallop!'

'*Oui, madame.*'

When the girl had gone, the dressmaker ushered Amy into a comfortable chair, and then she paused for a moment, looking down at Amy. 'It will be good that Miss Olivia has someone to talk to at last,' she said slowly.

Amy looked up in surprise. 'But surely she and Lady Chalbourne — '

'She could not commune with Lady Chalbourne, Miss van Allen. Oh, I know it is not my place to say anything at all, but Lady Chalbourne was a strange one — *oui*, very strange. She was very pretty, very unusual with her big brown eyes and bright golden hair, and when first one saw her one was taken by how striking she was. But her character was odd. Sometimes she comes here with Miss Olivia and mostly sits in that chair where you sit now, staring at the floor and not letting a single word pass her lips. Then at other times she comes in and all the while she chatters away like a magpie, about all sorts of things from Miss Austen's latest book to the quarrels of Princess Caroline and the Prince Regent or the death of Princess Charlotte. Talk, talk, talk, and no one else can make a comment at all. It was most disconcerting, and Miss Olivia did not feel happy about it, that I could tell. There could never have been companionship between the two of them, even though they were of an age.'

Amy sat back. She knew nothing of Alice Chalbourne, for Livvy's letters had been too full of her love for Charles Pemberton for there to be any room for mention of Alice. Or of Lord Chalbourne. 'Madame, do you know Lord Chalbourne?' she asked at last, knowing that it was indiscreet to talk to a chatterbox like the little Frenchwoman, but she was curious to know what sort of man her host was.

'Why yes, such a handsome man, such presence and such *flair*.' The dressmaker's hand twirled expressively in the air. 'I think the Bond Street tailors must fight together for the honor of serving him. His clothes are always perfection, so very fashionable and in such exquisite taste — I think even Mr Brummell himself would have envied Lord Chalbourne's cravats. And with his black curly hair and big gray eyes — ah, the ladies' heads turn when he approaches. First they are drawn by how fine he looks, and then by that air of sadness. A handsome face, a charming manner, and that gentle sadness in his eyes — Miss van Allen, such things all together in one man become a fatal mixture for us poor ladies, *non?*'

Amy smiled, raising an eyebrow. 'No man is *that* devastating,' she said firmly.

'They say that the bad Lord Byron was the most beautiful of men, *n'est-ce pas?*'

'I believe so.'

'Lord Byron was here in Bristol once and I saw him — he was not as fine as Lord Chalbourne. There was no *strength* in Lord Byron — there is great strength in Lord Chalbourne. A man with beauty but no strength is effeminate, a man with beauty and strength is a *man*. That is Lord Chalbourne. How he came to marry a woman like — ' The dressmaker broke off, embarrassed suddenly. '*Pardon, mademoiselle*, already I have spoken out of turn and it is not right that I should speak further ill of the dead. Where is that Monique? *Monique!*'

'*Oui, madame?*' Monique's voice was muffled as she staggered in with drawers of gloves and reticules, and the black chenille day dress draped precariously on top. She could hardly see where she was going and the cross dressmaker tutted as she rescued the things from the girl.

'Idiot!'

'*Pardon, madame —* '

'*Allez-vous-en!*'

Monique hurried to do as she was told and Madame Secherell closed her eyes faintly as the curtains swung violently to and fro with the force of the girl's passage.

'*C'est à ne pas y croire,*' she murmured weakly. 'It's beyond belief!' But then she recovered and picked up the day dress. 'This will be perfect for you, I think, mademoiselle. I had thought of a similar design for Miss Olivia's wedding gown, the drawstring is so pretty a method of fastening the bodice, do you not think? But then I remembered the sapphires and knew I would have to think again.'

'The sapphires?'

'Why yes. The Chalbourne sapphires. Have you not heard of them?'

'No.'

'Oh, they are very famous, Miss van Allen, a beautiful sapphire and diamond necklace, a priceless heirloom which has been in Miss Olivia's family since the time, I believe, of Queen Elizabeth. Every Chalbourne bride wears them on her wedding day, it is a tradition. They are magnificent — and very difficult to design around because the lower sapphires hang so very low on the bosom. It would be easy to make such a neckline positively indecent, *non?*' The dressmaker smiled. 'The necklace came from Constantinople many hundreds of years ago. It was originally for a sultan's favorite concubine — *she* can have worn nothing with it at all!'

Amy smiled, 'Well, no doubt you will design the perfect gown for such a piece of jewelry, madame.'

'Of course.' The two short words were

spoken with absolute and unquestioning confidence. 'But now, you will wish to wear the black chenille now, Miss van Allen.'

'If I may.'

'I will take you to the dressing room.'

'About the bill — you will send it to me at Chalbourne Park?'

'*Certainement, mademoiselle.*'

A short while later Amy was dressed in the soft black chenille and she buttoned the corduroy pelisse slowly, looking at her reflection in the gold-framed cheval glass in madame's dressing room. After the light-hearted green and yellow she had worn on entering the little room, the black looked heavy and forbidding, but how it brightened her red hair, making it gleam in the dull light. She pinned the military hat into place and donned the gloves, and then she transferred all the things she carried in her reticule to the new black one — her ivory comb, a tiny pair of scissors, a phial of scent, a handkerchief, and, most important, a needle and some thread for any emergency which might arise.

Madame Secherell escorted her through the shop as if she were royalty, and Monique carried out the boxes for Daniels to load onto the landau.

As the door closed on her again, the sunlight was once more blotted out by the blinds, but as the carriage lurched away from the curb, she snapped the nearest blind up. If the landau halted at all it would be a simple matter to lower the blind again, but in the meantime she meant to see all there was to see of England.

The landau soon reached the outskirts of the city and she saw new villas with gardens which stretched down to the road. A short while after that Bristol seemed well behind, and the only houses she saw were the occasional cottage or turnpike tollhouse. After driving for an hour or more, Daniels turned the team to the right and the carriage entered a narrow lane between high hedges. In the distance Amy could see a line of hills rising from the vale, and above them some burgeoning yellow-gray clouds which promised the first snow of winter.

Her head lolled against the landau's upholstery as she stared at the hills. What had Livvy said they were called? The Cotswolds? Yes, that was it — the Cotswolds. How suddenly and sharply they rose from the floor of the wide Severn valley. Her eyes began to close, and the landau bowled on toward the hills, taking her to a house at which she was sure she would no longer be welcome. No one wanted outsiders at a time like this, and she was about to be forced upon Lord

20

Chalbourne, who would surely wish her anywhere but under his roof at the moment.

★　★　★

The landau jolted over a deep rut and Amy awoke immediately. Outside the sunlight was watery and fading fast as clouds smothered the last of the warmth, leaving the wooded countryside dark and cold. The wind was more blustery now, buffeting the carriage as it toiled up the long incline toward the top of the Cotswolds. She could hear the sound of chilly air soughing through the bare branches of the beech trees which loomed on either side of the narrow, steep way. She wondered how much further they had to travel, for the coming night promised to be wild and wintery. She shivered as she stared out, for there was something lonely and eery about the deserted woods where the dead leaves of autumn scuttered across the ground, sometimes rising to brush against the landau's windows as if trying to find a way in.

Daniels halted the tired team just before they reached the summit where the woods ended and the land was more exposed and open, and he climbed down to open the carriage door. The weepers on his hat flapped around his head and his long coat lifted

21

slightly as the wind caught it. 'I'll just rest the horses a while, madam, and light the lamps.'

'How much further have we to go?'

'Ten miles or so, madam.'

'Ten miles of *this* road?' She was horrified. 'Is there no suitable turnpike?'

'The village of Great Chalbourne does not lie on a turnpike, madam, and this *is* the most direct route. In a moment we'll be out on the top of the hills and the road's straighter then.'

Cold air was sweeping into the carriage and the wind's moaning was frightening. Daniels went to the rear of the vehicle and returned with a thick woolen rug which he tucked around her knees, and then he lit the japanned lamps. The arcs of light shone palely in the gathering darkness, and as she looked she saw the first flurries of snowflakes diving and twisting into the light.

The snow was still falling as the landau moved on at last, and the wind rose audibly as they emerged from the shelter of the woods onto the naked crest of the hill. The dimly seen landscape was crisscrossed with dry stone walls, and occasionally she could make out the shapes of sheep huddled in the fields. This part of England was famous for its wool and she knew that some of Lord Chalbourne's revenue came from the prosperous woolen mills lining the lower

Chalbourne valley where the river tumbled swiftly down to the Severn vale. She wiped a clear space on the misty window. The snow tumbled past the glass and she could see that it was beginning to settle, a thin layer of white lying on the adjacent fields.

Another hour passed and the darkness was complete, an inky blackness where the clouds obscured the moon and stars. The horses toiled slowly, heads low against the wind, and Amy's feet were frozen as she looked out at the bitterly cold night. There were lights through the trees of a nearby wood and she thought that there must be a large house there, but as she looked the landau suddenly slid violently sideways, a splintering sound cracked through the night, and Amy screamed as the carriage pitched over to one side and lay still.

She had been thrown heavily against the far door and lay there winded for a moment. The floor stretched almost vertically away from her and she was pressed against the glass. She could feel the wheels still spinning and hear Daniels struggling to soothe the terrified horses. Then he was clambering up to the door, opening it, and looking in with the aid of a lantern. 'Miss van Allen? Are you all right, madam?' His face was anxious as he looked down at her.

'Yes. Yes, I'm all right.' She struggled to get up, reaching out to take the hand he offered. Snowflakes swirled into the wrecked landau and touched her face with cold, damp fingers as she climbed down into the road. The wind caught her skirts and the snow sank into her light shoes. 'What happened, Daniels? Did we go over a large stone?'

'I believe so, madam. The axle's broken, that is certain.'

'Oh, no! But how far are we from Chalbourne Park still?'

'About three miles, madam. Those woods ahead mark the beginning of the descent through Devil's Elbow to Great Chalbourne village, and the house is about a mile beyond the village.'

She stared at him by the light of the swaying lantern. 'The descent through *what?*'

'Devil's Elbow, madam. It's a very steep hill, with a tremendous drop on one side and a tight bend like a lady's hairpin halfway down.'

She swallowed. 'Really? And what do you suggest we do now?'

'I can take the lead horse, madam, and ride on to the house to return with the barouche to convey you to your destination well in time for dinner.'

She nodded patiently. 'Meanwhile leaving

me here alone in the middle of nowhere? No, Daniels, that I will not do. It will take you a goodly time to ride three miles in this weather, and then you have to prepare the barouche to come all the way back again.'

'But, madam . . . '

'What house is that over there through the trees?' She pointed at the lights she had been looking at when the axle broke.

'That? Oh. It's — it's Oakleigh Hall, madam.'

'Oakleigh Hall? Isn't that where Miss Olivia's fiancé lives?'

'Mr Pemberton lives there, yes, madam.'

'Then I shall seek shelter there for the night. Mr Pemberton will no doubt be more than delighted to be of assistance.'

He cleared his throat in a way she had come to recognize as meaning he was uncomfortable and embarrassed. 'Madam, I do not think we should — '

'Nonsense! I refuse absolutely to sit out here while you go all the way to Chalbourne Park. What if you should have an accident? I would have to remain here all night on my own! There are such creatures as highwaymen, Daniels, and I have no wish to encounter one.'

'Highwaymen don't bother with this small road, Miss van Allen.'

She was beginning to feel irritated by him now. 'Daniels,' she said coldly. 'I am going to Oakleigh Hall to ask for shelter for the night, and I suggest that you do the same. This — er, Devil's Elbow sounds dangerous enough to me on a warm summer's afternoon, but on a night like this it sounds positively the gateway to hell! So, if you will find me my small handcase?'

'But Miss van Allen, I don't think His Lordship would want . . . '

'Want what?' Her foot was tapping and she felt almost faint with the cold. What was the matter with the fellow? It was just a simple matter of asking Mr Pemberton's hospitality for one night!

'I don't think he would want you to break your journey so close to home, madam.'

'Really. Maybe he would prefer me to risk being frozen to death overnight in the landau while I wait for you? Or maybe it would be more sporting of me if I were to take the second horse and ride willy-nilly down that drafted Devil's Elbow with you? I hardly think, Daniels, that any reasonable man would wish either course upon a guest, do you?'

'No, madam.'

'So, *if* you don't mind, I think we'll ask for Mr Pemberton's help.'

'Yes, madam.'

'Look, what exactly is the matter with you, Daniels?' she snapped, losing her temper a little as the cold bit through her clothes when the wind's howl rose to a crescendo among the nearby trees. 'Is that or is it not Oakleigh Hall?'

'It is, madam.'

'Very well, the matter is settled. I will carry my handcase and you can unharness the team and lead them. The landau can be attended to in the morning, the nonexistence of highway-men apparently making my luggage safe. Then, when all is attended to in the morning, we can negotiate your Devil's Elbow in the relative safety of daylight.'

'Yes, madam,' he said reluctantly, turning to do her bidding.

They walked slowly through the driving snow which was forming drifts now against the nearby walls. The lantern swung wildly to and fro, casting shadows on the stone gate pillars and on the beech-lined drive as they made their way toward the house. The drive swept into a circle before the entrance, which was reached by a wide flight of stone steps. Unicorns stood on top of the balustrade lining these steps, and there were lamps kindled everywhere shining out in a bright, welcoming manner. There were symmetrical

27

windows ranged on either side of the huge, classical portico, and through them she could see chandeliers glittering in elegant rooms.

Daniels waited at the foot of the steps as Amy climbed to the great doors, but as she reached the top step, the doors opened suddenly and a man in brown came out. The light from behind him streamed out over his powdered periwig, and his expression was suspicious as he looked at her. 'Who are you? What do you want?'

She bridled a little at his disagreeable manner. Did she look *that* disreputable? 'My name is Miss van Allen. I'm on my way to Chalbourne Park but the landau has met with an accident and I wish to seek shelter here for the night.'

'Chalbourne Park, you say?' There was no softening of his expression or tone.

'Yes,' she said testily. She felt more cold than she had ever felt in her life, she was tired and homesick, and beginning to be more than a little angered by the odd attitude of these English servants. '*Would* you be so kind as to inform Mr Pemberton of my presence?'

'Miss van Allen, you say?'

'Shall I spell it?'

His eyes flickered. 'No, madam.' He glanced past her. 'Have you a maid?'

'No, I have not.'

The eyes flickered again. 'If you will step inside, madam.'

'Thank you.' She entered the huge, echoing hallway which was tiled in gray and white and had clear, pale green walls decorated with moulded plasterwork, but the cold colors did not matter — anything was warmer than the night outside. She remembered Daniels waiting patiently outside with the horses. 'Oh, Lord Chalbourne's coachman is out there.'

'All will be attended to in due course, madam. I will inform my master that you are here.'

She stood alone in the hall, glancing up at the ceiling so far above. It was painted in gold and gave a startling richness to everything. The butler walked away slowly, his steps sounding loud on the tiles, and he ascended a black marble staircase which stretched up from the far side of the vestibule, vanishing at last between immense marble columns at the top. A large gilt clock ticked on the wall nearby, the mechanism whirring suddenly as it prepared to strike six, and the melodious chimes rang out softly over the silence.

After a while the butler reappeared at the top of the staircase. 'If you will come this way, Mr Pemberton will receive you in the library, madam.'

It was warmer on the first floor, the

warmth encouraged by the crimson carpeting which had been laid in all the passages. Unsmiling portraits of long-dead people hung on the walls and each window Amy passed allowed the sound of the stormy night to enter the house. By two gold and white doors the man stopped. 'This is the library, madam.'

'You will not forget Daniels, will you?'

'A man has already taken him to the stables, madam, and in due course he will be accommodated with the other servants for the night.'

'Thank you.'

He inclined his head gravely, pushing open the double doors and announcing her.

Charles Pemberton stood by the fireplace, a glass of cognac in his hand. He was not much taller than Amy and he wore a gray coat and beige cord trousers. The opened buttons of his blue gambroon waistcoat allowed the frills of his white shirt to push through and his cravat was plain. His fair hair was cut *à la Titus*, a style which Amy approved, and his eyes were a deep gray-green as he walked toward her. She guessed that he was in his late twenties, and his easy, amiable smile was one to which she could immediately respond. He took her hand and raised it to his lips.

'Welcome to Oakleigh Hall, Miss van Allen. I only wish your arrival here could have been under more pleasant circumstances.'

'Thank you, sir. I trust that I am not inconveniencing you in any way?'

'Not at all. You were not injured in the accident?'

'No, merely a little shaken.'

'Good.' He led her to a deep leather chair by the roaring fire. 'May I offer you some refreshment?'

'I'm not at all hungry, I had a very large luncheon, but I would appreciate some ypocras if at all possible, for I'm very cold.'

He nodded to the butler. 'Some ypocras for our guest, Gibson, and then if you would take her maid to the main guest room so that she can prepare it.'

'Miss van Allen has no maid with her, sir.'

Charles looked at Amy in surprise. 'No maid?'

'I fear not. My maid was married quite suddenly as I was about to leave New York and I'm forced to make this long journey alone.'

'How very unfortunate. However, we have maids here. See to it, Gibson, and make sure the girl is *au fait* with all that's necessary. We don't want Miss van Allen to be attended by a ham-fisted laundress.'

The butler bowed and left the library.

Amy looked around the room with its countless shelves of books from floor to ceiling. A small chandelier hung from the center of the ceiling, and a large mirror was above the white marble fireplace. The chimney breast was adorned with Christmas evergreens, myrtle and ivy, holly and yew, and the tingling freshness crept through the room to where she sat. There were several book-strewn tables and another leather chair, and everywhere there was that oddly comforting smell of old leather bindings and musty paper which was the mark of libraries the world over. She was reminded suddenly and jerkingly of the library in her rebuilt home on North Capitol Street. So very, very far away right now. Christmas in America, and for the first time in her life she would not be there to enjoy it. The belles of Washington would be circling around Winfield, intent upon making what hay there was to make while the van Allen woman was safely on the other side of the Atlantic . . .

Charles sat in the other chair, and while they waited for Amy's ypocras to come, they talked of her voyage, of her plans during her stay, and any intention she had of visiting London to maybe see Carlton House, Hyde Park, Almack's, and all the other sights of

England's capital. Gibson returned at last with the spiced wine, and he informed his master that the main guest room was ready and a maid in attendance.

Amy sipped the wine and Charles smiled at her. 'Are you a little warmer now, Miss van Allen?'

'I'm beginning to thaw, I believe.'

'This is one of the few rooms in the house where it is possible to remain comfortable on a night such as this. You must forgive the English weather, Miss van Allen, its welcome is truly ungracious.'

'It is a little unfriendly, isn't it?' She smiled at him.

'You will soon discover that the single most popular topic of conversation in our drawing rooms is The Weather and its multitudinous vagaries.'

She liked him, admiring Livvy's choice. 'Livvy did tell me that, but I chose not to believe her. How is she, Mr Pemberton?'

His smile faded abruptly. 'I should imagine that she is well enough under the circum-stances.'

Amy felt immediately uncomfortable at the change in him. Had she said something wrong? Something to offend him? But what could it possibly be? And besides, his reply to a perfectly ordinary inquiry was surely odd in the extreme. Didn't he *know* how Livvy was? 'Have — haven't you seen her then, Mr Pemberton?'

'I haven't seen her since the night of the Chalbourne Hunt Ball, Miss van Allen, and that was the evening before Lady Chalbourne's death.'

She was staring at him, and she knew she was, but she couldn't help herself. He was engaged to marry Livvy, and yet when a tragedy of such proportion as Alice Chalbourne's death struck, he stayed away.

He smiled faintly at her obvious confusion. 'Perhaps I should explain, for things have happened of which you can know nothing. To begin with, your entire trip here has been wasted, I fear, for there is no longer to be a wedding.'

'A postponement of course — '

'Not a postponement, Miss van Allen, a complete cancellation.'

There was silence, and the smell of evergreens seemed suddenly stronger. 'But why?' she asked at last. 'What's happened?'

'On the day Alice Chalbourne met her death, a note was delivered to me from Olivia. With the note was my ring. It was a simple message she had written, just that she no longer wished to see me.' He swirled the cognac, speaking lightly as if the whole affair mattered but little to him.

'I'm so sorry,' she said hesitantly, 'truly I am. But *something* must have happened to make her do that, sir, for when she last wrote to me her letter was filled to capacity with glowing references to you.'

'Her heart has undoubtedly changed, for she apparently feels nothing of the kind now.'

'Have you attempted to see her?'

'No. And nor will I, Miss van Allen, for if she chooses to behave as she has done, then that is entirely up to her and I wash my hands of her.'

Amy was aghast. 'But you *know* it's not like Livvy to behave like that!' she cried.

'Forgive me, Miss van Allen, but I really don't wish to discuss it any further. There is to be no wedding and that is the end of it.'

'And you don't care? You'll just sit back and do and say nothing to put things right?'

'No, Miss van Allen, I do not care.'

She didn't believe him. The pain was there in his eyes, even if he strove to hide it. Slowly she got up, putting the empty ypocras glass on a table. She felt uncomfortable in his presence suddenly, and she was aware of her damp clothes and still cold feet. 'I — I'm really very tired, sir,' she said lamely. 'I seem to have been traveling forever. Would you think it ill-mannered of me if I retired to my room now?'

He was instantly concerned, getting up quickly to pull the bell rope to call the butler. 'Forgive me, Miss van Allen, how very inconsiderate of me to forget.' He took her hand then. 'And forgive me for what I've said to you tonight.'

She smiled faintly. 'And you forgive me, sir, for not believing you when you say you no longer care.'

'Good night, Miss van Allen,' he said as the butler came.

'Good night, sir.'

★ ★ ★

Later, after a warm bath by the fire, Amy sat on the rug before the flames, her knees clasped tightly as she gazed into the heart of the glowing coals. Her hair was brushed free, hanging long about her shoulders, and she wore a white wrap. The fire shifted lazily in the hearth and the smell of roses was released from the open pot-pourri jar standing nearby. The wind moaned in the chimney and tiny flames sprang into life with each drawn breath of draught, and sparks winked and flashed for a moment before dying away again.

She mulled over all that had happened since she'd arrived in England. First of all there had been the shock of Alice Chalbourne's death. Poor, strange Alice, sometimes morosely silent, sometimes irritatingly talkative . . . And now there was the further shock of Livvy's broken engagement. She sighed, getting to her feet and crossing to the four-posted bed with its golden velvet hangings. 'Oh, Winfield,' she whispered, 'how I wish I'd listened to you, and how I wish I was back in Washington with you right now.'

3

The sound of slow footsteps woke her from a troubled sleep, and she lay there for a moment listening to them. A man was coming toward her door. She leaned up on one elbow, watching the flicker of candlelight beneath the door, but then the footsteps passed and the hinges of the long gallery doors squeaked loudly in the night. The footsteps echoed on the gallery's highly polished wooden floor, becoming fainter as whoever it was walked further away from her.

Wide awake and suddenly curious, she slipped from the bed, straightening her crumpled wrap and hurrying from the room and along to the gallery. The man's silhouette was black in the moving light, and the candleflame gleamed on his fair hair. It was Charles Pemberton. The light illuminated the face of a clock and she saw that it was four o'clock in the morning, and yet he was still dressed. His gray coat hung loose and unbuttoned and as he turned at the far end of the gallery, she saw that his cravat was undone. He entered a small room and left the door open so that the light shivered and

38

moved out into the cold, dark gallery for a moment and then was still as he set it down somewhere.

Hesitantly Amy began along the gallery, passing the many marble statues which shone a dull white in the darkness, and past the rows of paintings hanging on the panelled walls. Beyond the windows the storm raged on, the wind whining and whistling in the eaves and making the long velvet curtains billow from time to time. She reached the pool of candlelight and paused on the edge, peering slowly around the doorway and into the room.

His shirt was startlingly white and yet his face was in shadow as he stood before a covered easel. The room was a small studio, with cold black windows in the ceiling where the upward light shone in the snowflakes as they flew past in the wild wind. Slowly he pulled the sheet from the painting, and Amy saw that it was an almost finished portrait of Olivia Chalbourne. The dainty, heart-shaped face had been caught so well by the artist that the warm smile seemed almost alive. She was leaning against a small plinth, a spray of roses in her hand, and she wore a plain white gown which became her dark prettiness very well. The background was incomplete but the central figure was finished in every detail, from the almond-shaped gray eyes to the short, curly black hair which framed her face so sweetly. Charles put out his hand to run his fingertips gently over the cold, unresponding paint.

'You cannot mistake Sir Thomas Lawrence's brilliant style, can you, Miss van Allen?' he asked without turning.

He'd known she was there all along! Ashamed at being caught so obviously prying, she came further into the candlelight, her cheeks burning with embarrassment. 'I didn't mean . . . ' she began lamely.

'It doesn't matter, for now you know that you were right, I *do* care about losing Olivia, I care very much indeed.'

'I should not have intruded so grievously.'

He smiled then, turning to look at her. 'No doubt if I were in your position, Miss van Allen, having journeyed halfway across the world for a wedding only to find the wedding canceled and a funeral taking its place in the jollifications, then I'd be curious as well.'

'It's still no excuse for my behavior.'

'If you feel so wretched about it, Miss van Allen, I feel encouraged to take advantage of your guilty conscience by asking you — no, *begging* you — to listen to my story of woe. I must talk to someone, and unfortunately for you, you would appear to be the only one near at hand.'

'Of course I will listen, Mr Pemberton.'

'We'll freeze if we remain here, but the fire will still be in the library and we can be more comfortable there.' His face was sometimes in shadow, sometimes alive with dancing light as he picked up the candle again.

After the cold air of the gallery and passages, the library was very warm, embers still glowing in the hearth. The silence of the books folded over them both as he went to coax the fire into life again, and the sweet, sharp perfume of the greenery seemed stronger than ever as Amy sat in the same leather chair again.

He poured two glasses of cognac, gave her one, and then sat down opposite. He smiled, 'I have need of fortification in order to tell you everything. The nights are always the worst, are they not, Miss van Allen?'

'They are.' She thought of those dreadful months after the British had raided Washington.

He nodded, guessing what she was thinking. 'It's ironic that an Englishman should seek sympathy and understanding from you, isn't it?'

'I want to help you if I can, because Livvy is very dear to me and I cannot believe that

41

she has just fallen out of love with you for no apparent reason. Livvy just is not like that.'

'She thinks she has very good reason for behaving as she does.' He avoided Amy's gaze then, and when he spoke again his voice was very quiet and he uttered the words with difficulty. 'Miss van Allen, I stand suspected of having been Alice Chalbourne's lover and of having conspired with her to steal the Chalbourne sapphires and put a fake in their place.'

Amy stared at him in stunned shock. 'You're *what?*' she gasped.

'I hasten to add that I am innocent on all counts. Chalbourne has no evidence against me, which is why I'm still a free man and not languishing in Gloucester gaol awaiting trial. How much longer I can hope for that freedom, however, is another matter.'

'How can you say that? If you're innocent, then — '

'Chalbourne is a very rich, very influential man with friends in high places. He's also a magistrate, and he believes I'm guilty. Many men in his position would not hesitate to lay false evidence against me in order to secure my arrest and conviction. Only Chalbourne's basic sense of honesty, for which I thank God, is keeping me free. Unfortunately for me, the only person who could have proved my innocence was Alice herself; that *she* was guilty there is little doubt, but *I* was not her accomplice.'

Amy put her untouched glass down. 'Why do they suspect you?'

'First of all because I knew Alice before and yet said nothing about it. She was Alice Brooking when I knew her then and I went to Oxford with her only brother, Michael. I visited the Brooking estate at Wildmoor in Lincolnshire, met Alice, and fell in love with her immediately. I cared nothing about how moody or unpredictable she could be, I bombarded her with letters and even proposed to her — only to be turned down in no uncertain way. I came to my senses then and left Wildmoor without delay — in fact, I left England for Bengal and stayed away for four years. The strange thing is that I'm sure she had not even *met* Jonathan Chalbourne at that time, and yet within weeks she'd married him and set society by the ears. Jonathan moved in court circles, Miss van Allen, and he'd always been expected to marry the Earl of Bendon's daughter, Lady Christabel, and therefore unite two of the largest estates in Gloucestershire. Instead, he suddenly married Alice Brooking, and left everyone standing open-mouthed with surprise.'

Amy looked a little uncomfortably at him.

'Could it be that she was — I mean . . . '

'No, I do not believe she was, Miss van Allen,' he said with a slight smile. 'But assuredly that is what the *monde* thought. Whatever the reason for the hurried marriage, it was not because the bridal pair had — er, anticipated the ceremony, shall we say? Anyway, I returned to England, bought this house, and settled down to run the small estate attached to it. I soon heard of the strange Lady Chalbourne whom no one ever saw and who attended no functions, but you can imagine my surprise on going there to leave my card to find that she was none other than Alice Brooking. The shock was even greater when she behaved as if she'd never set eyes on me before — which I naturally put down to Jonathan's being a jealous husband. I followed what I thought was her lead, Miss van Allen, and I never did reveal that previous acquaintance, not even to Olivia.'

'You — you didn't tell *Livvy?*'

'No, to my present eternal regret I did not. Only two other people could have revealed the truth anyway, and one was her maid, Mary Danthorpe, and she was hardly likely to divulge such a thing. The other person was Alice's brother, but I soon discovered that not long after the wedding, he and Jonathan had quarreled very bitterly and that Michael was still *persona non grata* at Chalbourne Park. I wish I had spoken up at the time, for now my silence looks so very incriminating when set beside recent events. At the time, though, I had what I considered to be more important matters on my mind — winning Jonathan's approval of my courtship of his beloved sister. Then, as now, however, he had a great many financial worries, and my presence did nothing to lighten his mood or improve his temper, for he did not approve of me in the slightest.'

'Jonathan Chalbourne has financial problems?' asked Amy in surprise, for she had thought him to be a very wealthy man.

'He has the same problems which beset every other landowner of note in this country at the moment. Since the end of the wars with both your nation and the French, the situation here has been very bad, the harvests have been poor, and there is a great deal of unemployment because of the huge numbers of discharged soldiers returning to the land. Prices are falling all the time, as are rents, and most estates find it virtually impossible to find new tenants or even to keep those they already have. To a certain extent I have those problems here too, but my estate is small — Chalbourne Park is vast and its problems ten times as great. Nothing matters more to

Jonathan than that estate, Miss van Allen, and he is in danger of having to sell part of it in order to carry on. He could also have decided to sell the sapphires in order to finance the estate during the recession.'

She stared at him. 'He would have considered selling them?'

'Yes, and in fact that is what he did decide. The land means more to him than the sapphires, Miss van Allen.' He smiled at her. 'So you see, at the time that I was trying to beat a path to Olivia's door, Jonathan was in no mood to be accommodating.'

'But why didn't he approve of you? You do not seem to be below the salt.'

'How kind of you to say so, Miss van Allen, but my father, it shames me to admit, was both a liar and a cheat, and as far as Jonathan was concerned bad blood would out, et cetera. He always acted in what he saw as Olivia's best interest, but he made our lives unbelievably difficult until he accepted that we were serious. He and I still do not see eye to eye, however.'

'Does *anyone* see eye to eye with him?' remarked Amy drily.

He smiled. 'There are times when I wonder that myself.'

She studied his drawn face for a moment. 'What happened that you are suspected of stealing the sapphires? I know you knew Alice before, but . . . ' Her voice trailed away. 'She died on the day after the Hunt Ball, I understand,' she went on then.

'Ah, the ball. And what a night *that* proved to be. My poor Olivia decided to take advantage of the fact that Jonathan would be away until after the ball had commenced — she determined that Alice should preside over the proceedings. This she did, to the extreme embarrassment of all.'

'Embarrassment? Why?'

'Alice was wearing the sapphires and was flushed and overexcited for most of the evening. Then Jonathan arrived and informed Olivia and myself of his decision to sell the sapphires instead of parting with some land. Alice happened to overhear him. She screamed, stamped her foot, and beat her fists on Jonathan, shouting incoherently. The ball, as you can imagine, came to an abrupt and early end. She was removed to her rooms by two footmen, and the guests all left, including myself.'

'It must have been quite a night.'

'It certainly was.' He leaned his head back against the chair. 'Everyone realized that Alice was unstable after that, Miss van Allen, but I think nevertheless she had a good reason for her hysterical outburst. I will explain. The next morning, I was leaving to visit my solicitor in Bristol when my barouche was halted because the coachman saw Alice riding across the park. I could see that she was still in that same overexcited state, as her first words on halting proved. She asked, Miss van Allen, if I would turn the barouche around and return to the house so that she could take tea with me! All I could think of was getting her into the barouche so that I could convey her safely back to Chalbourne Park! When I said so, she became hysterical again, turned her horse, and rode like the very wind toward the gates. Naturally I gave chase, for she was in no state to handle a horse or even to be out on her own. The doctor's gig was passing the gates at that very moment, her horse reared, and Alice was thrown against the stone pillar. She struck her head and died instantly.'

'What a terrible way to die,' breathed Amy, the scene all too clear in her mind's eye.

'It was indeed, but at least she did not linger in agony. But as for the reason for her hysterical outburst at the ball — when she died, the Chalbourne sapphires were found in her reticule and it was discovered that the fastening on the necklace had not been mended. The necklace was a fake, because the real necklace had been repaired by a jeweler only the week before. I think Alice knew perfectly well that she was wearing a fake and at the ball that Jonathan's decision to sell the sapphires threw her into terror about being caught — hence the hysterics. Sometime between the jeweler's visit and the night of the ball, the real necklace was taken and the fake put in its place.'

'That still does not explain why you are implicated, sir.'

'The discovery of the fake meant an immediate search of Alice's rooms. Of course, the real necklace was not found, but what was found was my old letters, written at the height of my passion for her.'

'She'd *kept* them?'

'So it seems, although why she should do so escapes me, but she *was* very strange. Suspicion followed suspicion after that. Why had Alice and I said nothing of our previous acquaintance? Why had she ridden to Oakleigh Hall with the false necklace? Why had she then been seen riding away from me as if all the hounds of hell were behind her? Oh yes, the good doctor saw that scene and put two and two together to make five. Then it appeared that there had been whispers in the village about Alice's having been seen meeting me in Chalbourne Woods at night. She had assignations with a fair-haired man who rode a dun horse which was exactly like mine — only the man was not me, Miss van Allen. But now perhaps you understand why *I* am accused.'

'I do indeed. But who saw this fair-haired man and thought it was you?'

'A local poacher.'

'Whose eyesight must be very keen,' she pointed out.

'Or very hazy with bad cider. It wasn't me — and I'll repeat that fact constantly until I am believed. Anyway, there the matter rests for the moment. I know Jonathan awaits a slip on my part, and I know Livvy believes I am guilty. I have not seen her, and do not know that I wish to any more for she has shown herself willing to believe the worst of me, which fact I find very hurtful. But I shall not creep away with my tail between my legs, for that would make me look guilty. I shall remain defiantly here, looking them all in the eye and daring them to accuse me outright. I shall brave the hatred of the villagers and attend Alice's funeral, as any innocent man would.'

'The *hatred* of the villagers?' Amy was taken aback.

'They fear that the loss of the sapphires will mean that Jonathan will allow the estate to fall into disuse until the recession is over rather than sell part of it. That will mean the loss of work, of their homes and everything else, whether they be farm laborers or mill workers, and they blame me for this new danger. My own servants here are loyal to me, but they are pathetically few when compared with the entire village.'

He got up and went to the window, drawing the curtains back. Outside it had stopped snowing and everything was still in the December dawn. The gleam of white was everywhere, changing the landscape and distorting distance. His breath lay mistily on the chilly glass. 'Soon it will be Christmas, the season of joy.' He laughed coldly. 'What joy will there be this year, mm?'

She lowered her eyes.

'Strangely enough, I was expecting Michael Brooking here shortly,' he went on.

'Alice's brother?'

He nodded. 'Alice must have informed him that I had bought this house because I received a letter from him. He's a captain in the Eleventh Hussars now and stationed at Hazebrouck in Belgium. He expressed delight at discovering my whereabouts again and asked if he could come here for Christmas to talk over old times. I wrote back with the necessary invitation. No doubt he will stay away once he learns what's been happening.'

'It could be that he will give you the benefit of the doubt.'

'The British flag will fly on the Capitol first, Miss van Allen.'

Sadly she went to stand next to him. His voice was so hollow, and she knew that she believed his story, Charles Pemberton was innocent. She put a hand tentatively on his arm. 'I believe your story, Mr Pemberton, and I know that Livvy would too if she heard it.'

He looked quickly into her eyes. 'You believe me?'

'Yes.'

'Bless you for saying that.'

'When I reach Chalbourne Park you will have a friend in the camp, sir, and I will help you all I can. I will certainly try to persuade Livvy to see you, and I will turn that house upside down in an effort to find the sapphires, I promise you.'

He smiled. 'Miss van Allen, I almost believe you will find them, too! But if you defend me in that house then you will be setting yourself against Jonathan. The pressures on him at the moment are immense and he holds me responsible.'

'He's wrong though, isn't he?'

He took her hand warmly, raising it to his lips. 'Thank Providence for the American nation, its sense of justice — and its so very beautiful women.'

'Sir, you may first thank Providence for putting that large stone in front of the landau's wheel, for without it I should have driven past your gates and never heard your side of the tale.'

4

After an examination of the landau the following morning, it was decided that it could not be repaired without the attentions of Lord Chalbourne's wheelwright, and so Charles Pemberton arranged for his own barouche to be made ready for the final part of the journey. Amy wore a warm crimson cloak over her somber mourning as her luggage was carried from the stricken landau, and she took her leave of Charles.

The day was bright and sunny, and the skies above were crisp and blue. The rolling Cotswold hills stretched away as far as the eye could see, the hidden valleys almost completely disguised by the thin blanket of unspoiled white which had fallen during the night. Rooks rose complaining from nearby elms as the dark red barouche pulled away from the great portico of Oakleigh Hall, and the men engaged upon clearing the drive stood aside for the slow carriage to pass. Amy waved farewell to Charles Pemberton as he stood by the doorway, and she watched his small, lonely figure until the curve of the drive took him from her sight. He seemed almost lost, against the vastness of the house, and she was reminded again of the terrible things of which he was accused. The sobering light of day had brought no change in her conviction that he was innocent; and she sat back against the cold gray upholstery knowing that she would not rest until she had proved him free of guilt and brought him together with Livvy again.

Outside the sun was dazzling on the snow, and the barouche rattled out between the stone gate pillars where Alice Chalbourne had met her death. Now that it was light she could see the countryside of dry stone walls and sheep fields. The animals huddled in the lee of the walls, scraping at the snow to find the sparse winter grass beneath. A shepherd trudged across one field, his crook swinging as he neared the woods. His sacking cloak seemed inadequate against the sudden cold as he passed from the sunshine into the chill shadows of the trees. Then the barouche entered the woods too and abruptly the sunshine disappeared, only filtering through from time to time between the thatch of overhanging branches. The road began the slow, steep descent to the Chalbourne valley, and to the left the land fell sharply away, dropping down to the foaming, splashing waters of the River Chalbourne far below.

The Devil's Elbow was even more tortuous than she had been expecting, and she felt quite sick inside to think that but for the broken axle she would have been driven down this dangerous hillside in the darkness. Once or twice she glimpsed the woolen mills through the trees, dull-red brick buildings built along the banks of the fast-running stream, twists of gray smoke rising from their tall chimneys.

The dark shadows of the woods meant that the snow was frozen hard on the road, and beneath it was a treacherous layer of black ice. The barouche slipped sideways once or twice and Amy closed her eyes faintly, listening to the horses slithering as they struggled to regain control of their heavy load. Their harness jingled and she heard the coachman's low, encouraging voice, at once soothing and urgent. Slowly the barouche continued on its descent, and the terrible drop was left behind at last.

At the foot of the hill, where the bushes hung low and heavy with their burden of snow, she saw the first cottages of Great Chalbourne village. The thatched or stone-tiled dwellings straggled along the floor of the valley, and next to the road ran the river, bubbling and brown with winter floodwater. Children were playing in the little front gardens of several cottages, and men and women were busy clearing snow away from the roads and paths, but they fell silent as the dark red barouche drove into sight. A small dog rushed yapping and darting around the horses' legs until the coachman flicked his whip to sting the little creature's back, and then it ran yelping away, its tail between its legs.

At the end of the village stood the church, the Chalbourne family crest on the flag which flew at half-mast from its square tower. In the churchyard the gravedigger was busy clearing the snow from the place which must be destined for Alice Chalbourne's grave.

The barouche went very slowly now, for an ox cart was turning in the road ahead, and then it halted altogether as the carter whistled and shouted at the lumbering beasts dragging the unwieldy vehicle. A group of men stood by the churchyard wall and Amy glanced at them. She could see the resentment in their eyes as they looked at Charles Pemberton's carriage. She didn't see who threw the pebble which cracked the barouche's window pane, for at that moment the way ahead was clear and the carriage began to move again, but an ugly cobweb of cracks distorted the view now. The coachman immediately urged the team into a trot and then a slow canter, and the barouche bowled swiftly away from the village. Amy's heart was still thundering with fear and shock and she stared in disbelief at the cracked window. Surely feelings did not run as high as that . . .

She sat back, taking a deep breath to steady herself. The road wound on beside the river, and the overhanging trees emphasized the hollow hissing of the water until the sound echoed all around. There were no cottages along the wayside now and the trees were thicker, making the way dark again, as it had been in the woods. Among the trees there began to appear ornamental evergreens, and she knew they were rapidly approaching Chalbourne Park itself. A moment later there was a wall along the road, topped at regular intervals by snarling stone griffins. Ivy leaves rustled against the stone as the carriage passed, and snow was dislodged from low-hanging branches by the draught. Wrought-iron gates straddled the road ahead, and as they were passed the land suddenly swept into a wide park, Chalbourne Park itself. Holly bushes marked the river's bed away to the left, their leaves dark and shining and their berries a burning scarlet in the sunlight, and everywhere was blinding with the dazzle of the snow. Deer wandered slowly among the trees, coming timidly closer and closer to some men who were breaking some bales of hay for them.

Amy's first sight of the house came not long afterward, and her breath caught at the beauty of the rambling old building. It was not magnificent and classical like Oakleigh Hall, it was low, with steeply-pitched roofs and many gables, and the small, mullioned windows caught the sunlight as the barouche swayed along the drive beneath the avenue of chestnut trees. A jutting stone porch marked the main entrance, and beside it was a huge oriel window which would not have looked out of place in a church, but which looked perfect on this old house. The gutters and eaves were adorned with gargoyles and above the porch snarled more of the fierce griffins, but even they enhanced Chalbourne Park's charm. Had a woman in Tudor dress stepped out of the house, Amy felt she would not have been surprised. The beauty of the house was timeless, and it did not seem possible that such a building had been put there by mere man — nature seemed responsible for it, for only nature could have fashioned something so flawless in its setting.

Two grooms were leading a team of horses back and forth outside the nearby stableyard as the barouche rolled to a standstill by the porch, and they halted their work in surprise on recognizing the carriage. After a moment they carried on with what they had been doing, but they glanced frequently at Charles Pemberton's carriage, whispering together as they did so. The coachman opened the door for Amy to climb down, and as she shook out the pelisse and pulled her gloves on more tightly, the door of the house opened and a butler in blue livery came out. He was a thin, stooping man wearing a heavily powdered white wig which was tied back with a black ribbon. Black weepers trailed from his upper arm and there were black knee ties on his breeches, as well as a black rosette on his breast to denote the deep mourning of the household.

His glance went suspiciously to the barouche as he came down the three shallow steps and approached her, his shoes crunching on the freshly cleared gravel. His suspicion served to remind Amy yet again of the terrible things of which Charles Pemberton was accused. 'Good morning, madam,' said the butler, bowing.

'Good morning. My name is Miss van Allen.'

His face cleared. 'Oh, yes, madam, welcome to Chalbourne Park. My name is Jeffreys and I am the chief butler. I fear Lord Chalbourne is not at home, but Miss Olivia is in the drawing room.' He turned to beckon to the two grooms, jerking a peremptory thumb at Amy's luggage.

Amy hesitated. 'Jeffreys, there was an unpleasant incident as I drove through the village; a stone was thrown at the carriage. In view of Mr Pemberton's great kindness in coming to my assistance, I think it only right and proper that someone well known from here should ride back with the barouche to ensure that no further damage is done.'

The butler blinked. 'I — er — very well, madam, I will attend to it now.'

As she waited for him to return, she looked up at the house. The curtains were drawn at all the windows and there was a heavy silence about everything as she gazed at the gargoyles which grinned so grotesquely from every corner. A light breeze blew across her face, catching the tassels of her hat and making them flutter a little. The oriel window was decorated with stained glass shields and emblems, and ivy was creeping slowly over the old stonework, mingling on the pillars of the porch with the thick, twisted stems of an ancient wisteria. Amy shivered suddenly. What awaited her in this house?

The butler returned and she followed him into the great hall where there was a smell of woodsmoke from the single stone fireplace.

The surround of the fireplace had been painted at some time far in the past, the stonework picked out with crimson roses and green leaves. The light was diffuse because of the drawn curtains, and the red and gray tiles on the floor looked hazy as she went to stand by the warmth of the fire while the butler went to inform Livvy that she had arrived.

Alone with only the crackling of the fire to break the silence, she removed her cloak and looked around. The paneled walls were dark and heavily carved, and everywhere there were portraits, countless faces looking down at her. A long table stood in the center of the red and gray floor, and on it was a large copper bowl filled with white hothouse roses. Beside the bowl lay two dress swords and next to them a silver dish containing black-edged mourning cards. High above, two wrought-iron chandeliers hung from the molded plaster ceiling. They were made of hoops of strap iron held together by decorative scrollwork. The impression of stepping back in time lingered with her as she stood there, and she jumped a little when the butler reappeared, bowing low to her again.

She followed him toward a low, dark doorway at the far end of the hall. The drawing room was wainscoted like the great hall, and was a long low room, strangely intimate in spite of the dark walls and heavy, old-fashioned furniture. The ceiling was smoke-marked, the intricate plasterwork trapping the smuts of countless fires over the years until the white was turned to a deep yellow. There were more wrought-iron chandeliers, their thick, creamy candles smoking a little in the rush of cooler air from the open door as Amy was shown in. Tapestries hung on the walls, their colors dulled by the lack of sunlight from the curtained windows, and firelight leaped over the walls and furniture, flashing briefly on the faces of more portraits, making the eyes glitter with life for a moment. Christmas greenery was arranged in every corner, and bowls of holly and white roses stood on the tables.

For a moment she could not see Olivia, but then a black-clad figure rose from a crimson velvet sofa in a shadowy corner, and taffeta rustled as she came toward Amy. Her face was pale and drawn and there were dark shadows beneath her almond-shaped gray eyes. Her voice was low and taut as she dismissed the butler after asking him to bring some coffee. There was nothing of the happy, carefree girl Amy had known in Washington; Olivia Chalbourne was sadly changed. The door closed behind the butler.

'Hello, Livvy,' said Amy, smiling gently.

'Amy. Oh, *Amy!*' Tears shone in Olivia's eyes and she ran the last few steps toward her friend, flinging her arms around Amy's neck and bursting into tears.

Amy held her tightly, stroking the short, curly hair soothingly. 'It's all right, sweeting, I'm here now.'

'I thought you'd never come, and I've been so desperately unhappy for this last week — '

'Before you go any further, Livvy, perhaps you should know that an accident forced me to spend last night at Oakleigh Hall.'

The tear-stained face was raised slowly. 'You — you stayed at Oakleigh Hall?'

'Yes.'

'So you know what's happened?'

'Yes. I do.'

'It's been such a shock,' whispered Olivia. 'I didn't believe it was possible to be so miserable.'

'My poor Livvy.'

'Which side of his character did he show you, Amy? The sweet, charming, debonair side? Or maybe his true colors were to the fore this time.' Olivia's voice was harsh and bitter.

'He was as utterly desolate and miserable as you are.'

'He lied to me all along! And to think that I felt sorry for *her!* I actually thought she should be encouraged a little, coaxed with a morsel of gentleness so that she could be much happier! Oh, *God*, how they must have laughed at me! That pathetic strangeness of hers was all an act — all the time she was being courted by my fiancé!' Olivia's eyes were bright with a mixture of anger and unhappiness, and she twisted a black lace handkerchief until it was crumpled beyond recognition.

'Oh, Livvy, you don't really believe that, do you?'

'What else am I to believe? They were seen meeting in the woods! I wish I'd listened to Jonathan — from the outset he warned me that the Pembertons had tainted blood.' The handkerchief twisted again. 'I keep wondering about those times when she accompanied me to Oakleigh Hall for sittings for Sir Thomas Lawrence's portrait. Where did they go when I was posing so obligingly? To his bedchamber? Or maybe they were together in the very next room to the studio! The very day before the ball, when I was planning to coax her to attend, were they making love and laughing at me?'

'Stop it, Livvy, you're only making yourself more miserable by speculating on completely nonexistent happenings.'

Olivia stared at her. 'You believe him, don't

you?' she breathed.

'Yes.'

'Then do not seek to defend him in this house, Amy, for he has no friends at Chalbourne Park!'

'You're condemning him unheard, and you're not even granting him any right of appeal. That's not justice, Olivia Chalbourne, that's not justice at all. You should have at least listened to what he had to say in his own defense.'

'He's too persuasive, Amy. If I allowed him to come close to me then he'd weave his spell all around me again and I'd want to ignore the truth, I'd want to be convinced. He told me such lies and — '

'He didn't lie to you, Livvy, he just omitted to tell you something. There's quite a difference. And *I* believe his reason for not telling you that he'd known Alice before.'

'And what eminently believable reason did he give you for his meetings in the woods with her? Were they picking wild flowers? Or maybe writing poetry?'

'He gave me no reason, he had no need when he denies those meetings altogether.'

'Poachers train themselves to take notice of things, even in the dark.'

'I still believe him, Livvy.'

The black taffeta rustled as Olivia went to

66

stand by the fire, the heavy folds of her skirts tinted with a blush of pink by the moving light. 'Why is he staying on at Oakleigh Hall? Everyone around here hates him so now.'

'I know they do; someone in the village threw a stone at his barouche when it was conveying me here. Why should he leave, Livvy — he's innocent and has no reason to go?'

Olivia glanced at her. 'I — I've always respected your opinions, Amy . . . '

'Then let this be no exception. You *should* see him, Livvy, you should listen to what he has to say.'

'To do that would be to hurt Jonathan.'

Amy stared at her. 'Not to do it is to hurt yourself. And Charles. And what if Jonathan is wrong about him? If Charles is innocent, then think of the dreadful wrong you are doing him. Olivia Chalbourne, you could be throwing away your future happiness because of a mistake! If that's what you want, then go on as you are now and face the prospect of a life spent in sorrow for what might have been!'

'Don't, please don't!'

'I must if I am to make you face what you've got to do. You *must* give him the chance of putting his side of things to you.'

'I need more time, Amy, I can't just change

my mind like that.'

'You did when you condemned him,' reminded Amy, knowing that she was being deliberately cruel. She continued then in a gentler vein. 'He'll be at the church tomorrow. Maybe seeing him like that will help you to decide what's right.'

The gray eyes were large and startled then. 'He — he's coming to the *funeral*?'

'Yes.'

'Oh no, he mustn't do that, Amy, it's very ill-advised when feelings are running so high against him.'

Amy smiled a little. 'You see. You *do* care about him.'

Olivia turned away agitatedly, leaning a shaking hand on the mantelpiece and fingering some carved shapes.

'He refuses to behave as if he's guilty, Livvy, and in his opinion staying away from the funeral would be the action of a guilty man. I admire him for his actions, Livvy, and I agree wholeheartedly with what he's doing. I like him a great deal, and I love you as if you were my own sister. I will *not* sit idly by and watch the pair of you spoil your lives like this.'

'I — I will think about what you've said, Amy, I promise I will.'

'Then that will do for the moment; a little

progress is better than none at all.' Amy smiled and went to sit in a chair by the fire, holding out her hands to the heat. 'Could the sapphires still be somewhere in this house, Livvy?'

'Everything here has been searched and searched and then searched again. If they're here, then they are most skillfully concealed. Jonathan believes that they were got well away from here, that they've probably been broken up and sold separately.'

'And what do you think?

'I don't know, and that's the truth. Although . . . '

'Yes?'

'Well, sometimes I have a feeling — just a feeling — that they're still close by.' Olivia smiled. 'It must be my Chalbourne blood responding to the precious family heirloom.'

'Probably.' Amy smiled at that. 'Livvy, where did Alice go during that last week? Who did she see?'

'Alice hardly ever went anywhere, and that week was no exception. She spent most of her time in her room, writing to her brother Michael or just reading — she was extremely fond of Miss Austen's books. Oh, and she came with me to Oakleigh Hall for my sittings — she was my chaperone!' A trace of bitterness returned to the soft English voice.

'Why didn't she go out much?' asked Amy curiously. 'I mean, I know she behaved badly at the ball, but then it was all new to her and she *did* have a dreadful shock about the sapphires.'

Olivia glanced at her. 'She didn't go out much because she was in poor health a lot of the time and had been since she first came here. She also stayed in because Jonathan insisted that she did so.'

'*Insisted?* Wasn't that a little strict?'

'It was, and I confess I was taken aback by it when I first came here from London, and I took him to task about it more than once, but he was adamant. Besides which, Alice herself did not seem to have any objections, so it wasn't really my place to grizzle. She remained in her rooms for days on end sometimes, with only her dreadful maid Mary Danthorpe for company. I was sorry for Alice and I blamed Jonathan for being less than kind, but when she behaved as she did on the night of the ball, well, I could understand for the first time why he kept her on such a very tight rein.'

'Charles told me about it, but it doesn't seem possible that she could have been so very bad.'

'She was, Amy, she truly was. I thought she'd gone completely insane.' Olivia lowered her eyes. 'To return to your question about who she met during that week — well, she was introduced to everyone who attended the ball. Including Charles again.'

'She could as easily have given the necklace to Lady Christabel Bendon, or Jeffreys, or an under housemaid or scullery boy — maybe she died before she could give it to anyone at all, come to that. The possibilities are endless. You'd think that the secluded life she led would make it easier, wouldn't you — but it doesn't seem to make the slightest difference, the world and his wife are suspects.' Amy sat back, suddenly daunted.

'I know,' said Olivia unhappily. 'And if she didn't appear to go out during the day, she could quite easily have gone out secretly at night — as she did when she was seen meeting Charles in Chalbourne Woods, although I don't think she was seen during that particular week.'

'She was seen meeting someone at night,' corrected Amy firmly.

'Very well — someone.'

'If she was going out at night, then I'd bet my last dollar that her maid knows about it.'

Olivia smiled. 'Yes, but if Mary Danthorpe knows anything, then she won't say. She was Alice's nurse originally and, has always been with her — she protected Alice like a lioness with an only cub.'

'By your tone, I would imagine you don't like Mary Danthorpe very much.'

'I don't, I find her thoroughly repulsive, and the thought of her hands dressing me or brushing my hair makes me feel positively ill.'

'What's she like then?'

'Clammy.'

'*Clammy?* How can a person be clammy?'

'She can somehow. She has always made little secret of the fact that she compares Chalbourne Park unfavorably with her precious Wildmoor — I sometimes think that neither she nor Alice ever wanted to leave that place in the first place.' Olivia turned the lace handkerchief slowly. 'We'll just have to accept that if Mary knows anything, then wild horses would not be able to drag it out of her. But how can she *not* know? She was *always* with Alice, so I fail to see how she could have missed anything.'

Amy was thoughtful. 'Livvy, my maid left me just before I left America — I need someone to attend me while I'm here.'

Olivia turned quickly to look at her, her eyes wide. 'You traveled all this way without a maid?'

Amy groaned. 'Oh, don't *you* start looking at me like that, I had quite enough of those looks during the voyage! I didn't really have much choice in the matter when a handsome Baltimore parson swept the wretched girl off her feet and up to the altar in the winking of an eye! Anyway, I'm here without a maid and it seems to me that if Mary Danthorpe was capable of attending Alice, then she's capable of attending me. And who knows, maybe I will be able to glean something from her.'

'She isn't exactly the talkative type, Amy, and I certainly don't think you'd find her agreeable.'

'I don't have to like her, do I?'

'Very well, I'll tell Jeffreys to inform her. Ah, when one talks of the devil . . . ' Olivia turned as the door opened and the butler came in with a tray of coffee. 'Jeffreys, Miss van Allen is without a maid. I wish you to inform Mary Danthorpe that she is to attend her.'

'Very well, Miss Olivia, I will speak to Danthorpe immediately.' The man bowed and left them again.

'That's settled then,' said Amy, leaning forward to pour the coffee from the elegant blue and white porcelain pot. 'But it's the only thing which is, for we're still no further forward where the necklace is concerned. I won't be defeated though. I fully intend looking for those sapphires myself.'

'Amy,' said Olivia patiently, sitting opposite to accept a cup of the thick black coffee, 'there cannot be anywhere on this estate that Jonathan's searchers haven't already turned inside out.'

'Your intuition says otherwise, Olivia Chalbourne.'

'I only said that I sometimes have a feeling — '

'You also once said that you *felt* that that footman of mine back in Washington was dishonest, and so he turned out to be. You also *felt* that Mary Lou Prescott and Vere Tarleton were doing things they shouldn't, and so they were; there was a *very* hasty wedding not long after you'd returned to London. So, you see, I take notice of your intuition, for it has proved uncannily correct in the past.'

'Well, it wasn't correct this afternoon when you arrived, for I was convinced that Jeffreys was going to announce Captain Michael Brooking, not you.'

Amy lowered her cup, surprised, for Charles had said that Michael Brooking was most definitely not welcome at Chalbourne Park. 'You're *expecting* him?'

'That is the problem, Amy — *I'm* expecting him, but Jonathan isn't. You see, Jonathan charged me to write to Wildmoor,

74

informing the captain of his sister's death, and the date and time of the funeral here. He expressly forbade me to invite the captain to this house as a guest — they had a most dreadful quarrel once and Jonathan even called Captain Brooking out.'

'But what did they quarrel about?'

'I don't know, Jonathan refuses to say. Anyway, it seemed to me a terrible thing that Alice's only living relative should not be offered the hospitality of this house at such a time, and so I defied Jonathan and wrote inviting Captain Brooking here. Now I dread his coming, because I know Jonathan will be furious and will probably refuse to allow him over the threshold.' Olivia gave a wan smile. 'Still, my second thoughts come by far too late, for the wretched invitation has been issued and I'll have to face Jonathan's wrath if Captain Brooking does indeed come.'

'Well, I think you can relax a little for the time being, Livvy, for if you sent the letter to Wildmoor then I doubt if the captain has received it even yet. Charles told me that he is with his regiment in Belgium.'

Olivia almost dropped her cup and saucer in relief, and she gave a nervous little laugh. 'Thank heaven for that! The evil day is put off for a while at least.'

Amy felt uncomfortable at the obvious

anxiety Olivia experienced at having to tell her brother what she'd done. 'Livvy — will your brother be returning here today?'

'Yes. He's in Cirencester on magisterial business, but he intends to be here for dinner tonight.'

Amy said nothing, for she was becoming increasingly apprehensive about meeting Jonathan, Lord Chalbourne, for the first time, but Olivia did not notice the silence. She put down her cup and got up, crossing the room to the window and holding the curtain aside to look out. The sunlight was blinding as it streamed into the darkened room, the shaft of bright sunbeams made brighter by the snow. 'Oh, Amy, you've only been here a little while, but already you've made me feel better — I was beginning to think that I would bend beneath the weight of all my problems.' She turned to Amy then. 'Did — did Charles say he would definitely be coming to the funeral tomorrow?'

'Yes.'

'I'm glad. You're right, Amy, I've treated him poorly and I *do* care so very much for him still.'

5

Amy went to her room not long afterward, feeling suddenly very tired after the long journey and the small amount of sleep she had had the night before. Her room was in the western wing of the house and had two windows, the smaller of which overlooked the walled kitchen gardens and part of the stableyard. The other window had a magnificent view over the park toward the distant dark outline of Chalbourne Woods, and beyond that the Cotswolds gleaming white in the sunlight.

Like the rest of the house, the room was wainscoted, the walls above the panels being hung with blue damask. The bed commanded the attention from the moment the room was entered, for it was very large and square, with carved posts and royal hangings. On the headboard she could make out a date — 1603. The year Queen Elizabeth died, she thought drily, prodding the old, lumpy mattress and wondering if it was the very one where Gloriana had last rested her head! It seemed old and uncomfortable enough, that was for sure! But any bed would have been welcome to Amy in her present tired state. Where was Mary Danthorpe, she wondered, crossing the room to the smaller window. The paths and formal flowerbeds were hidden by the snow now, but she could imagine what it must be like in the summer when insects droned in the sweet-smelling herbs and bees were busy in the rambling rose which grew against the wall below the window. The old latticed glass made strange uneven patterns of light all over the room as she turned to look around again, studying it all carefully, for it was to be her home for the next months.

A crystal bowl stood on the dressing table and in it someone had arranged some pink and white carnations from the hothouse, and the heavy perfume filled the warm air. The fireplace was similar to that in the drawing room, carved of dark, old wood, and the newly-lit fire crackled and spat as the bed of sticks shifted beneath the weight of the coal. It was then that her attention was drawn to the room's only painting, not another portrait this time but a view of a large, old crenelated house which was dominated by a hexagonal belvedere tower, and beyond the house was a landscape of flat marshes, dikes, and the distant sea. The name of the house was clearly written on the gilt frame: Wildmoor.

So this was Alice's home, the family seat of the Brookings . . .

The door opened suddenly and Amy jumped. A woman in a gray wool dress and white mob cap came in. She was thin and almost wiry, her chest was flat and boyish, and her face somehow flat, too. Her nose did not seem to protrude very far and her chin was smooth and a little receding. Against her brown skin her pale eyebrows were almost invisible, and the wisps of hair which fell from beneath the cap were a dull gray. Only those stray wisps and the sagging of her chin gave a hint of her age, looking at odds with the lithe, still-slender body which moved so quickly as she turned to close the door again without seeing Amy by the far window. She was not an attractive person by any means, and her face would have been entirely unmemorable had it not been for the quick dark eyes which shone with bright intelligence as she suddenly saw Amy and halted abruptly.

'Beggin' your pardon, madam.' Even the voice was flat and uninteresting.

'Don't you knock before entering a room?' asked Amy a little crossly.

'I thought as you was still down with Miss Olivia, madam.' The woman bobbed a belated curtsey. 'Mr Jeffreys said as I was to attend you.'

'Yes. You must be Mary.'

'Mary Danthorpe, madam.' The face was wooden.

Amy did not like her, as Olivia had said she would not, but there was no point in starting off the relationship on a bad footing. 'I hope you are used to dressing long hair, Mary.'

'My lady's hair was long. I'm used to it.'

Amy glanced at the painting. 'Is Wildmoor really like that?'

A light passed through the sharp eyes as the woman looked at the canvas. 'Wildmoor's Wildmoor.'

'Will — will you be returning there now that . . . ?'

'Not yet. But I will when the time comes.'

Amy cleared her throat. 'Yes. Well, I intend resting now, Mary, so if you will attend to my hair and so on . . . ?'

'Very well, madam.' The woman drew out the stool by the dressing table and stood waiting for Amy to sit down. The pins tinkled into the little dish as the maid silently did Amy's long red hair. The woman's smooth, flat face was reflected in the mirror, all feeling and emotion disguised by the expressionless mask, and suddenly Olivia's use of the word *clammy* to describe her seemed very apt. Amy conquered the urge to shiver as the woman's fingers brushed the nape of her neck.

A little later Amy was dressed in her warm, comfortable wrap and preparing to lie down on the bed.

Mary folded the top coverlet back. 'Shall you take any luncheon, madam?'

'No, I think not — I need to sleep. Oh, and I would like a bath before dressing for dinner, Mary.'

The maid straightened. 'A bath in the *evening*, madam?'

'That is what I said.'

'My lady *never* bathed in the evening.'

'Really,' remarked Amy coolly. 'Well, I do — so, if you please, I would like a bath made ready for me.'

The wooden expression returned. 'Very well, madam.'

The royal drapes enclosed the bed like a cocoon and Amy lay back thankfully, finding the mattress surprisingly comfortable and soothing in spite of its irregular surface. She closed her eyes, wishing that when she awoke she would be miraculously preparing to dine with Winfield back in Washington, listening to his amusing anecdotes about his political colleagues and rivals, rather than facing the prospect of dining across the table from Jonathan Chalbourne, a man whose character she felt sure contained all the very worst of male traits. Her thoughts returned to Winfield

Kenney. She missed him, oh, how she missed him . . . As she drifted into a deep, almost motionless sleep, she decided that she would write to him shortly, accepting his proposal.

★ ★ ★

It was dark and someone was waking, her. 'Madam? It's time to wake.'

Amy opened her eyes and saw that across the room a plump young maid was dragging a lacquerwork screen before the fire to shield the bath from view.

Mary Danthorpe's curiously flat voice spoke again. 'Shall I put out the bombazine gown, or the radzimir, madam?'

Sleep finally fled and Amy sat up. 'The bombazine, I think. Yes, the bombazine. Good heavens, have I slept through the noise of them bringing in the bath and filling it?'

'There was no noise.' Mary turned away to tie back the velvet drapes against the bedposts, carefully arranging the thick cords and heavy golden tassels so that they hung in just the precise way she wanted. The younger maid hovered for a moment, her nervous gaze following the older woman all the time. Mary snapped her fingers once and the maid almost ran from the room.

Amy luxuriated in the rose-scented bath,

82

lying back in the deep water and watching the lazy flames in the fireplace for a while. She felt relaxed and refreshed now, catching up on her lost sleep had restored the energy and vigor she had lost since leaving Washington all those days ago.

Later, the bombazine gown felt cool against her skin, and the shining black beads stitched all over the black material made it heavy. Mary had dressed her hair expertly, pinning it up in careful coils and curls through which dainty strings of tiny pearls were threaded, and as Amy surveyed her reflection in the mirror, she was very agreeably surprised at how well the effect of graceful high fashion had been achieved with so little effort. 'Thank you very much, Mary,' she smiled, pulling the grenadine shawl around her shoulders. 'I'm really very pleased.' Perhaps the well-earned praise would soften the woman a little.

But Mary's face did not show any emotion. 'My lady always expected to look well, madam,' came the lifeless reply.

Amy abandoned any further attempt at conversation, accepting the reticule the woman held out. Mary opened the door for her and Amy inclined her head briefly as she left the room, and as she walked down the dark passageway, the dinner gong echoed through the old house for the first time.

Candles smoked in wall brackets as she descended the steep, wooden staircase where griffins snarled on the top of each newel post and gold leaf gleamed richly on the balusters. Portraits of past members of the Chalbourne family hung on the smoke-marked walls, and a mahogany, long-case clock chimed as she reached the foot of the stairs.

A footman opened the dining room door for her, and she stepped through into a room of mirrors. Her own reflection looked back at her ten or twelve times from all sides, and the already large room was made to seem even larger. Deep crimson curtains were drawn at the windows, and a Persian carpet which must have been woven specially for the room covered the floor. A white-clothed table stood down the center, garlands of winter greenery arranged around its edge, and more greenery, where the rich scarlet of holly berries could be seen, standing in a silver-gilt bowl in the middle of the crisp white cloth. The porcelain was gold and white and there were tall crystal glasses sparkling in the light from the chandeliers above. Two fireplaces warmed the vast room, and Olivia and her brother sat by the far one. All this Amy noticed in the few seconds as she paused to adjust her shawl before crossing the room toward the far fireplace.

Jonathan Chalbourne stood immediately, coming to meet her. He was as Madame Secherell had described him, although if anything he was even more strikingly handsome than Amy had been expecting. He was tall, his shoulders broad and well made, and his hips slender, and at about thirty or thirty-one he was in his prime. Like his sister, he had dark curly hair and gray eyes, his hair worn a little bit longer than was fashionable, although that did not detract from his appearance, rather it enhanced it. His eyes were dark-lashed and almost beautiful, but there was no trace of effeminacy in him. He wore black velvet, his coat having the high, stand-fall collar which no fashionable Bond Street gentleman would be seen without, and his frilled white shirt was very startling against the somber darkness of the velvet. His waistcoat was dove gray, and his neck cloth full and complicated, and it must have taken his valet a considerable time to perfect, she thought as she smiled politely at him. He took her hand to lead her to a chair, and she thought him quite one of the most arresting men she had ever seen.

'Forgive me for not being here to greet you when you arrived earlier, Miss van Allen, but I was unavoidably detained in Cirencester.' His voice was light and soft, and not at all deep and assertive as she had been expecting.

'I'm only sorry, sir, that my arrival here has been at such a very sad time.'

'Sad? Yes, indeed. However, already you've managed to considerably lighten my sister's heavy spirits, so I am in your debt, am I not?' He held her hand a moment longer than was necessary and she looked quickly at him, sensing — something, she didn't know exactly what, she only knew that although his voice was warm enough, his eyes were cool. He smiled faintly as she sat in the chair next to Olivia. 'May I offer you an aperitif? Some dry sherry maybe?'

'Thank you.'

Olivia sat forward. 'Are you feeling better now that you've had a good rest?'

'Much better. I think I would have slept right through until tomorrow morning if Mary had not woken me.'

'How do you find her?' Olivia smiled a little.

'Oh — clammy.'

The smile deepened. 'I told you so.'

'I loathe people who say that. Anyway, whatever else she may be, she really is an excellent maid, and she's very clever with hair.'

'Alice was very particular about her hair — wasn't she, Jonathan?'

His dark eyes were mildly uninterested. 'So it would seem. I gather then, Miss van Allen, that you've had very little sleep since arriving in England.'

Again she caught the edge in him, and this time she sensed that it was connected with her night at Oakleigh Hall. 'The English weather made certain that the last miles of my journey were uncomfortable, to say the least,' she replied, holding his gaze and silently challenging him to come out with whatever was on his mind. But he said nothing more for the moment.

Throughout the fine dinner he was the perfect host. The food was excellent, from the asparagas soup with its delicate flavor to the lamb cutlets served with fresh rosemary, and much as Amy would have liked to taste the apricot tartlets, she was far too full to try even one mouthful. All the time, however, she was aware of Jonathan at the head of the table. He kept the conversation flowing, although there was no mention of Alice or of the missing sapphires. In fact, had it not been for the mourning clothes they wore, there would have been no way of telling from their conversation that the lady of the house had so recently met her death, or that Jonathan Chalbourne had been a widower for less than a week. It was almost as if Alice Chalbourne had never been, although Amy could sense her shadow all around the old house. Amy felt uncomfortable, watching Olivia's studied brightness as she tried to be an entertaining hostess, and Jonathan's cool politeness which made Amy more and more aware that for some reason he had taken a dislike to her — and that that dislike was there because she had spent the previous night under Charles Pemberton's roof.

Jeffreys brought the coffee on a silver tray which he set on a small table by the fire, and the three diners adjourned to the more comfortable chairs. Olivia waved the butler away. 'I will attend to the coffee, Jeffreys, that will be all for the moment.'

'Very well, Miss Olivia.'

Olivia began to pour the coffee into the pink and gold Sèvres cups, and Jonathan looked at Amy. 'Tell me, Miss van Allen, your name is surely of Dutch origin?'

'My great-grandparents were from Amsterdam; they settled in New York. My parents came to Washington when the city was first begun and there have been van Allens there ever since.'

'So, you can remember Washington when it was little more than a few poor hamlets, a great number of alder trees, and vast stretches of swamp?'

She nodded. 'Yes, I recall a childhood spent surrounded by a great deal of mud.'

'My father had occasion to go there in eighteen hundred, when John Adams was President. The White House was at that time still unfenced and the plaster still wet on the walls — and Mrs Adams complained that she had to hang the washing up in the East Room.'

Amy laughed. 'I think he would find that things have improved since then.'

'I know, for I was there myself six years later.'

'You've been to Washington?' She was taken aback, for Olivia had said nothing.

Olivia smiled sheepishly. 'I did not think you would find my brother's political activities very pleasing, Amy, you being so very fiercely patriotic.'

Amy looked at him. 'Political activities, sir?'

'I had occasion to go with a British commission which was hoping to make exploratory soundings concerning a treaty between your country and mine.' Jonathan smiled suddenly. 'I remember that the north wing of the Capitol was on the way to completion, but the roof leaked and the sound carried so badly in the main chamber that many of the speeches were virtually inaudible. But that did not prevent one young man from making an impassioned speech against any understanding with Britain. He thought that the British and the French should be left to squabble in Europe, and America should carry on without either. His name was James van Allen.'

Amy sat back slowly. 'My brother.'

He nodded. 'Our opposing views, however, did not prevent us from taking a very enjoyable dinner together later. I was to have visited your home, Miss van Allen, but I was suddenly sent back to London and had to forego that pleasure. Who knows, we might have come face to face all those years ago.'

'I was staying with an aunt across Washington at that time, sir, so we would not have met anyway.'

'Which, no doubt, you would have found a welcome relief.' His smile faded. 'I was sorry to hear of his death at Bladensburg, Miss van Allen. We were on opposing sides of the fence in many ways, but I enjoyed his company and I like to think that he enjoyed mine. He was a great loss — to you and to his country.'

'Thank you,' she said slowly.

'He was such a fiery and convincing exponent of the Republican anti-British feeling that I was somewhat relieved to discover that he was not to be one of your representatives at the subsequent talks in

London when I returned from America.'

'You were involved in those talks too?'

'Peripherally, no more than that. I became acquainted with your present President, however — would to God he had been President instead of Jefferson.'

Amy sat back at that. 'Do I sniff a challenge in your words, sir?'

'Challenge?' He gave a short laugh. 'No, Miss van Allen, you do not. Monroe was in favor of the treaty which was decided upon and his signature one of the four appended to it — Jefferson chose to sit on that treaty for a year and a half before throwing it out without explanation and deciding instead to escalate matters toward a war. That is why I would have preferred Monroe to be holding the reins at that time, for it would have avoided a totally unnecessary war which merely made life difficult on both sides of the Atlantic and achieved nothing.'

'I do not know that the war was unnecessary,' she replied, 'for at that time the British Navy was seizing an American ship every two days, on the pretext of searching for British deserters. If they found none, they took other seamen instead. It was piracy and the vast majority of the American people were angry about it.'

'We were prepared to make concessions on

the point, Miss van Allen.'

'How vastly benevolent of you, sir. But I wonder how it would be in Britain if we Americans behaved in such a fashion on the high seas? Would the British sit back and want to sign a convenient treaty? Pigs would fly first, I fancy. The so-called concessions in that treaty meant nothing, for any British captain could still behave as he had done before on the high seas; there would still have been impressment.'

'And after the war, Miss van Allen, the eventual peace treaty changed nothing. All those lives lost — for nothing. The war was unnecessary and I have always firmly believed it. It was that conviction which brought about my abrupt decision to end my career in government. I found it singularly sad that two nations, two cousins if you like, could not settle their differences in a more civilized manner. The fault lay on both sides; I do not pretend that Britain was blameless. It was still very sad, though.'

She stared at him, for she had not expected him to say anything like that. She had thought she detected a definite enmity toward America, and yet she had been wrong. But there was still a coolness about him, and it was directed personally at her. He smiled, but the reserve was there, and he talked easily

— but all the time she knew that she had offended him. She glanced at Olivia, noticing the new lightness in her since their first meeting earlier. It could only be because she had been influenced to think again about Charles Pemberton.

Olivia refilled Jonathan's cup. 'So, Amy, after all that I presume that you are still moving in the very highest of Washington circles.'

Amy smiled. 'Where else would you find a van Allen? Such a leading Republican name would hardly be in the lower echelons — even if I am the sole representative of my family now.'

'Oh, I beg your pardon, I'm sure,' giggled Olivia. The wine she had taken during dinner had brightened her whole face and she was feeling almost exuberant for the first time since tragedy had struck the household. Her cheeks were flushed and she smiled a great deal. 'Jonathan, it just could be that Amy's present standing in Washington will one day be considered very small fry — I have a notion that she will one day be America's First Lady.'

His dark eyes moved to Amy. 'You are contemplating marriage, Miss van Allen?'

'Livvy's intuitive guesses are becoming tiresome, sir, for she seems to know what I intend before I do.'

Olivia pulled a face. 'It's a foregone conclusion that you will accept Mr Kenney, Amy — it needed no intuitive guessing.'

'Kenney?' Jonathan spoke again, 'Winfield Kenney, I presume.'

'Yes.'

'I understand that great things are predicted for him; he is a rising star of some magnitude. I congratulate you.'

'Amy, when did you accept him?' asked Olivia.

'I haven't yet. I decided only today that I would, and so I will write to him.'

'And *I* shall be able to say that I'm a close friend of the President's wife!'

'You are rushing things a little,' said Amy, laughing. 'He is far from being President at the moment, and there's many a slip 'twixt cup and lip.'

'Nonetheless, I shall look forward to putting that particular poke on Christabel Bendon's unpleasant little snout! *She* won't be able to claim such an exalted friendship!'

Jonathan put down his cup. 'I hadn't realized you disliked Christabel as much as your present tone would seem to suggest, Olivia.'

Olivia's face was still flushed and she was unwary. 'I find the way she's come over here since Alice's death a little distasteful, if you must know. She comes under the guise of offering comfort to me, but all the time she's hunting for your hide again!'

There was a moment's embarrassed silence and then he smiled faintly. 'I think that's enough said on that point, don't you, Olivia?'

Olivia flushed and Amy quickly asked for another cup of coffee, which Olivia hurried to pour.

Jonathan toyed with the frill at his cuff. 'Miss van Allen, I do not know if you wish to attend this charade tomorrow, but I shall quite understand if you do not.'

'Charade?' What sort of word was *that* to describe his wife's funeral? Amy stared at him. 'I shall attend the funeral, of course I shall, sir.'

Olivia put the coffee pot down suddenly, the unwary flush staining her cheeks again. 'So — so will Charles,' she said, looking straight at her brother.

His steady eyes did not waver. 'Indeed?'

'Yes.'

'Then you, my dearest Livvy, will not. You will remain here, well away from him.'

'But Jonathan — '

'No, Livvy! You'll have no dealings whatsoever with Pemberton, is that not finally clear to you yet? I forbid it absolutely, and if he has the audacity to come to the church, then I'll have him run off my land like the felon he is!'

'But — but he may not have done anything,' whispered Olivia in a small, broken voice, tears glistening in her gray eyes as she stared at his angry face.

He glanced coldly at Amy and then returned his attention to his sister. 'There is no doubt in my mind about his guilt, Livvy, and if you are not prepared to be sensible about this, then the best thing you can do at this very moment is to take yourself to your rooms immediately!'

With a choked cry Olivia got up and ran across the dining room, her black silk skirts rustling. Amy got up to follow her, but he put a hand on her arm. 'Leave her, Miss van Allen.'

'I will not, sir — can't you see how very upset she is?'

'Miss van Allen, *I* am master in this house,' he snapped, 'so, *if* you please, sit down again, for there are things which I wish to discuss with you.'

Slowly she sat down again, suddenly disliking him intensely, and suddenly conscious too of the wide gulf which separated her American spirit from his cool English pride. 'I do not see, sir, that there is anything for us to discuss,' she said in a voice which shook with anger.

'To begin with, there is the matter of your unfortunate sojourn at Oakleigh Hall, a sojourn which has resulted in your considerable interference in matters which do not concern you, madam!'

'Interference?'

'You have seen fit to plead Pemberton's case with my sister, thus causing her to nurture hopes again where he is concerned! How very fortuitous for him that fate brought you to his doorstep, affording him the chance of putting the full, embroidered tale to you, a tale colored with threads of *his* careful choosing and bearing little resemblance to the truth! And you duly arrived here with your carefully learned party-piece, making Livvy doubt again and thereby causing her even more heartbreak than she already endures! I trust you are well-satisfied with yourself, madam!'

She stared at him, silenced for a moment by his outright attack and by the fact that he made no attempt at all at being polite. Then her anger rose again. 'And what, sir, if you are wrong about Mr Pemberton — which God forbid of course, you are always correct, and are a veritable *oracle* of informed knowledge! But supposing, just *supposing* you've made a tiny mistake and are placing the blame upon an innocent man?'

'Have a care, madam, for in this matter I have no sense of humor whatsoever! While you are a guest under my roof, you are forbidden to have any contact at all with Pemberton, or anyone else from Oakleigh Hall! Is that quite clear?'

'It is, and what else is abundantly clear is that being your guest entails bowing to your every wish, no matter how wrong or how arrogant that wish may be!' she cried, knowing that she was breaking every rule in the book of etiquette by losing her temper so completely with her host, but she was unable to prevent herself from standing up to him.

'You are enjoying my hospitality — ' he began coldly.

'*Enjoying* it? You flatter both yourself and your so-called hospitality!'

'You are enjoying my hospitality,' he said again, speaking slowly and deliberately as if to a child, which infuriated her all the more, 'and under that particular circumstance I expect a certain standard of behavior and conduct from you, madam.'

'And what of the standard to be expected from you, sir? Do you always behave in this ill-mannered, despotic way? I am not a scullery maid to be ordered about, nor am I your inferior, sir, and I will *not* be spoken to as if I am!'

'You have already demonstrated to me that you are capable of disregarding the niceties of decent behavior, madam, just as you have demonstrated that you are, to say the least, a snake in my bosom. You've chosen to uphold Pemberton's side of this miserable affair and to put that side to my sister — while at the same time you lodge beneath *my* roof. I fail to see how you can reconcile all these things in any satisfactory manner, Miss van Allen, but no doubt you can enlighten me.'

'If you're wrong about Mr Pemberton, sir, you are guilty not only of casting aspersions upon the good character of an innocent man, but also of ruining your sister's happiness — or does that not occur to you at all, even for the most fleeting of moments?'

'It does not, madam, because I am not wrong about him. If there was any room for doubt, then I assure you that I would not be as implacable as I am.'

'Aren't you *ever* wrong? If you're so perfect, sir, why are you not prime minister instead of Lord Liverpool?' She was close to losing her composure completely, the remnants of her ruffled calm severely agitated by his oblique reference to her traveling unchaperoned. She had been goaded into virtually forgetting every tenet of good behavior and she was painfully aware of the fact. Never, in all her seasons in Washington society, had she been guilty of such poor conduct — and yet a short time in the company of Jonathan Chalbourne had brought her to this sorry pass. She took a steadying breath and looked at him again. 'You have no proof against Mr Pemberton,' she said quietly.

'I need no proof when the facts speak so clearly for themselves.'

'Circumstantial evidence, sir. As a magistrate you must surely know the worth of such evidence — or would you find a man guilty simply because he *could* have committed a crime? Obviously you would — the gaols of Gloucestershire must be full to overflowing with men unfortunate enough to have appeared before you.'

'I think, Miss van Allen, that you fail to grasp the importance of what has happened. Have you *any* idea how valuable those sapphires are? Or how necessary at the moment for maintenance and welfare of this whole estate? I think you have not, for if you had then you would not spout such vapid rubbish! What has happened here during the last week is sufficiently important for me to seek, and indeed strive for, evidence which will convict Mr Charles Pemberton — and, by God, if I can find anything which will put a damned noose around his pretty neck, then I will do so! Circumstantial evidence does not hang a man in this country, madam — I cannot speak for what passes for law in your own land — and I am an honest man, I think *only* in terms of genuine, undeniable evidence! In the meantime, however, I will *not* have Pemberton's nonexistent virtues extolled to this house, and neither will I have you beavering away at undoing the good already done by my sister's ending her engagement to him. Livvy has enough misery to cope with at the moment without you blasted well adding to it!'

'I still believe he is innocent,' she said stubbornly, her voice shaking.

'God *damn* it, woman, I didn't want you here in the first place, but now that you're here I want your solemn word that you will desist from this interference! Now then, do I have that word?'

'Didn't want me here . . . ?' she began, his words settling over her like ice.

'*Do* I have your word?' he interrupted.

'Sir, if you are a prime example of an English lord, then I am sorely sorry for the English people! No, you do *not* have my word. I am not in the habit of giving my promise to people like you, sirrah! It seems to me small wonder that your late wife chose to spend so much of her time in the peace and quiet of her own rooms — as far as she could get from you as possible!'

He said nothing for a moment, turning away sharply. 'And what would you know of that, Miss van Allen?' he asked at last. 'I think, don't you, that this conversation should end right here?'

She closed her eyes, horrified at what she'd said, for no matter how heated the argument had become, she should never have brought up the subject of his painfully unhappy marriage. 'Sir,' she began hesitantly, 'I — '

'Good night, Miss van Allen,' he said coolly, without turning.

The moment of regret evaporated instantly at the chilly dismissal, and she left the dining room without looking back.

Slowly she went up the dark staircase, pausing at the top with one hand on a griffin. She was still shaking a little, and she felt drained of all vitality as the sudden bitterness of her quarrel with Jonathan Chalbourne swept over her like a shock. She had never in her life lost her control or her temper so completely as she had tonight — she was miserable, alone, in a foreign land, and so very far away from her home suddenly. His precise English voice seemed to be ringing in her ears still, and she was conscious of the silence of the house all around her. She longed to hurry to her own room, to curl up in the immense bed, hidden and safe behind the royal curtains — but first she must see that Olivia was all right.

Olivia's diminutive maid, Sally, opened the door a crack as Amy knocked.

'May I see Miss Olivia?'

'I don't rightly know, ma'am — she's that upset still . . .'

But at that moment Olivia's tearful voice came from the room beyond. 'Is that you, Amy?' The words were tearful and muffled.

'Yes, Livvy.'

'Come in.'

The room was larger than Amy's, and furnished in the French style, the colors all various shades of Olivia's favorite pink. The floral wallpaper was soft and pretty, and the thick Axminster carpet picked out the same range of shades. The brightest splash of color in the whole room came from the deep rose satin hangings of the gold and white bed where Olivia lay face down, her black silk dress creased and her hair tousled. Her eyes were red from weeping as she raised her head to look at Amy.

Amy sat on the edge of the bed beside her,

taking one of the cold little hands. Her own troubles paled into insignificance as she saw the deep unhappiness on the tear-stained face. 'How are you now, sweeting?' she asked gently, determining to say nothing of the harshness of her words with Jonathan.

'I don't know any more — oh, why, *why* did I have to blurt out about Charles going to the funeral?'

'It can't be helped now, Livvy.'

'I should have know how Jonathan would be about it.' More tears welled down the pale cheeks. 'After I spoke to you this morning, I thought a lot about Charles, and I knew that after I'd seen him at the church I would want to meet him again. I do love him so, Amy, in spite of everything. I've never loved anybody before — when I was in London I met so many eligible gentlemen, and I had many proposals of marriage, but I didn't want any of them. They left me uninterested and cold, but after my first meeting with Charles I knew that I was falling in love because it was so different.' The cold hand twisted in Amy's. 'He knew Alice before he knew me, and he'd proposed to her. When he met her again she was still very pretty, and also unhappily married to my brother. How will I ever be sure that his love didn't grow again, that he didn't meet her once or twice — that he didn't become her lover? I can't be sure of that, can I? Can I?'

'Oh, Livvy . . . '

'I don't believe for one moment that he was involved in taking the sapphires — that isn't Charles. But what of the other thing? What if he was my sister-in-law's lover? I couldn't bear that, Amy.'

'It's something you have to make up your own mind about, sweeting,' said Amy carefully, mindful of Jonathan's accusation about her interference in things which did not concern her.

'I know. That's why I have a very great favor to ask of you.'

'What is it?'

'I want you to give Charles a note from me tomorrow at the funeral.'

Amy stared at her. 'Oh, Livvy, I don't know about that.'

'Please, Amy! *Please!* Just a little note asking him to meet me somewhere; with you to be my chaperone it would all be perfectly correct.'

In the face of such imploring and heartbreak it was almost impossible to heed Jonathan's warning, but in her heart Amy knew that he was justified in expecting her to refrain from active involvement in his family's affairs. Slowly she got up. 'Livvy, I'm already in your brother's bad books; he and I have had — words — tonight, and I would rather not risk crossing him again while I'm here.'

'You won't help me?'

'Is there anything to prevent you from sending a letter to Oakleigh Hall with the letter carrier?'

'It will take so long! Oh, Amy, I thought that you of all people would help me, especially after the way you defended Charles this morning!'

Amy looked away miserably. 'I know I defended him, and I still do, but Jonathan has expressly asked me not to interfere in any way. I just don't think I could try to slip a note to Charles right under his nose like that, not at a funeral. Please try to understand, Livvy. And surely the letter carrier does not take that long?'

Olivia looked at her for a long moment and then she smiled, squeezing her fingers gently. 'I understand, Amy — I know how Jonathan can be sometimes.'

Amy returned the smile. 'I think I'll go to my room now, I want to write a letter.'

'To inform Mr Kenney of your decision?'

'Damn your intuition.'

'I'm sorry your stay here has got off to such a bad start, Amy. I'll try to be a better hostess tomorrow, I promise. The funeral is early, and

I'm not allowed to go, but maybe afterward we can take a ride together?'

'I'd like that. Good night, Livvy.'

'Good night, Amy.'

But when Amy returned to her room and the silent Mary had undressed her and brushed her hair and then placed the writing implements on the little escritoire in the dressing room, Amy found herself sitting staring at the empty page. She had so much to say, but the words wouldn't come, and she knew that she was still in a turmoil because of her confrontation with Jonathan. Slowly she put the quill down again and closed the silver lid of the crystal inkwell. Maybe tomorrow evening the words would flow more easily — yes, maybe tomorrow . . .

6

The next morning Mary brought Amy's breakfast to her room on a tray. The only sign that for the maid this day was in any way different from all the others was the way her hands trembled slightly as she set the tray on the little table before the newly-kindled fire. Then she went to draw the curtains, snapping them angrily back and standing there for a moment in the bright sunlight which streamed in from the clear morning outside.

'He's ordered that the curtains shall be back during the day already,' she said, her voice shaking.

Amy stared at her from the bed. 'Who has? Lord Chalbourne?'

'Yes.'

Amy said nothing more, for one did not discuss such things with the servants, but even so she was inwardly shocked that Jonathan should order a lessening of mourning on the very day his wife was to be laid to rest.

She sat by the fire, but she didn't have much appetite, contenting herself with only toast and coffee. Outside she could see icicles had formed above the window and they caught the light, shining and glistening like crystal in the early morning. Mary was laying out the clothes Amy was to wear to the funeral, and Amy watched her. She wanted to say something comforting to the woman, but there didn't seem anything suitable — and anyway she doubted if Mary would welcome any such approach. But the trembling was still there in the busy hands which smoothed, plucked, and fussed over the clothes.

After breakfast Amy dressed in silence, and she stood by the window as she pulled on her gloves. A solitary carriage rattled in the stableyard, and she looked at the glass-sided hearse. Its team of two black horses was draped in black, and they shook their heads, which carried filmy black ostrich plumes, and stamped their hooves while the groom held them. A small building at the far end of the yard drew her attention then as the door slowly opened, and for the first time she realized that it was a tiny chapel. Four men carried Alice Chalbourne's coffin across the yard to the waiting hearse.

A slow intake of breath beside her made Amy realize that Mary Danthorpe was watching too. The maid's bright eyes were fixed on the polished coffin, and then without a word she turned and left the room, not

109

asking permission and not taking her leave in any way.

The men eased the coffin into the hearse and one of them then carefully arranged a black pall on top while the others brought several wreaths of white flowers.

Amy left the window then, picking up her reticule and hurrying down the stairs past the griffins. Jonathan was waiting for her by the stone fireplace, his figure swathed in a voluminous black cloak. A black crape weeper trailed from his tall silk hat and he was motionless as she crossed the red and gray floor toward him.

'Good morning, Miss van Allen.' He seemed detached, uninterested.

Memories of the previous evening were sharp for her still, however. 'Good morning, sir,' she said, wondering if an apology would set matters on an easier footing, but his next words dispelled the thought, for his voice was cool and did not invite.

'I trust you will not find my company too odious, for we are forced to travel together in the same landau.'

'I will, no doubt, endure with as much fortitude as you, sir.' She was satisfied that her voice matched his in every way.

'Then, if you are ready . . . ?' He offered her his arm and without saying anything

110

more they walked from the house and out beneath the porch.

A procession of carriages and wagons was drawn up before the house, the servants filing into some, while others seemed already to have their full complement of passengers. The only sound was the shuffling of boots and shoes on the snow-cleared gravel, and the occasional call of the rooks as they soared around the rooftops of the house. Mary Danthorpe stood at the end of the column of waiting servants, a little apart, her eyes downcast, and no one made any attempt to speak to her.

The hearse drove out of the stableyard as Amy was climbing into the completely repaired landau, the crunch of the iron-rimmed wheels sounding unnaturally loud as it drove slowly down the outside of the waiting carriages to take its place at the head of the procession. The wreaths inside bobbed and trembled with the motion, and Amy found herself staring at the black-palled coffin and wondering again about the enigma of Alice Chalbourne. She glanced at Jonathan, but he did not look at the hearse as he took his seat opposite. The footman closed the door then and the sunlight was gone, leaving a half-light as the day tried to pierce the lowered blinds.

Along the valley, as if alerted by some sixth sense, the bell at Chalbourne church began to toll, and the landau lurched as the slow funeral procession moved away from the house. One by one the other mourning carriages followed, until they were all making their slow way toward the great wrought iron gates where the valley narrowed and the River Chalbourne's splashing roar could be heard in the silent landau. Gradually the tolling of the bell became louder and louder, and Amy held the blind aside a little to look out. Silent groups of villagers stood by the roadside, their eyes lowered respectfully as the hearse passed, but there was resentment on their faces as they raised their eyes again to watch Alice's coffin beneath its shivering wreaths. She was as guilty as Charles Pemberton, more so maybe — and she'd betrayed Chalbourne, endangered them all; let her rot . . .

As the carriage came to a standstill at last, the air seemed to throb with the sound of the bell, and the light was blinding as the door was flung open again. Jonathan helped Amy down, and she shook out the heavy corduroy pelisse and adjusted the veil over her face. A long path led from the lychgate between overhanging yew trees, and there was black crape twisted all around the gate itself.

Occasionally some powdery snow drifted down from the yews as the breeze played through them, and at the end of the path by the church's wooden porch, the parson waited, his vestments fluttering. She looked at Jonathan and their eyes met for a moment before he offered her his arm again and they walked slowly up the path.

The church was empty, the air smelling of molten wax and lilies. The sun shone through the stained glass window above the altar, and the colors were jewel-bright and lovely. The organ was playing a funeral march and Amy and Jonathan walked down the aisle to the Chalbourne pew at the front. Amy knelt to pray, but Jonathan did not; he sat silently beside her, staring straight ahead at the altar where the colors lay in shafts across the cloth and the golden vessels. The cross shone, gleaming brightly against the cold gray stone. The servants from the house took their various places behind her, and soon the small church was almost full. Charles Pemberton had not come . . .

The pallbearers carried the coffin in and everyone stood. Amy held her breath for a moment, biting her lip as the organ played the same music which had played at her brother James's funeral. Then she had been so overcome with grief that friends had had to support her, but as she glanced around the congregation, she saw that no one really grieved for Alice Chalbourne. Except Mary Danthorpe, for there were tears on the woman's smooth cheeks, Amy could see them shining behind her lowered veil.

As Amy glanced at the maid, the door of the church opened again and a man's heavy steps sounded on the stone flags. Charles Pemberton walked slowly in and gasps rippled around the church as everyone turned to see who it was. Charles took his place across the aisle, and Jonathan turned then to see why the stir had gone through the servants. Anger leaped swiftly into his gray eyes and he made as if he would leave the pew and cross the aisle to where Charles stood, but Amy put a quick hand on his arm, her fingers digging in urgently.

'This is the House of God, sir,' she whispered, 'Do not profane it.' Still she held him, her eyes anxious as she looked up into his angry face. Gradually he relaxed, turning to face the altar again, and she took her hand away.

The service was short and the parson's address brief and lacking in most of the usual eulogies attendant at such occasions. Amy felt that the poor man was unsure of what to say about Alice, that he felt uncomfortable and restrained officiating at a funeral which should have been a grand and important occasion, but which instead was slipping by almost without a murmur.

When the short service was finished and the coffin was carried out again, Amy put her hand back on Jonathan's arm, seeing the burning anger on his face as he again looked at Charles Pemberton.

'Please, sir,' she said quietly, 'this is neither the time nor the place!'

'Pray do not set yourself up as the voice of sweet reason, madam!'

'The occasion of your wife's funeral is hardly suitable to begin a common brawl!'

'Common brawl, madam?'

'What else would you term it? I tell you this, sir, the settling of your differences with Mr Pemberton here would be considered oafish and unseemly even among the rustics of America!'

He stared at her for a moment, and then slowly he nodded, and unbelievably she thought she saw a trace of humor in his eyes. 'Very well, Miss van Allen, I shall conduct myself with suitable decorum, I promise you.'

They walked out behind the coffin, and Amy was conscious of Charles Pemberton immediately behind them. In the church porch, she glanced around, and he smiled briefly, doffing his black hat politely and then walking past without saying anything. His dark red barouche was waiting at the lychgate, and she watched as he climbed in and the coachman whipped the team up to a smart pace on the road toward the Devil's Elbow.

She glanced at Jonathan. 'Do — do you wish me to come to the graveside with you?'

'If you wish, Miss van Allen.'

'It is hardly a matter of what I wish, sir, it is a matter of whether *you* wish.'

'Then thank you, Miss van Allen, I should be glad of your presence.'

Once and only once during those moments by the graveside did he allow any emotion for Alice to show through, and that was when he bent to pick up the first handful of cold earth to throw over the wooden casket. He hesitated, gazing down at the polished mahogany surface, and everyone waited expectantly. The moments passed and Amy glanced quickly at him, and in that brief second she saw the pain in his eyes — then he swiftly tossed the earth over the coffin and turned on his heel to walk away, leaving the parson murmuring the words, 'Ashes to ashes, dust to dust . . . '

Amy hurried after him and he handed her quickly into the landau. The journey back to

Chalbourne Park was accomplished at a much swifter pace than the outward one. There were clouds in the sky now, and from time to time they hid the sun, turning a bright, sparkling day into one which was suddenly chill and gray. The wind rose a little, too, sighing in the trees and rippling across the rushing surface of the river.

Jonathan leaned his head back, his eyes closed. There was a great weariness in his face, and she thought she saw again the man beneath the studied veneer of fashionable ennui. She wondered about the expression she had seen in his eyes at the graveside. What did he really feel about Alice? He was not immune, not entirely cold toward her, for if he had been, then there would not have been that hesitation, or the hurt and pain in his eyes. No, whatever he felt, it was not hatred or indifference, and that was in spite of all she had undoubtedly been guilty of.

Amy held the blind aside to look out as the landau moved along the driveway toward the house, and so it was she who caught the first sight of the elegant britschka drawn up by the stone porch, its team of matched bays held by a patient groom.

'I believe you have a visitor — or visitors — my lord,' she said.

117

His eyes opened quickly. 'A blue britschka?'

'Yes.'

'Goddamn it,' he breathed, 'On this of all days . . . '

'Who is it?'

'The Earl of Bendon — or more probably just his daughter, Christabel.'

The landau drove the final yards to the front of the house, drawing to a standstill alongside the britschka, and when the door was opened, Jonathan climbed down, turning to offer Amy his hand. His fingers closed unexpectedly around hers for a moment. 'Miss van Allen, would you consider it the better course to forfeit my freedom again, or to forfeit part of my inheritance? Neither course holds much appeal, so which should it be?'

'I — I'm afraid I don't understand . . . '

'No matter, the decision is, as always, mine.' He released her hand.

Lady Christabel had come alone, and she was waiting in the hall on a sofa by the fire. She was tall and graceful, with honey-colored hair and pale blue eyes, and she wore a mauve velvet pelisse and a high-crowned hat adorned with three very flouncy ostrich feathers. The bright smile of welcome she extended to Jonathan became a little fixed as she saw Amy.

Her voice was surprisingly husky. 'Why Jonathan, I would not have come had I realized you had guests.'

'Nonsense, Christabel, I have yet to discover a set of circumstances which would deter you from your purpose.'

The light blue eyes flickered critically over Amy's clothes, as if mentally pricing each item. There was a curve of disapproval on her lips as she met Amy's gaze at last. 'Well now, you must be Miss van Allen.'

'So I must. And you have to be Lady Christabel Bendon.' Amy disliked the simpering smile and the patronizing tone.

The two eyed each other, the dislike flowing equally between them. It was not often that Amy experienced such an instant aversion to anyone, but this was just such an occasion, and she could see by the other's eyes that the feeling was completely mutual.

Jonathan handed his cloak, hat, and gloves to Jeffreys, and Christabel smiled warmly as she went toward him. 'Jonathan, do forgive me for coming here today, but I just felt that I *had* to.' Her eyelashes fluttered seductively and her smile was adoring as she slipped her hands into his.

He returned the smile, leading her toward Amy. 'Christabel, allow me to present to you Miss van Allen of Washington. Miss van

Allen, Lady Christabel Bendon.'

'*Enchanté,*' murmured Christabel.

'Charmed.'

Amy found Jonathan's manner a little disconcerting. His first reaction on knowing that Christabel was calling had definitely not been one of unmitigated pleasure, and now he was suddenly all agreeability. As she watched him, the meaning of his strange question before they had entered the house became abundantly clear — he was considering marrying Christabel, and through her fortune safeguarding the future of Chalbourne Park.

Tweaking the fingers of her kid gloves one by one, Amy looked at the patient butler. 'Jeffreys, is Miss Olivia up yet?'

Christabel turned smoothly before the butler could reply. 'Poor, dear Olivia is indisposed, Miss van Allen.'

'Really — well, I think I'll just go visit 'poor, dear Olivia' and see how she's feeling.'

'She really isn't up to visitors, Miss van Allen,' insisted the other, moving just that little closer to Jonathan as if to emphasize her superiority.

Amy did not deign to say any more. 'If you will excuse me . . . ' She turned and walked away, but Jonathan followed her.

'Miss van Allen?'

'Yes?'

'I feel I should thank you for attending the funeral.'

'There is no need, sir.'

'Will you at least take some refreshment with us?'

She lowered her voice. 'With you *and* sweet li'l ole Christabel? My lord, I believe my feeble colonial stomach would not be able to take the cloying atmosphere.'

'Your claws are showing, madam.'

'And so, sir, are your empty coffers *and* your abysmal sense of decency. And now, if you will excuse me . . . ?'

His eyes were dark with anger. 'Oh, pray do not let me detain you a moment longer than is absolutely necessary.'

Inclining her head coolly, she walked on, and a footman opened the door to the staircase for her.

Christabel's tinkling laughter rang out as the door closed behind her, and she shuddered at the sound. The woman had no shame, no shame at all — descending upon Chalbourne Park on the very day that Alice Chalbourne was laid to rest! A vulture in fine clothing, fluttering down on her prey. *Prey?* Amy pulled a wry face at one of the griffins, for Jonathan Chalbourne hardly warranted *that* description. If anything, he was just as much a vulture as Christabel, fully intending to sink his talons into her inheritance in order to protect his own! They deserved each other. Again Christabel's dainty laughter echoed from the hall. Amy gritted her teeth and gathered her skirts to go a little faster, and when at last she was walking along the passage toward Olivia's room, she could no longer hear the sound.

There was no reply to her knock at Olivia's door, and so she opened it quietly to peer inside. The room was in darkness, the curtains drawn, and it was almost unbearably hot because of the roaring fire which crackled in the hearth, the flames leaping almost up the chimney. Olivia sat on the rug before it, her knees drawn up and her arms clasped around them. She wore a loose white robe and was staring so intently into the fire that she didn't hear Amy until the door closed again. Then she gave a gasp and turned quickly. 'Sally?'

'No, it's me — Amy.'

'Oh — oh, I thought it might be my maid.' Olivia's eyes slid away, and Amy couldn't help noticing how agitated she seemed, although she was striving to hide it.

'Is everything all right, Livvy?'

'Yes — yes of course. 'Oh, if you must know, I'm trying to avoid Christabel. She came up once when she knew I was here, and I had to tell her I was feeling unwell, that I had a dreadful headache — well, I *had* to give some reason for not attending the funeral . . . ' She smiled wanly. 'And now I *have* got a headache, which I suppose is poetic justice for telling fibs in the first place.'

'Is it a very bad headache?' asked Amy, unbuttoning her pelisse and draping it over a chair before sitting on the rug beside Olivia.

'Bad enough. I get them sometimes, especially when I'm worrying about something, and the Lord knows I'm worrying enough at the moment. It will go away in the end.'

Amy accepted the reply, but she was unconvinced somehow, because Olivia seemed so loath to meet her gaze, and she toyed continually with a fold of the white robe.

'Was — was Charles at the church?'

Amy nodded. 'Yes, and a fine stir he caused when he arrived. He left immediately afterward, he didn't come to the graveside or anything like that.'

'How was Jonathan?'

'Furious.'

'Oh, no!'

'Well, I prevented the actual sacrilege of blood being shed in the church, and Charles took himself back to Oakleigh Hall swiftly enough afterward so they didn't actually exchange a word. Livvy — I wouldn't have been able to give him a note anyway, there just wasn't a chance.'

'Note? No, no I suppose not.'

Amy glanced at her curiously, but Olivia stared steadfastly into the fire again, the light moving over her pretty face and burnishing her dark hair until it was almost coppery.

'Have you met Christabel yet, Amy?'

'I have.'

'Isn't she awful?'

'Yes.'

'She'll regard you as a possible rival for Jonathan's affections, and she'll treat you accordingly.'

'I don't think she needs to worry on that particular score,' remarked Amy drily. Nothing could be further from the truth.

'She's not to know that. As far as she's concerned you're beautiful, you're unmarried, and you're not exactly impoverished. She's *bound* to be wary of you. She's very brazen about wanting him, she always has been, even after he'd married Alice. I sometimes think that if she'd been a little less shameless and forceful, then maybe she'd never have lost him in the first place. Jonathan does not like forward women, and Christabel can be very forward at times.'

'I noticed.'

'He's always viewed her with tolerant amusement Until now.'

'What's different now?'

'Well — today is hardly the day to talk of such a thing, I know, but he and Alice meant nothing to each other and hadn't for a very long time, if ever they did in the first place. No one can pretend that he's the grief-stricken widower, not by any stretch of the imagination.'

For a second Amy thought again of the moment of hesitation by the graveside.

Olivia continued. 'One thing and one thing only has ever meant anything to my brother, Amy, and that's Chalbourne Park. He needs capital right now, and he needs it badly if the estate is to be saved in its present form. Christabel is very rich — and she's made it abundantly clear that for Jonathan she is most definitely *available*.'

Jonathan's words on alighting from the landau a little earlier echoed in Amy's head as she watched the flames dancing above the coals.

'Oh, Amy, I can't bear the thought of Christabel being here all the time, being mistress of this house . . . '

'It may not come to that.'

'I pray not.'

They were silent for a moment. 'Have you written your note for Charles, Livvy?'

'I . . . No, not yet.'

Again Amy noticed the oddness in her friend's voice and manner. Something was wrong — but what? 'When does the letter carrier call?'

'Tomorrow. I'll write it in time, I promise.'

'Good. Maybe I'll have written my letter by then, too.' Amy got up, picking up her pelisse. 'I suppose your headache precludes you from taking that ride you promised me?'

The gray eyes swung quickly to her face. 'I'm sorry, Amy, I really couldn't.' Already Olivia's gaze was wavering away though; it was as if she could not meet Amy's eyes . . . 'I think I'll go to bed for the rest of today, and maybe the headache will be cured by the morning.'

'And if Lady Christabel stays, you'd leave me to endure her and your brother across the dinner table by myself?' teased Amy lightly, but she was uneasy. Olivia was behaving very strangely.

'Forgive me, Amy. Please forgive me.'

'It's only a little teasing, sweeting,' began Amy, seeing the sudden tears in the other's eyes.

'I know, but I feel guilty. You've come all this way and . . . '

'Don't worry about it, Livvy, I quite understand.'

'Do you?' whispered Olivia. 'I pray you do, and that you will continue to do so.'

Outside the wind blustered against the windows suddenly, and Amy saw that the sun-shadows on the curtains were no longer as clear and bright. 'I think I'd better take that ride now,' she said. 'It was beginning to cloud over when we returned from the church, and if I wait too long then maybe there'll be no sun left for me to enjoy at all. I'll blow the cobwebs away and then maybe I'll be able to write that letter to Winfield.'

'Give him my regards, won't you?' Olivia was staring into the fire again, her fingers playing constantly with the folds of her robe.

'Yes, I will. I'll come and see you later, to see how you are.'

'I — I intend taking some rosemary tea, it always makes me sleep very heavily, so maybe . . . '

'All right, I'll leave you to do it then. I hope I'll see you tomorrow morning.'

'Yes.'

★   ★   ★

Amy saw nothing of Jonathan or Christabel as she slipped downstairs a little later after taking a light luncheon in her room. She wore a wine-red riding habit, and after the unrelieved black she'd worn since leaving Bristol, the color seemed oddly bright and garish as she caught a glimpse of her reflection in a small mirror. But the Countess of St Victoire had not had the foresight to order a black riding habit, and so Amy's own would have to suffice. At the foot of the stairs she paused — the last thing she wanted was to come across either her host or his other guest . . .

The hall door opened suddenly and she turned with a squeak of fright, relief flooding immediately through her when she saw that it was only the butler, Jeffreys. 'Oh, Jeffreys!'

'Did I startle you, madam? Forgive me.'

'I was wondering — where exactly is Lady Christabel at the moment?'

'She is with His Lordship in the orangery. Shall I show you the way?'

'No! No, I want to avoid her.' Amy decided that honesty was the best policy.

The butler smiled. 'Of course, madam, so if I can be of any help?'

'Can you take me to the stables? Mary should already have informed them that I want a good riding horse saddled.'

'She has indeed, madam. If you will come this way, I think we can safely avoid the orangery.' He bowed politely, standing aside as he indicated a doorway behind the staircase.

She followed him through the kitchens, the buttery, the laundry, various larders, the gun room, and finally the butler's pantry, and thence out into the walled garden she could look down into from her window. The air was cold and fresh outside, the breeze catching the gauze scarf around her beaver hat and fluttering it behind her as she walked. She paused just before they reached the doorway in the wall, for some low, pale flowers were growing up through the snow, their creamy petals looking so delicate and out-of-place in such cold weather.

She bent beside them, removing a glove to touch them, and Jeffreys returned from the doorway. 'They are Christmas roses, madam.'

'How lovely they are, all alone like this.'

'I can have some taken to your room if you wish.'

'No. No, leave them where they are, they'll last so much longer that way.' She straightened, sighing. 'Christmas, and yet I don't think I've ever felt less festive in my life.'

'It is not a joyous season at Chalbourne Park this year, madam.'

'What is it like usually? I mean — what happens?' Amy was suddenly inquisitive about what had happened in the past, when Alice Chalbourne had been alive.

The butler cleared his throat. 'Oh, there was not a great deal of entertaining, madam, but His Lordship always saw to it that the servants enjoyed themselves. He provided food and drink, and he hired traveling players to come and perform for us. And he always arranged for us all to go to the Theatre Royal in Gloucester to see the pantomime.'

'Maybe everything will be the same again this year,' she said, thinking of the speed with which Jonathan was discarding mourning.

'It would not seem right, madam.'

'What did Her Ladyship do?'

'Every year His Lordship would take her to London, and she would buy souvenirs for every servant here at the house.'

'*All* of you?'

'Yes, madam, from myself and Mrs Brocket, the housekeeper, right down to the smallest kitchen boy. No one was left out. She liked to come to give the gifts to us on Christmas Eve, and His Lordship would help her. Christmas was always a good time here, madam, and His Lordship was always so kind and thoughtful with her — that's why we ... Forgive me, madam, I should not speak out of turn.'

'No, go on Jeffreys — that's why you what?'

'That's why we cannot understand why Her Ladyship did what she did, madam. Why did she take the sapphires when she knew that it would almost certainly destroy Chalbourne Park, and that it would hurt His Lordship more than anything else in the world?'

Amy stared at him for a moment, and then the wind rose again a little and the watery sun went behind a small cloud.

'Perhaps, madam, we should go on to the stables, for the weather may not hold.'

'Yes, of course.'

A roan mare was waiting in one of the loose boxes, and a groom was still quickly brushing the long winter coat. He led the mare out when Amy arrived.

'What's her name?' asked Amy, rubbing the mare's velvety muzzle.

'Jasmine, ma'am. She's very spirited, mind, she don't need much telling.'

'I'll remember.'

Jasmine was indeed mettlesome and highly-strung, and her responses to the lightest command were instant and light. She had a springy gait which was a joy to a horsewoman as competent as Amy as she urged the mare across the park toward the wrought-iron gates where the valley narrowed and the trees closed over the way.

The wind was rising all the time as she rode past the first houses of the village, and it made the treetops sway, and a mist of fine white snow was blown above the woods like low clouds trapped by mountains. The long village street was deserted, everyone observing Lady Chalbourne's funeral day in the peace of their own homes now. There were no children playing on the frozen pond and no dogs to yap around the mare's heels as she cantered easily past the churchyard. The hooves clattered on the ice-hard road, the sound echoing around the silent cottages, and from time to time the sucking of the wind brought the smoke down from the chimneys into the street where it stung Amy's eyes and made the mare toss her fine head.

On she rode toward the beginning of the climb up through the Devil's Elbow, and the noisy river swerved away from the road to tumble down between the rocks past the still woolen mills and on toward the distant vale. The sound of the river and the wind seemed to be everywhere as the mare began the slow, tiring climb, and Amy's heart began to beat more swiftly as she reached the Devil's Elbow itself and the land suddenly dropped steeply away down toward the river so very far below. Occasionally she could see the water between the trees, but if she could not see it, then the splashing, thundering roar could be heard all around. A solitary crow wheeled in the air high above, its melancholy call grating on the wind.

The clouds were thickening all the time, and when she glanced up she recognized the familiar yellow-gray tint in them — there was more snow on the way. She thought that she would just have time to ride to the small crossroads a little way past the entrance to Oakleigh Hall, and return to Chalbourne Park before the weather closed in.

She smiled to herself as she urged the mare up the last of the incline past a holly bush which was heavy with swollen, scarlet berries. Christmas was only a short time away now, and yet she hadn't even unpacked her gifts since her arrival. Maybe they'd been damaged during the voyage . . . But somehow, she could not imagine giving any gifts this year, for who would want a souvenir of this particular Christmas? Back in Washington, by now she'd have been in a whirl of excitement, accepting invitations and issuing those of her own; she'd have taken delivery of at least three new evening gowns to dazzle everyone with; and she'd be spending every possible moment she could with Winfield. Instead, she was here, in England . . .

As the mare emerged from the shelter of

the trees, the full force of the wind snatched at Amy's hat and skirts, and the icy air cut through the riding habit as if it were made of muslin. The mare broke into a slow canter, and Amy's cheeks tingled with the cold and with the exhilaration of the ride. She had told Olivia she would blow the cobwebs away, and so she was. There was nothing quite like a ride on a good horse for restoring the spirits and making life seem less wearisome. She urged Jasmine a little faster, and the hooves drummed on the hard road. Two shepherds in one of the fields glanced up. They were sitting by a stone-ringed fire, their dogs beside them, and the sticks they held over the flames speared pieces of bacon for their midday meal. The sweet smoke and delicious smell drifted over the road as Amy rode past, making her feel hungry again in spite of the light luncheon she had taken before leaving.

The gates of Oakleigh Hall loomed ahead, and a short way on she reached the small crossroads she remembered from the night-time journey from Bristol, and she reined the mare in, dismounting to allow the animal a well-earned rest before attempting the home-ward ride. There was an elm tree at the crossroads, its branches winter-bare, and Amy leaned back against the trunk to gaze across the rolling countryside which was so white with snow and so cold, and yet so very beautiful. After the wide openness of the American landscape, this was so quaint, the fields so small and patchworked since enclosure, and the roads so winding and narrow, and so reluctant somehow to get to their destination, as if eager to show off the loveliness of the scenery rather than adhere to their proper function of conveying the traveler from one point to the next in the shortest possible time. Even the hills were small and rounded, softened by time — there were no towering, snow-capped peaks or jagged rocks to pierce the skyline. It was all so rambling and oddly attractive, and so very appealing even in the heart of such a bitterly cold winter. She was an American, proud of her own nation and fiercely patriotic, and so maybe she could understand how Jonathan Chalbourne must feel about this land. Christabel's brittle laughter seemed to carry on the cold winter wind as it blew across the hillside, and Amy lowered her eyes to the frozen earth. Was he really prepared to enter a second unhappy marriage in order to save his inheritance? Was he? She looked up again quickly — why should it matter in the slightest what his intentions were? Why should *she* care anyway? Why should anything Jonathan, Lord Chalbourne, thought, said, did, or intended to do have any bearing whatsoever on the way she felt?

She was annoyed with herself for allowing him to so encroach upon her thoughts, and crossly she gathered Jasmine's reins and remounted, carefully arranging her cumbersome riding habit. Kicking her heel, she urged the mare back along the road toward the entrance to Oakleigh Hall. Just as she reached it, a cloaked figure ran out of the driveway, the cloak flapping wildly, and Jasmine reared, almost dislodging Amy, who clung on in terror. She screamed as the frightened horse plunged once more, but then she regained control and Jasmine became more quiet. The cloaked figure stood as if frozen, and then slowly pushed the hood back, and Amy saw with surprise that it was Sally, Olivia's maid.

'Sally?'

'Oh, Miss van Allen! You terrified me, I thought as you were — were — Her Ladyship's ghost.'

'You thought I was?' Amy was having difficulty keeping Jasmine still, for the mare was anxious to be away from the gates.

'She was riding through here when she . . .'

'I know. But what are you doing here, Sally?'

'I — I've got a young man as works at Oakleigh Hall, ma'am.' The maid avoided Amy's penetrating gaze.

Amy knew when she wasn't being told the truth. 'That's a fib, isn't it, Sally?'

The maid continued to avoid her gaze, and quite suddenly the truth came to Amy anyway. 'You've delivered a note from Miss Olivia to Mr Pemberton, haven't you?'

'No! Oh, *no*, ma'am!' cried the maid, her eyes huge.

'That's too much protesting! You *have* taken a note to Oakleigh Hall!'

Sally stared miserably at her. 'Yes, ma'am,' she said in a very small voice.

So, Olivia's strange behavior was explained; she had a guilty conscience because she'd used her poor little maid, thereby risking Sally's position at Chalbourne Park if Jonathan found out. Although, even so, Olivia's behavior had been very odd. Maybe there had been something more in the note than Amy suspected. 'Sally, what did Miss Olivia tell you about the note?'

'Just that she was asking Mr Pemberton to meet her and you — '

'Me?'

'Yes, she said you'd be there to be a chaperone so that everything would be all right. I took the note there, but Mr

Pemberton is away until tonight; he had some urgent business in Dursley — so I left the note with Mr Gibson, the butler. Oh, Miss van Allen, you won't tell Lord Chalbourne what I've done, will you? Only I couldn't bear to see Miss Olivia so unhappy, and when she asked me if I'd leave the note here on my way to see my mam this afternoon . . . '

'It's not your fault, Sally.'

'I don't think Mr Pemberton did anything bad, Miss van Allen, truly I don't.'

'No, nor do I.'

'Then you won't tell on me?'

'No, Sally, I won't tell.'

'Oh, thank you, ma'am! Only, you see I feel bad about doing what I've done today, on account of it's something Lord Chalbourne wouldn't like one bit, and he's always been a good and fair master.'

Amy felt cross with Olivia — she should be thoroughly shaken for involving her maid like this, and all because she couldn't wait another day for the letter carrier to call!

Sally smiled. 'Reckon if only someone could up and find the necklace, then everything would come all right again, wouldn't it? I mean, the estate wouldn't be in all this trouble and folk would know again that there was work for everyone, and Miss Olivia would be happy again, still getting

138

ready to marry Mr Pemberton like she always wanted to.'

'Yes, finding the necklace again would certainly solve a few problems,' agreed Amy, thinking again of her resolve to conduct her own search for the missing sapphires.

'I think they're still somewhere at Chalbourne Park, if only we knew where to look,' said the maid.

'Do you think they are? Why?' Amy leaned forward on the pommel.

'Oh, don't rightly know *why* I think it, I just do. Any road, I'd best be gettin' on my way to my mam's, or I won't be ready when Mr Jeffreys sends the dog cart for me tonight.'

'Have you far to walk then?'

'No, Mam only lives in that cottage over there.' Sally pointed across the field on the other side of the road.

Amy turned and she could just make out the roof of a small cottage, built close against the lee of the hillside where the Chalbourne valley slope began. She hadn't noticed it before, for it was hidden among the trees.

Sally pulled her cloak more comfortably around her shoulders, glancing up at the skies. 'Reckon we'll have more snow before the day's out. This's been an awful winter so far, first off there was all that rain in

November, and now we've got snow, already. Mam said it'd be a hard winter on account of there was so many berries. Well, good-bye, Miss van Allen, and thank you for saying you'd not tell His Lordship what I've done today.'

'That's all right, Sally. Good-bye.'

Amy watched the little maid hurry across the road, climb a stile over the dry-stone walling, and then almost run across the snowy field toward the cottage. The wind blew icily over the hillside, ruffling Jasmine's mane and making the tree by the gate rustle as Amy rode away.

7

She rode quickly back through Great Chalbourne, for the short winter afternoon was already coming to a close as the dark clouds gathered more and more overhead. When the house itself came into view ahead, she saw that the servants were lighting the heavy brass lamps by the porch so that the bright light shone out into the gray gloom of the December day. It was hard to remember now that only that morning the sun had shone brightly down from a clear blue sky. The wind whined constantly through the naked trees, and as she rode into the shelter of the stableyard, the first flurries of snow were carried spinning through the air.

Amy dismounted and a groom led the mare away, but as she turned to hurry back toward the house, she saw the Bendon britschka standing in one of the coach houses. The coachman was hanging the harness and traces on the wall, and by the swinging light of an oil lamp she could see the freshly groomed team in a loose box. The scene meant only one thing to Amy — the certainty that Christabel was staying and that the evening meal would therefore be an even more strained and awkward affair. The luggage waiting to be carried into the house was proof that Christabel had even had the audacity to come fully prepared for a possible sojourn.

Mary Danthorpe seemed to have recovered entirely from the morning's ordeal, and there was no sign at all on her still face of the tears she had shed for Alice. The maid undressed Amy without a word, laying out the bombazine gown ready for dinner. The way she assumed Amy would wear that gown irritated a little, and Amy decided that for the moment she had had enough of the woman's odd and almost rude ways.

'I will wear the radzimir tonight.'

The eyes didn't flicker. 'Very well, madam.'

'And in future I would prefer to be consulted about what I am to wear.'

'Yes, madam.' Dislike gleamed in Mary's eyes for a moment and then was concealed.

When she was dressed, Amy went to spend the time before dinner with Olivia, but when she reached the bedroom, Olivia was asleep. Amy could see her huddled shape in the shadowy bed as she held the rose satin curtains aside, and she guessed that Olivia had indeed taken some rosemary tea, for there was not the slightest stir in the bed when she whispered her name. 'Livvy?' Amy dropped the curtains back into place. There was a little time yet before the dinner gong would summon everyone to the dining room, and she had no intention of spending any longer than was absolutely necessary with either Christabel or Jonathan — but how to while away those minutes, that was the question. She still had to write her letter to Winfield, but she had already decided to use that as an excuse for not remaining downstairs after dinner. She closed Olivia's door, glancing along the passage to the door which she knew to be that of Alice Chalbourne's room.

Well, Amy van Allen, she told herself, you've been promising to start searching for those sapphires, and now would seem to be as good a time as any.

Returning to Olivia's room, she picked up the candelabra which stood on the mantel-piece, and she carried it carefully along the passage to the other door. The hinges squeaked as it swung open to her touch, and chilly, damp air swept out over her as she paused for a moment. The quivering light swayed and leaped over the pale green damask wall hangings, and flashed on the unlit crystal chandelier as the droplets moved in the sudden draught. She closed the door behind her and looked around the silent room. It was a luxurious room, shining and exquisite, and quite unlike any of the other rooms in the house, for it would not have looked out of place at Versailles and so seemed incongruous in this lonely house hidden in a Gloucestershire valley. The furniture was inlaid with ivory, and there was a magnificent Persian carpet on the floor. The fireplace was of white marble which was carved and gilded with a pattern of rose leaves, and above it was a mirror around which golden cherubs twined. There was no wainscoting in this room, the green damask stretched from floor to ceiling, and there were no beams. A smell of musk hung in the air and the only warmth came from the candelabra. Amy could see her breath in a silver cloud as she walked slowly into the room, the shadows advancing and then fleeing as the little flames fluttered, and the light winked and flashed on the little silver-gilt caskets on the dressing table. Slowly she looked around, almost holding her breath at the splendor of the room, and it was then that she saw Alice's portrait. Holding the candelabra a little higher, she went to look more closely at the woman who was the cause of so many difficulties.

The pretty, youthful face smiled silently

back at her. Madame Secherell had said that Alice Chalbourne was unusual with her dark brown eyes and golden hair, and so she was for the combination was startling and caught the attention. But for all that, the face was characterless. The smile was not one of pleasure, nor was it one of amusement, it was just a smile, as if those sweet lips were permanently curved in that vacantly pleasant way. There was no expression in the lovely dark eyes, no hint of quick intelligence or hidden depths, and the artist's skill had not imbued her with any individuality. Just as all Amy had heard of Alice revealed little or nothing of the true woman, so the face similarly failed to communicate anything to the beholder.

Outside the wind gusted suddenly, and as it moaned through the eaves, Amy shivered, for the portrait's eyes seemed alive as the faint draught made the flames move. With a deep breath, Amy turned away. She had come here to search for the sapphires, not to ponder upon Alice Chalbourne, but where to begin?

Crossing the room to the door of the dressing room, she opened it and looked around the small space. She put the candelabra on the second dressing table, which stood before the misty, night-blackened window where she could see the snowflakes dancing through the

145

air. One wall was entirely taken up with wardrobes, and she opened the first one, looking at the array of fashionable and costly gowns which hung there. She ran her fingertips over the rich fabrics. Jonathan Chalbourne's marriage may not have been a happy one, but he did not stint his wife's dress allowance, that much was for sure. There were delicate cashmeres, silk culgees, shining silver damasins, and fine watered gauze, and even the very latest barege which made Amy quite envious as she lifted the oyster-colored gown down and held it against herself. The golden fringes and spangles glittered in the candlelight, and with a sigh she returned the gown to the rail and smoothed it into place again. It was a magnificent gown, splendid enough to wear at court — and yet Alice Chalbourne had hardly ever left this house . . .

Crouching down by the hat boxes on the floor of the wardrobe, she opened the nearest one. Inside lay a leghorn bonnet, its bright yellow ribbons and posies of artificial daisies as pretty and fresh as if Alice herself had but a moment before removed it and handed it to Mary Danthorpe to put away.

Amy's teeth were chattering with the cold, for the chilly dampness seemed to seep right through to her bones. She opened box after box, but the constantly moving light made it difficult to search properly, and outside the wind was whistling, rattling the windows and making the bedroom curtains move as if someone were hiding behind them. The candle flames smoked and shook, setting the shadows looming all around, menacing her as they suddenly stretched up from nowhere to darken the pale green walls, and then a sudden bitter draught from the bedroom extinguished the candles completely, and a shroud of inky blackness descended over her.

She froze, her heart thundering in her breast. A door closed in the other room, and as her eyes became accustomed to the darkness, she realized that someone was in the bedroom. Another candle flickered in there, the light leaping and dying as whoever it was crossed the room, and then the flame became steady as the candle was set on a table. Silently, Amy crept toward the dressing room doorway and looked stealthily into the room beyond.

Mary Danthorpe stood at the foot of the bed, and the light of the single candle was so feeble that she didn't see Amy's pale face in the doorway. The maid was looking at Alice's portrait.

'Oh, my lady, my lady,' she whispered, stretching out a hand almost in supplication.

'It was all in vain, all in vain . . . What did you do?'

Amy stared at her. Mary continued to gaze at the portrait, her shoulders slumped and her whole bearing one of dejection, but then the dinner gong sounded and the woman stiffened, turning to pick up the candlestick from the nearby table and hurrying out of the room. As the door closed behind her, the blackness returned and Amy could see nothing. For a moment she could not move, but then she felt her way across the room to the door and as she opened it the welcome brightness of the lamps in the passage flooded in.

There was no sign of the maid, and Amy glanced back into the silent rooms. What had Mary meant? What was 'all in vain'? She began to walk along the passage toward the stairs.

The griffins seemed more lifelike tonight, their snarling faces threatening, and beyond everything there was still the sound of the wind as it howled mournfully around the old house. Rearranging her shawl around her shoulders, she began to descend the staircase, nodding to the footman who waited by the dining room door.

The mirror-filled room had only one occupant apart from the butler, and that was

Christabel. She was dressed in a silver muslin gown which clung revealingly in a way which strongly suggested that it had been dampened. Diamonds glittered in her honey-colored hair and a brightly-colored Indian shawl was draped loosely over her arms. Her magnificent shoulders were bare, allowing everyone the full benefit of her flawless white skin, and her lips were curved in a cool smile as she looked at Amy. The dislike born earlier in the day was still there in her haughty, almost contemptuous expression, and as Amy crossed the room toward her, an invisible gauntlet was thrown down.

'Good evening, Miss — er — van Allen.' The voice seemed even huskier.

'Good evening, Lady — er — Christabel.'

Jeffreys bowed. 'Will you take an aperitif, madam?' Amy saw the amusement in his eyes as he looked at her.

'Yes, Jeffreys, some dry sherry, I think.'

'Yes, madam.'

Amy took her seat directly opposite Christabel across the fire-place. The battle lines were drawn as Amy folded her hands neatly in her lap and waited for the first salvo. Jeffreys brought the glass of sherry on a silver tray and then retreated to his position by the sideboard, well out of hearing of any conversation by the fireplace.

Christabel's eyes were hooded. 'Well now, Miss — er — van Allen,' she murmured patronizingly, 'you really *must* tell me all about America and how you manage over there.'

'We've made a little progress since the time of the Founding Fathers, Lady — er — Christabel. I believe we've actually dispensed with the *Mayflower* now. And would you believe, we actually have a road or two these days.'

The aristocratic nostrils flared a little. 'Really?'

'Why yes,' went on Amy, beginning to enjoy herself, 'and we have a navy, but then you British already know that, don't you? I mean, your Royal Navy has come across the American men-of-war from time to time, has it not?' She smiled innocuously, but she felt triumphant. Yes, she thought, the British Navy with all its tradition of superiority over the waves had been forced to have a very healthy respect for its American counterpart during the recent war! Make what you can of *that*, Lady Grisly Belle!

Christabel's fan snapped open crossly and her lips were a straight line. She gave Amy one of her most withering glances, but Amy only smiled even more irritatingly.

The fan wafted to and fro for a moment.

'Miss van Allen, I understand from a friend that Creole women make *the* most excellent ladies' maids. Tell me, is *your* maid a Creole?'

Amy's feathers were unruffled. You know perfectly well that I haven't got a maid, she thought, and I suppose the next shot will be a raised eyebrow! 'My maid?' she answered smoothly, 'Why, no, I do believe she comes from Lincolnshire. She was Lady Chalbourne's maid at Wildmoor, I believe.'

'That's *not* what I mean!'

'Oh. Oh, *now* I follow! You mean the maid you know I haven't got,' cried Amy, sitting back and smiling as if the light had dawned brilliantly over her.

The fan moved so swiftly that it became almost a blur, and the lips tightened until they virtually disappeared altogether. 'Very droll,' said Christabel huskily. 'If drollery is your forte, Miss — er — van Allen, perhaps you can amuse me further with a humorous explanation of your lamentable behavior in spending a night alone and unchaperoned at Oakleigh Hall with Mr Pemberton.'

It was a monstrous insult, deliberately and calculatedly so, but Amy's outward composure remained the same. She slowly swirled her sherry, her lips pursed a little. 'Well, how news does travel,' she said softly. 'And really, you know, you *do* surprise me, Lady

Christabel — as I understand it, you are not in a position of authority here, you are merely a guest, as I am, so I do not see that I owe you an explanation of anything. And I most certainly do not feel any need, not even the very vaguest, to attempt to amuse you. As to *my* behavior being lamentable, well it seems to me that *yours* is hardly likely to excite scholars of etiquette, is it? You are very vulgar, Lady Christabel, *very* vulgar and *very* obvious. I once saw a celebrated demimondaine in a dress such as the one you are almost wearing, but her conduct was in no way as decidedly tasteless as yours. Lady Chalbourne was only laid to rest this morning and yet here you are, out hunting for her husband. You even came with extra clothes. I find that very vulgar, my lady, and I have little doubt that Lord Chalbourne finds it so too.'

The fan clacked shut furiously. 'How dare you! How *dare* you presume to speak to me like that!'

'You set the standard, Lady Christabel, and I merely follow in your well-bred footsteps.'

'I *won't* be spoken to like that! And certainly not by a — a — '

'Lady Christabel, I would advise you not to attempt to better me, for in my time I've taken on the *chiennes* of Washington's drawing rooms, and I've come out on top. A considerable achievement, though I say so myself. You really are not in the same class and will only succeed in making yourself look even more foolish than you already are in that atrocious toggery. Now then, I suggest that we behave with a little more dignity and decorum — if you are tolerably polite to me, then I shall be tolerably polite to you. That way you can devote the rest of this evening to attempting to win Lord Chalbourne's affections — you can flutter your eyelashes, whisper seductively in that odd voice of yours, and heave your considerable bosom to your heart's content. I promise to *try* not to laugh if your conduct becomes a little too ridiculous, truly I do.'

Christabel trembled from head to toe and her face was hot and bright with impotent fury. She had thought Amy would prove to be easy to dispose of, and exactly the reverse had proved to be the case.

Amy sipped her sherry, rolling the pale golden liquid deliciously around her tongue and taking a sweet delight in watching the myriad expressions which moved over the other's crimson face. Perhaps that will teach you to keep your unpleasantness to yourself in future, she thought savagely. That's one up to the Stars and Stripes if I'm not mistaken.

At that moment the door opened to admit

Jonathan. He wore a dark gray velvet tailcoat and pale gray trousers, and his waistcoat was peacock blue, and as he walked toward the two women, Amy was conscious quite suddenly of just how very attractive a man he was. Handsome, rich, titled, and eligible — what more could any woman want if she was searching for the perfect man?

He bowed before them. 'Good evening, Miss van Allen,' he said politely, 'Christabel.'

Christabel struggled to regain her lost calm, returning his greeting in an oddly strangled voice. 'G-good evening, Jonathan.'

'Is something wrong?'

The pale blue eyes shot a venomous glance at Amy. 'No, nothing's wrong.'

He looked quickly at Amy's bland face, his expression suspicious, but she smiled and raised her glass. 'Good evening, my lord,' she murmured sleekly, and she could almost hear the purr in her voice as she gloated over the complete devastation of Grisly Belle's poise.

Jeffreys bowed to them. 'Dinner is served, my lord.'

'Very well, Jeffreys.'

Christabel was beginning to recover, leaning on Jonathan's arm as he escorted her to her seat and allowing her hand to linger on his sleeve for just that moment too long. Amy looked away in disgust — how could any woman be *that* obvious?

Jonathan returned to escort Amy. There was a faint amusement in his eyes. 'Do I detect an overpowering air of easy *camaraderie* between you and Christabel?' he asked softly.

'Well now, you really just might — but if you blink you'll probably miss it.'

A footman brought a silver tureen of mulligatawny soup and Jeffreys began to ladle it out.

By the time they were halfway through the first course, Christabel's former aplomb had fully returned, and she set about deliberately excluding Amy from the conversation by the elementary ruse of constantly referring to people about whom Amy knew nothing. Jonathan brought the conversation back to more general topics each time, and Amy meekly sipped her soup, enjoying watching Christabel struggle. Christabel's dislike flowed across the table to the almost silent figure in black radzimir, but her hopes of disturbing Amy's equilibrium were disappointed. Amy sipped the soup and smiled from time to time, knowing perfectly well that she was getting under Grisly Belle's skin more and more with each passing minute. Jonathan glanced at Amy and their eyes met, and she could see the hint of humor in his face.

At last Christabel could not bear it any longer, she *had* to try to belittle Amy somehow. 'I must say, Miss — er — van Allen, that I do so admire how well you've managed with that gown.'

'Managed?'

'To make it a little — different.'

'Different?' Amy put her spoon down carefully and sat back. 'In what way exactly?'

'The Brussels lace, of course. It's so difficult, I would imagine, to vary a gown made of so popular a fabric as *ras du more.*'

'*Ras du more?* I was under the impression that it was called radzimir.'

'That is the common term for it, I grant you,' purred Christabel, 'But I do so much prefer the old name for it.'

'How quaint.'

The pale blue eyes flickered. '*Ras du more* for mourning has become a positive bore, don't you think?'

'Oh, indeed I do, Lady — er — Christabel, but then beggars cannot be choosers and I, unfortunately, was in the role of beggar when it came to acquiring suitable mourning on my arrival here. I would never have chosen radzimir myself, it is such a common and vulgar fabric, but then I understand that the lady for whom the toggery was made was herself common and vulgar.' Amy's voice became rich and creamy as she prepared for Christabel's final extinction. 'Only someone of very low character would be forced to flee the country because of bad debts, and that is just what that *dreadful* Countess of St Victoire did, would you believe?'

Christabel's face reddened. 'The Countess of St Victoire?'

'Did I say that? Oh, how very lax of me to go mentioning names. Do you know her? Only you seem to know so many people I do not, that it is quite possible that you've been forced at some time to converse with such a *low* person.'

'She is my aunt,' said Christabel frostily.

'Really? Oh, how very embarrassing for you! One can choose one's friends, but one cannot choose one's family, can one? Still, I have your aunt to thank for this gown, and although I agree with you that it is somewhat common, I still feel I should be grateful to her.' Amy smiled sympathetically, picking up her spoon again. 'This really is delicious mulligatawny, Lord Chalbourne, your cook is to be congratulated.'

There was the merest pause. 'Thank you, Miss van Allen.'

'Not at all — credit where credit is due, sir.'

Christabel slowly put her napkin down beside her unfinished soup. 'I really don't think, Jonathan, that I feel able to continue dinner when my family name has been so grossly insulted.'

'Christabel . . . '

Amy glanced up. 'But my lady, *I* did not criticize the Countess's taste — if I recall correctly, you did.'

Jeffreys had no time to pull Christabel's chair back, and it scraped as she stood. '*If* you will excuse me, Jonathan.'

He got up hastily. 'Christabel . . . '

'I'm going to my room.'

He turned to Amy. 'Miss van Allen, I . . . '

Amy smiled sweetly. 'Oh, my manners again. Good night, Lady Christabel.'

In a flurry of furious silver muslin, Christabel marched from the room, and the hapless Jeffreys had to run in order to open the door for her.

'And you *look* as if butter would not melt in your mouth, Miss van Allen,' murmured Jonathan, looking down at her.

'I *was* quite good, wasn't I?'

'Vitriol masquerading as milk and honey.'

'When I'm bitten, I bite back.'

He sat down again. 'Madam, you don't bite — you savage.'

'She asked for everything she got.'

158

'No doubt.'

'*Absolutely* no doubt.'

'It's your capacity for going in for the kill which astounds me most.'

'A mildly wounded Christabel obviously does not learn — *ergo* a virtually slaughtered one will think twice before attempting the same foolish mistake again.'

He seemed amused. 'That is a somewhat doubtful philosophy, Miss van Allen.'

She was silent for a moment. 'Very well, if we're criticizing philosophies, let us consider yours for a while.'

'I have no philosophy.'

'Yes, you do.'

'Pray enlighten me then.'

'You're of the belief that the continuance of this estate in its present form is worth everything. At any price. Even a second lousy marriage. *That*, sir, is a most doubtful philosophy if ever I came across one.' She held his gaze. Had she gone too far? 'Shall I retire now, my lord, or shall I wait for your command?'

'Miss van Allen, you appear to possess more knowledge about my future plans than I do myself. Am I to presume that you think I intend making Christabel my second wife?'

'Yes.'

'Very well, let us inspect that in more

detail, shall we? Christabel is rich and very well-connected.'

She smiled at that. 'Not entirely well-connected, sir. We must not forget the rather doubtful Countess of St Victoire.'

'I think we may dispense with the Countess for the remainder of the evening, Miss van Allen, for the poor woman's name has been maligned more than sufficiently already. Whatever else she is, she is a woman of exquisite taste where clothes are concerned — taste to which that excellent gown you are wearing more than bears witness.'

'I am already aware of that, sir.'

'I realize that you are, Miss van Allen, for a woman like you would not deign to wear anything less than perfect. Indeed, I would go further and say that that gown becomes you more than it would the Countess, for she does not have the benefit of your magnificent red hair to set it off.'

The unexpected compliment took her aback slightly. 'Why — I thank you.'

'Not at all, Miss van Allen — after all, credit where credit is due.'

She looked suspiciously at him then.

He leaned back in his chair. 'So, we are considering a hypothetical marriage between Christabel and myself. As a proposition she has much to commend her — she is not only very rich in her own right, she is also from an extremely blue-blooded family and is therefore accepted everywhere, the court not excepted. She also happens to dote on me and is flatteringly faithful. Those points would all have to be placed to her credit, would you not say?' There was a faintly mocking smile on his lips. 'So, in her I would have an adoring, obedient, exceedingly wealthy, and exceedingly malleable wife.'

She stared at him, her anger sparking into instant fire. '*Malleable?* Oh, there speaks the pompous, overbearing, conceited male of the species if ever I heard him! Sir, you need a servant, not a wife!'

'Miss van Allen, we are discussing a purely supposed match — please do not allow emotion to color your otherwise superb judgment.'

'You and she deserve each other, sir — I wish you well.'

He ignored the remark. 'So, given that I intend proposing to her, then I rather think that there are a sufficient number of benefits to be gained to justify what you are pleased to term 'my philosophy.' '

'A philosophy which requires sufficiently lowered standards in order to accommodate it but, all must surely be well, for on the present evidence your standards are obviously

161

capable of the required depth.'

He was reasonable. 'I merely point out, Miss van Allen, that *if* I decide that 'a second lousy marriage' is necessary, then indeed I must give due consideration to Christabel.'

'Then you had best take yourself to her right now, to soothe the undoubted pet she is in and to do all you can to placate her and make certain that she remains available if necessary in the future!'

'My dear Miss van Allen, I think I can safely leave all the pursuing to Christabel, don't you?' He smiled infuriatingly. 'However, we are digressing a little from the main point of this exercise. We were discussing what I would be prepared to do in order to secure the future of my estate. Very well, if it is a wealthy wife that I need, then maybe I should look no further than yourself.'

She sat back. '*Me?*'

'Well, why not? After all, you have all the qualities necessary — you are beautiful, wealthy, of excellent family, and you are available.'

'Sir, maybe I should point out that the availability does not extend to you.'

He continued as if she hadn't spoken. 'But you are also some-what forthright, headstrong, outspoken, and endowed with fearsome claws — so maybe I could not face that prospect with the necessary fortitude.'

'In other words, my lord, you are afraid of a woman who can think for herself and stand up for herself. Well, I suppose I can understand the insecurity and timidity which obviously result from an inherent weakness in your character. But if you feel you lack the necessary fortitude, then let me assure you that even my *considerable* fortitude could not uphold me if I should ever find myself unfortunate enough to be your wife. You do not arouse any of the necessary instincts in me, sir, whether that instinct be one of acquisition, predation, or anything else! I could *never* become your obvious ideal of meek, servile womanhood, scurrying around in a futile attempt at anticipating and accommodating your every mood! Nor could I rush constantly to satisfy your male self-esteem by complimentary words, admiring glances, and general abject groveling. And finally, I could not then face the thought of having to creep submissively into your bed at nights, whether merely to warm the sheets for you or to perform any other conjugal duty!' Her face felt hot; and she knew that she'd again allowed herself to be goaded beyond the bounds of propriety when she'd made that last remark. She looked away quickly, angry with herself and angry with him. In

Washington she was one of the undisputed first ladies, renowned for her poise and mettle, and yet this one man, this *Englishman* seemed so easily able to disturb her calm, and able to stir the fiery van Allen temper which was usually under such precise and rigid control. Damn him! *Damn* him!

He gazed across the table at her, toying a little with the ring on his finger as he smiled. 'What a vastly entertaining vision you conjure in my mind, Miss van Allen, but I do not see you creeping anywhere submissively, least of all into my bed.'

Her flush deepened. 'Should — should we not continue with dinner before the cook decides to leave?'

'By all means, do let us continue dinner.'

★　★　★

Later she sat before the escritoire in her room trying to begin the letter to Winfield, but the quill lay untouched beside the equally pristine sheet of writing paper. She stared thoughtfully at the gently moving candle-flame, listening to the howl of the wind beyond the window, and then she got up slowly, pulling her wrap closer around her shoulders. Holding the curtain aside at the window, she stared out. Her reflection gazed back at her from the blank, black glass, her hair very red as it tumbled past her white-clad shoulders. She had tried to write to Winfield, but she couldn't, and again it was because of Jonathan Chalbourne. On the previous occasion it had been because she was too upset and angry after their argument on her first night, but this time it was because she was too disturbed. Why she allowed him to affect her so she didn't know, for he was everything she most loathed in men.

She turned away from the window, and immediately her glance went to something white on the floor by the door. Crossing the room she picked it up. It was a folded square of paper with her name written hastily on it in Olivia's writing.

Slowly she unfolded it. '*My dearest Amy, Please find it in your heart to forgive me for deceiving you, but I cannot bear it any more. I am going away with Charles. I love you so and I know I have done badly by you, but I pray you will understand — even eventually forgive. Yours, with deep and sincere afection. Olivia.*'

Amy stared at the note, a sudden coldness going through her veins. The note Sally had delivered, it had contained so much more than a mere assignation . . . At that moment she heard the sound of a horse's hooves on the cobbles of the stableyard, and she ran across the room to the window again, opening it quickly to look out. A solitary saddle horse was being led across the yard, and by the light of a swaying lantern on the corner of a store, she saw a heavily hooded and cloaked figure preparing to mount. A sudden gust of wind lifted the hood and it fell back from the figure's face. There was no mistaking Olivia's heart-shaped face and short dark hair.

'Livvy!' cried Amy desperately. 'Livvy, come back!'

The figure turned quickly, staring up at Amy's window, and then Olivia hurriedly mounted, urging the horse beneath the clock tower and out into the wildness of the stormy, winter night.

'Livvy!' called Amy again, leaning out of the window so that the snowflakes clung to her face and hair, but her voice merely drifted into the empty darkness where the snow muffled the sound of the horse.

Sally was standing in Olivia's room, her cloak still on as she gazed at the carefully placed bolster in Olivia's bed. She turned, her face terrified as she heard Amy come in. 'Oh, Miss van Allen,' she whispered, 'she's gone! Miss Olivia's gone!'

'It was the note, Sally, it can only have been the note. I'll have to tell Lord Chalbourne.'

'Not that it was me, Miss van Allen! Oh, please, don't let on as I done anything like that!'

Amy stared at her for a moment and then turned to run along the passage toward Jonathan's room. At his door she hesitated — knocking might arouse Christabel, whose room was only a little way further on. Deciding immediately, Amy pushed the door open and went in.

'Here, ma'am, you can't come in here!' cried the outraged valet, who hurried through from the bedroom. 'This here's a gentleman's room!'

'Then will you kindly inform Lord Chalbourne that I wish to speak with him and that it's urgent? Well, get on with it, man, or I'll go in there myself!' Amy's heart was thundering and she glanced through the inner door at the clock on the wall. The pendulum swung slowly to and fro, and with each swing it took Olivia further and further away.

Jonathan came through the door, tying a green brocade dressing gown around his waist. 'Miss van Allen? What on earth . . . ?'

'It's Olivia, she's run away.' She held out the note.

His face was still as he took it, and when he'd finished reading he looked coldly at her. 'And how did she manage to make the necessary arrangements?'

Sally's frightened face flashed before Amy's eyes for a moment. 'I took a note to Oakleigh Hall for her this afternoon when I went for my ride,' she said, meeting his gaze with her chin raised defiantly.

'God *damn* you for your presumption!'

'She hasn't long gone — only about five minutes. We can still catch her.'

He nodded at the valet 'Get my riding things ready, James, and then rouse some of the more trustworthy grooms. I'll take a search party with me. And be discreet, I don't want Lady Christabel, her maid, or her damned coachman to discover what's happened.'

The valet nodded. 'I understand, sir.'

Jonathan looked at Amy again. 'I trust you're satisfied now that your interference has achieved my sister's certain ruin, madam!'

Amy said nothing.

'What in God's name do you imagine awaits her now? What manner of man would stoop to *allowing* her to run away with him like that? A saint? A reliable prospect as a husband? And what price her good name if Christabel should sniff out tonight's work? Go to your room, madam, I think you've more than caused enough trouble by your activities, don't you?'

She stared at him. 'I intend coming with

you,' she said firmly, her chin raised defiantly.

'No, Miss van Allen, I want you as far as possible away from me for the time being!' he snapped, turning on his heel and walking back into the other room, leaving her standing there.

She ran back toward her own room, not sending for Mary Danthorpe to help her but merely putting on her heaviest winter cloak and some ankle boots. She pinned her hair back from her face and then pulled the cloak's hood up before running from the room again and down through the kitchens where the startled staff watched her in silence as she opened the outer door and ran out into the night.

Her boots crunched on the snow-covered path as she ran across the dark garden, through the door in the wall to the stableyard where already the small search party was mounting. Torches flickered on the cobbles, the light falling across the piles of cleared snow and across the fluttering flakes as they continued on their endless twisting, curving dance through the darkness.

She caught a groom's arm. 'Saddle me a horse, if you please.'

'You're going with them, ma'am?' His mouth dropped.

'I am, so if you please — a saddled horse!'

She was mounted when at last Jonathan reached the stables, and as he took the reins of his own horse, he did not see her at the back of the small group of waiting horsemen. But as he mounted, some of the torchlight fell on her and he turned his horse angrily.

'I thought I made myself clear!'

'You did, but I fully intend helping to look for Livvy, sir, and each moment you spend arguing with me merely takes her further and further on her way!'

He pressed his lips angrily together, and then he flicked the reins of his horse, riding out beneath the clock tower and across the park in the direction of Oakleigh Hall.

Olivia's tracks were still visible in the torchlit snow, but already the storm was softening the outlines, filling in the cavities, and disguising the fact that a horse had passed that way at all. The torches flared and hissed, their light picking out stark branches and trunks, and the snow was driving into their faces as they rode slowly through the dark night. Behind them the lights of the house were hidden from view now, and the winter night closed around them, flapping at Amy's cloak and dragging at her hood so that it soon flew back from her head and her hair tumbled down from its pins and streamed wildly behind her.

The snow flew against her eyes and mouth and she was shivering with cold when at last Jonathan reined in, dismounting to inspect the tracks which were fast disappearing beneath the heavy flakes. 'She's changed direction, she's not riding toward Oakleigh Hall any more. Able, you take Matt and Bob to Oakleigh Hall just to make certain, the rest of us will continue to follow the tracks.'

'Yes, my lord.' Able turned his horse toward the southeast, followed by the two others, and Jonathan remounted, continuing on the southerly course which Olivia's tracks now took.

For a long while the horses trudged through the snow, until at last the tracks finally vanished beneath the fresh fall and nothing could be seen in the light of the torches. Jonathan halted again. 'It's no use, we can't go on without knowing if we're going in the right direction or not.'

Amy looked quickly at him. 'But we can't just give up!'

'What would you suggest then?' he snapped angrily, 'That we trust she keeps to the present course? Don't be foolish, Miss van Allen, we cannot hope to find her without tracks to follow, and even you must have noticed that the storm is getting worse with each moment now.'

171

She glanced around at the wild night where the wind shrieked through the trees and the snow was blown almost horizontally through the ice-cold air. 'We can't leave her like this,' she cried, tears filling her eyes as she gazed at him. 'We can't!'

'We have to — to carry on now is to risk our own lives. Now then, turn your horse around, madam, or as God is my witness, I'll use force to make you do as you are told!'

Tears were on her cheeks as she obeyed him, and as the tired horse turned at her command, the wind was suddenly behind them and it was easier to ride. Her hair fluttered damply across her cold face now and her cloak lifted around her shoulders to reveal the flapping whiteness of her night robe, and she could feel the snowflakes as they touched her bare legs. Her teeth were chattering when at last the lights of the house appeared through the trees ahead, and the horses picked up their pace to move those last yards between the wind-torn trees toward the haven of the stableyard.

The other half of the search party had already returned from Oakleigh Hall, and the man called Able was waiting. 'My lord?'

'Is there any news?'

'No, my lord. Mr Pemberton left Oakleigh Hall immediately he had been given Miss

Olivia's note, and he'd been gone ten minutes when we got there. He took his barouche, and we lost his tracks by the main gates to Oakleigh Hall because the doctor's gig and another coach had passed within several minutes and we just couldn't make out which was which. He must have driven back along the crossroads, but after that we don't know where he went, my lord.'

'You're sure you were told the truth?'

'Oh yes, my lord, the butler Mr Gibson is by way of being my cousin, and he'd not dare lie to me about sommat this important — he knows as it's more'n his fool life's worth.'

Jonathan dismounted heavily, handing the reins to a waiting groom. 'Thank you, Able, we'll go out again in the morning.'

'Ah, mayhap someone saw Miss Olivia, or saw the barouche . . . '

'Yes. Maybe. Good night, Able.'

'Good night, my lord.'

The man touched his cap and walked away, vanishing quite suddenly in the flurries of wild snow which swept constantly across the yard. The cobbles were covered with a sheet of white again, and as soon as it was light, everything would have to be cleared again.

Jonathan reached up to help Amy down, and he looked swiftly at her cold, pinched face when he felt how icy her hands were. As she slipped down from the saddle, the wind caught her cloak, lifting it to reveal the flimsy white robe beneath, and beneath that the bareness of her legs. 'God above, woman, you've come out in your undress!'

She stared at him without answering. His face seemed to swim before her and she couldn't really concentrate on what he was saying. Quickly he took off his coat and put it around her, and then with his arm tightly around her waist, he helped her back through the walled garden and into the house.

Jeffreys followed them to the drawing room, hurriedly tossing fresh logs on the dying fire as Jonathan led Amy to a chair. 'Bring some caudle, Jeffreys.'

'Yes, my lord. Did you find . . . ?'

'We couldn't follow the tracks any more. Pemberton's gone too, though, we ascertained that much.'

'I'm sorry, sir.' The butler looked sadly at him, and then left the room to bring the caudle.

Jonathan tossed his coat aside and removed Amy's damp cloak, before kneeling before her and rubbing her frozen hands in his. 'Are all American women as mulish as you, Miss van Allen?' he asked gently. 'Or are you completely unique?'

The numbness still gripped her, deadening

her responses so that she could only look at him. He became anxious, reaching out to put his hand to her cheek. 'Miss van Allen?'

His hand seemed to burn suddenly on her skin, a hot flame which dispelled the numbness as if it had never been. His gentle words and manner were so different, so at odds with the way he had been until now when with her that it came as a shock. With sudden insight she knew that this was how she had wanted him to be, she had wanted gentleness and warmth from him. Startled at the force of her own unexpected reaction to him, she stared into his face without a word.

Disturbed by her continued silence, he took his hand slowly away. 'Are you all right?'

'Mm?'

'Are you . . . ?'

'Yes. Yes, I'm all right.'

He got up. 'There's only cognac in here, would you . . . ?'

'No. But please, you have one if you wish.'

She watched him as he went to the decanter. How could she not have realized before the truth of how she felt about him? How could she have been so blind to the reason for the flare of anger he always wrought in her? It was a moment of clear self-knowledge, an explanation for her inability to write to Winfield Kenney, although she had tried so hard. How could she write to Winfield when all the time she was attracted so fiercely to this other man? How could she even think of accepting Winfield when it was Jonathan Chalbourne she wanted? Desire had flared into life from that first moment, and she had denied her own feelings, stubbornly refused to see the obvious, and closed her eyes to the real reason why she was so aware of him, why every nerve was so alert to everything he said or did. The hopelessness and irony of the situation would have made her laugh had she not been so utterly miserable as she watched him. She had come halfway across the world only to fall for this one man, this Englishman who so obviously felt none of the emotions which now tumbled so distressingly through her. Oh, Amy van Allen, she told herself, you fool, you *fool* . . .

He returned to sit wearily in the chair opposite her, lounging there with an easy grace in spite of his tiredness. He smiled. 'Your silence confused me, Miss van Allen, I have come to expect sparks, not a faint glow.'

'I will endeavor not to disappoint you again.'

Jeffreys returned with the caudle, but first he went to Jonathan with a charred piece of paper. 'Excuse me, my lord, but the maid Sally found this on the hearth in Miss Olivia's room. She believes it was originally placed on the mantelpiece but that it fell down in a draught. It's in Miss Olivia's handwriting and it's addressed to you.'

Jonathan took the paper and carefully unfolded it. Amy accepted the hot silver goblet of caudle, watching Jonathan's face as he read his sister's note. 'It seems Olivia has run away to a distant cousin of ours in Oxford.'

Amy stared. 'She's actually said where she's going?'

'She's said where she would have us *think* she's going!' He screwed the paper up angrily, tossing it into the fire where it blackened and curled, rows of tiny ruby sparks glittering and flashing around its edges before the heat of the fire sent the flaky ashes fleeing up the chimney. 'If she had wanted to visit Oxford, she had only to ask. I know my sister well enough to guess that Oxford is not her destination, but I dare not act on that assumption. I'll have to go there in the morning if the weather allows any travel. God *damn* her for her foolishness! Jeffreys, that will be all for tonight — if you could just inform Daniels that I shall require the landau immediately after breakfast in the morning?'

'Very well, my lord.'

'And I still wish to keep Lady Christabel as

unaware as possible that anything is wrong.'

'Yes, my lord. I have taken the precaution of setting a maid to watch her room, but so far there has been no sign that Her Ladyship is aware of anything untoward.'

'Well, that's one small mercy, at least.' Jonathan's tone was heartfelt. 'Good night, Jeffreys.'

'Good night, my lord. Good night, Miss van Allen. I trust that you will feel a lot better by the morning.'

'So do I, thank you, Jeffreys.'

When the butler had gone, Amy sipped the hot brew of wine, cereals, and saffron for a moment. 'Do — do you want me to come with you tomorrow?'

'Come with me? I hardly — '

'It's just that if Livvy *is* in Oxford, she may be upset, distressed, and might be glad of the comfort of another woman.'

'As distinct from that of a bear of a brother?'

She smiled faintly. 'Something like that.'

'I thank you for the kind thought, Miss van Allen, but I would rather you remained here. I intend to be gone before Christabel rises in the morning, and I wish things to appear as normal as possible. If you hurry off with me in such a strange manner, she is bound to wonder what is going on.'

'You don't really think Lady Christabel would spread rumors about Livvy, do you? I mean, Livvy's *your* sister!'

He swirled his cognac for a moment. 'Miss van Allen, we earlier discussed Christabel's attributes, but now I am talking of what is definitely one of her worst points. She cannot keep a close tongue in her head, and she would rattle about my sister's antics until the whole of Gloucestershire was rattling too. There is still a chance that my sister's good name and character can be salvaged, *if* she can be rescued with only those I can trust being aware of what has happened. I would like you to — er — entertain Christabel in my absence.'

'*Me?*'

He smiled. 'At least I fancy I can be sure that Christabel will not remain a moment too long, especially if you inform her that I intend to be away for several days. If she believes that, and that Olivia is still indisposed and in bed, and that she will have only your company to look forward to, then I think she will take herself back to Papa as swiftly as possible.'

She took a long breath. 'I don't know if I should seek a compliment or an insult in that, sir. However, I'm glad I can be of *some* service to you.'

'I'm trying to protect my sister's reputation, Miss van Allen. Her association with Pemberton may not yet have ruined her, and so there is a chance that she will still make a good match one day if I can do all I can now. I think you too have only her welfare at heart, so I ask you if you will do this for me.'

'In spite of my lack of cooperation hitherto?'

'I didn't say that.'

'No, but it's what you're thinking. I'll do as you ask, my lord, for Livvy's present predicament is undoubtedly the result of my interference and unwise counsel. And on top of that, I'm conscious too that you've not wanted my presence here in the first place, so my sins in your eyes must surely be doubled.'

'Please, Miss van Allen, don't remind me of my gross ill manners. I shouldn't have said what I did, not even in the heat of the moment.'

'Words uttered in the heat of the moment are frequently the truth, sir, and you were speaking the truth that night.'

He looked at her for a long moment without speaking, and then he put down his glass. 'Miss van Allen, I was speaking the truth, I admit it, but my reason for not wanting you here was nothing I held personally against you, believe me. How could it be when I did not know you? Please forgive me for what I said.' He paused, and she remained silent, knowing he was going to say more. His gray eyes swung to meet hers again. 'I've always discouraged people from visiting Chalbourne Park — because of Alice. My wife's — health — did not permit her to lead a strenuous social life.'

'I understand,' she murmured, knowing that there was a great deal he had left unsaid about Alice. She got up. 'Well, I think I had better go to bed now. Otherwise I will not be fit to take Christabel on in the morning.'

He smiled, standing and taking her hand. 'I think the verbal mauling she received at dinner will keep her in line, Miss van Allen.'

She turned to leave, but then halted. 'How long will it take you to reach Oxford, do you think?'

'If I leave early tomorrow morning, I trust I will have returned by this time tomorrow night.'

'Even if it is that late, you will come and tell me if there's any news of Livvy, won't you?'

He nodded. 'I promise that I will, Miss van Allen.'

'Good night.'

'Good night.'

8

'Has Lord Chalbourne left yet, Jeffreys?'

The butler turned from the sideboard as Amy entered the breakfast room the next morning. 'He has indeed, Miss van Allen, and he charged me to tell you that he had not forgotten and that he would come to see you directly he returns.'

'And Lady Christabel has yet to come down, I take it?'

'That is correct, madam, but she sent a maid a short while ago to see that a fresh pot of Souchong was waiting for her, so no doubt she will not be long.' He watched as she went to look out of the window. 'Are you recovered this morning, madam?'

'Yes, thank you, Jeffreys.'

Outside the English weather, as perverse as ever, was once again bright with sunshine and blue skies, the fresh whiteness of the new snow glittering and sparkling in the morning light. There was no breeze to bring that extra chill to the air, and from the warmth of the breakfast room the scene looked cheerful and inviting. There was only the fresh snow to remind her of the stormy night, and it seemed unbelievable now that the gale had blown so fiercely over the hill. A single set of carriage tracks marked the passing of the landau taking Jonathan to Oxford, and already those marks were being cleared away as the men once again shoveled the snow from the drive. They laughed and talked as they worked, their breath hanging in white clouds, and their light mood did not blend with the happenings of the night, or of the past few weeks.

Amy stared at the trees with their branches bowed down by the weight of the snow. Where was Livvy now? Had she reached her destination in safety? Or was she lying out there somewhere, injured in a fall from her horse, frightened and alone. Dying in the cold ... Amy shivered and turned abruptly from the window. Of what use were such thoughts? There was nothing she could do; she did not know the countryside and there were no tracks to follow. 'Jeffreys, do you know if any of the men have gone out again this morning to search for Miss Olivia?'

'Oh yes, madam, His Lordship made certain before he left that the search would continue, in case a mishap had befallen her. He also had a party ride over to Oakleigh Hall to ascertain if there was any news there, but nothing has been heard from Mr

Pemberton since he left so hurriedly last night on his return from Dursley.' The butler moved to draw out a chair for her at the table. 'Would you like some bacon, madam?'

'I don't think I could eat anything this morning.'

'The bacon is most excellent, a little crisp. I urge you to try to eat, madam,' he murmured kindly, 'for worrying on an empty stomach is surely far worse than worrying when your stomach is satisfied.'

She smiled at him. 'Very well, some bacon and some black coffee.'

'Yes, madam.'

He was just setting the coffee on the table in front of her when Christabel arrived in a flurry of pale pink silk. Her fan was wafting busily to and fro, and her smile froze as she saw that only Amy sat at the table.

Amy smiled. 'Good morning, Lady Christabel.'

'Miss van Allen,' came the curt reply. The silk whispered as Christabel crossed the room to where Jeffreys held her chair for her. 'Is His Lordship down yet, Jeffreys?'

'He has left for Oxford, my lady.'

'Oxford? But . . . '

Amy smiled sweetly. 'Unexpected business, my lady. He does not expect to be back for several days.'

'Indeed. He said nothing to me.'

'You left last night before he had time.'

Christabel's face was a dull red, and she looked at the butler again. 'Where is Miss Olivia?'

He cleared his throat. 'She is remaining in her room, my lady. She is feeling far too unwell to rise at the moment. She asked me to express her sincere apologies to you, and to beg you to forgive her.'

Amy's smile was sweetness personified. 'And you and I can be such good company for each other, can we not?'

Christabel's pale blue eyes were icy. 'I hardly think that there is any possible common ground between us, Miss van Allen. I found your whole manner extremely offensive last night and have no hesitation in telling you so this morning.'

'Oh dear,' murmured Amy, stirring her coffee very slowly, 'how the days are going to drag for us.'

'Jeffreys, will you see that my carriage is ready to leave directly?' snapped Christabel, shaking her head as the butler inquired upon her choice for breakfast. He held her chair again as she stood. 'I will not eat with a creature like you, Miss van Allen, and I give you due warning that if you intend to stay here, then things will be said of you in the neighborhood, which will make any social gathering you may be thinking of attending over Christmas an extremely unpleasant and embarrassing experience for you. You'll regret your miserable triumph over me last night, I promise you that, and if you entertain notions of snapping Jonathan up for yourself, you may forget it, for by the time I have finished with you he would not touch you with a pair of tongs!'

'Lady Christabel, your voice has risen to a squeak — are you perhaps wearing something a little too tight?'

Words failed Christabel at that, and with an odd sound deep in her throat she stormed from the room, and this time Jeffreys had not time at all to open the door for her. It crashed behind her as she slammed it.

Amy sat back with a sigh. 'Jeffreys,' she said softly, 'I wish to God I'd never left Washington.'

He said nothing as she sat gazing at her untouched bacon which was beginning to cool and congeal on the plate.

She drank the strong black coffee slowly, thinking not of Christabel and her threats, but of Jonathan. Her feelings of the night before had had something of a dreamlike quality, but on waking this morning, they had still been there. She must face up to it, she

186

was in love with him — with all the pain and heartbreak that love must inevitably bring. He felt nothing for her beyond a certain irritation and impatience, and she had done little to foster any change of feeling on his part. She had been outspoken, she had argued, defied, criticized, and insulted, and, in short, had proved herself to be a combination of all those female traits he most disliked.

'The sooner you go back to Washington the better, Amy van Allen,' she murmured absently.

'I beg your pardon, madam?' Jeffreys turned at the sound of her voice.

'Oh, nothing, nothing at all, Jeffreys. May I have some more of that excellent coffee?'

★　★　★

The morning seemed to drag by with leaden feet. She thought of taking another ride, but that prospect held no pleasure, and the snow was just that little too deep to make a walk seem possible. It was then that she remembered her abandoned search of Alice's room. Picking up her warm shawl and pulling it firmly around her shoulders, she left the drawing room's warm fire and went up the dark staircase.

The candelabra still stood where she had left it in the dressing room, but the darkness, the shadows, the strange stealthy noises that all houses make, all were gone now as she knelt by the wardrobes again to continue her search for anything which might lead her in the end to the sapphires. She sat back on her heels, inspecting each hat box, thrusting her hand into each pair of shoes, into every pocket of every pelisse or spencer. She went through the seemingly endless drawers, taking out, folding and unfolding, turning things over, undoing and then patiently doing up again. Everything she could think of was gone over with the same finetooth comb, but at the end of two hours she was not only at a loss for anywhere else to search, she was also frozen to the bone in the ice-cold rooms where the sun no longer shone as the day wore on.

The shadows had begun to return with the grayness of the early afternoon, and she was shivering when at last she sat on the edge of Alice's bed, looking around for a last time for some inspiration.

On the dressing table all the caskets stood in a row, the one which had obviously contained Charles Pemberton's old love letters being the only one which was empty. The others contained necklaces, rings and bracelets, brooches and hat pins, pieces of lace, ribbons and handkerchiefs. The drawers were full of Alice's things, the wardrobes full of her clothes, but the woman herself still remained as mysterious as ever. Strange, solitary Alice, with her odd moods and lonely life — what was the real truth about her?

With a heavy sigh, she huddled deeper into the grenadine shawl, her breath billowing in a cloud in the still, freezing air. She remembered a time as a child when she had searched and searched for a favorite doll, and she had almost given up with a similar feeling of hopelessness — until her nurse had come in and helped her, finding the doll in the end when she had removed every drawer from the toy cupboard, and there was Gretel, lying almost crushed behind them all . . . Amy pondered the childhood incident for a moment, and then her gaze went to the white and gold dressing table and she wondered if anyone had removed those drawers to search behind. Slipping from the bed she knelt before the dressing table, taking out all the drawers one by one. At the bottom of the cabinet she found a book.

Sense and Sensibility by Miss Austen. She flicked through the pages. Well, here was the sole fruit of her long search, Miss Austen's first novel, and one which Amy had not yet read. She replaced all the drawers and stood, the book in her hand, as she looked at Alice's portrait again. 'Well, Alice,' she murmured, 'if this book is as good as *Pride and Prejudice*, then I shall be well pleased. I hope you don't mind if I read it.' How foolish, she thought to herself as she stood there looking at the portrait, talking to a painting as if it were flesh and blood. The expressionless brown eyes gazed back at her. Amy left quietly, closing the door as softly as possible so as not to disturb Alice's peace.

She decided not to return to her own rooms, just yet, for there was a risk of finding herself with Mary Danthorpe again, and that she wished to avoid if at all possible. Holding her skirts, she hurried down the draughty staircase, intending to reach the warmth of the drawing room as soon as possible.

At the foot of the stairs she almost collided with a group of maids who emerged from the kitchens, and in the confusion the book dropped to the floor. One of the maids picked it up immediately. 'Oh, ma'am! Oh, I'm ever so sorry!'

Amy took the book. 'That's quite all right, it was my fault for being in too much of a hurry.'

The maid smiled shyly, the smile fading as she looked beyond Amy to see Jeffreys slowly descending the staircase. In a moment the maids had melted away, and the butler went to open the hall door for Amy.

'Thank you, Jeffreys.'

'Shall I bring some tea to the drawing room, Miss van Allen?'

'Tea? Oh, yes, if you please, Jeffreys.'

He bowed, and she went through the door into the hallway. Her slippers tapped on the red and gray tiles as she hurried on toward the drawing room.

She sat in the chair she had occupied the night before, sitting forward to hold her cold hands out to the welcome warmth. The memory of the chill, damp air in Alice's room made her shudder. She glanced across at the chair where Jonathan had sat, and then with a deep breath she sat back to begin the book. The gold-embossed cover glittered in the dancing firelight, and outside the afternoon was drawing in, the wind beginning to moan around the house, its soft breaths lonely and low. The fire drew and sparks shone like golden diamonds in the hearth as the logs shifted, the smoke curling and writhing up the chimney. She turned the pages one after another. The problems facing the unfortunate Dashwood family at the beginning of Miss Austen's story seemed hard indeed, but as she read on she became engrossed in the differing characters and loves of the sisters, Marianne and Elinor. Jeffreys brought the tray of tea and she continued to read as she ate.

She did not notice the passage of time, or how dark it had become, until quite suddenly she was startled out of the book by the door closing as a maid came in to light the candles.

'Oh, excuse me, ma'am!'

'Please carry on, I was just going to my room.' She closed the book carefully and got up.

Mary was waiting in her room, her face as flat and uninteresting as ever.

'Good evening, Mary.'

'Good evening, ma'am. What shall you wear for dinner?'

'Well, as Lord Chalbourne has not returned yet, I don't think I wish to dine alone. I will stay here in my room and would like a tray brought here a little later.'

'If you wish, ma'am.'

'I do wish.' The woman's manner grated immediately. Amy put the book down on the dressing table. 'That will be all for the moment, Mary.'

'Yes, ma'am.'

The woman went quietly out, and Amy turned to pick up her reticule, and for the second time the book was knocked to the floor. This time it fell heavily on its spine and she crouched quickly with a gasp as she saw how the fine leather had been buckled slightly. As she picked it up, though, she saw the small fragment of paper which was protruding from the spine now.

She removed it and saw that it appeared to be a piece torn from a letter, for there was sloping handwriting, penned in black ink, on the plain white paper. On one side were the words ' . . . and then things will be as they always were before . . . ' and on the other ' . . . but whichever place you decide upon, you must tell me *exactly* . . . .' There was another hand on this side too, a rounder writing in blue ink, where someone had scratched with a poor quill '3 4L Cupbd.'

She gazed at the paper in puzzlement. What did it mean? Why would anyone go to the trouble of carefully folding up a piece of a letter and pushing it into the spine of a book? It had to be a deliberate act, for the book was new and the spine tight, and the paper had only been revealed by the force of the heavy fall which jerked it from its hiding place. She picked up the letter knife which lay on the dressing table, poking it carefully down the spine to see if there were any more papers there, but there was nothing.

Sitting on the stool, she looked at the paper

again . . . *but whichever place you decide upon, you must tell me exactly* . . . . Could it possibly be that beyond all her wildest expectations, she had actually found the very thing she had been searching for? A clue as to where the sapphires were? *3 4L Cupbd.* Cupbd. was obviously short for cupboard, but what did the cryptic figures mean? Slowly she took a clean handkerchief from her reticule, unfolding it and carefully placing the piece of paper in it, and then replacing the folded handkerchief in the reticule. There was no need for anyone to know about what she had found just yet, not until she had had time to think a little. Maybe she was just being extremely silly, for it was surely a rather unbelievable coincidence that she should have found something which was just enigmatic enough to maybe be important.

She was sitting in a chair reading again when Mary brought a tray containing a light dinner and a glass of good red wine. She spent another hour reading after she had eaten, but her concentration on the activities of the Dashwood sisters had gone now, and all she could think of was the strange paper.

The wind continued to moan around the eaves. It sounded petulant, as if it could not manage a full-throated gale. The drift of cold air carried the sound of Great Chalbourne's church bells, a vibrant, joyful sound as the bellringers practiced their most intricate peals. It reminded her suddenly of Christmas Eve back in Washington, sitting around the fire listening to the church bells ringing out as midnight approached. Again it struck her how lacking in any festive spirit she was — she still hardly gave it a thought. But now she wondered about Winfield. Was he preparing to go out tonight? Maybe he was going to the theatre ... She glanced across at the escritoire where her untouched sheet of paper still lay where she had left it, the quill dipped neatly into the inkwell.

She had been so certain of her decision, she had been sure that she should marry Winfield. Well, what was really so different now? She would soon return to America and she wouldn't see Jonathan Chalbourne again — and why should that concern her so? He would never glance at her with love in his eyes, he would never whisper her name as if it were a caress ... She could never mean anything to him, not as she meant to Winfield, and had it not been for that moment of insight the night before when Jonathan had touched her cheek, then even now she would not have been aware of the truth.

With sudden determination she got up. She

would have to forget this hopeless, pointless yearning as quickly as she had discovered it! She went to the escritoire and took up the quill. '*My dearest Winfield . . .*'

★　★　★

The nightmare engulfed her, and she was imprisoned by sleep.

She was cowering back from Alice's portrait, and a chilling mist enveloped her as she tried to stay beyond Alice's reach. The brown eyes were alive now, shining malevolently as they laughed at Amy's abject terror, and the breath of that laughter stirred the mist around her. She couldn't move, she couldn't move . . . With a silent start, Amy was suddenly awake, lying there in the bed where the sheets were creased and untidy from her restless sleep. The night candle she had set beside the bed before retiring had gone out and she could still smell the acrid, waxy smell of the lingering curls of smoke. The room was in complete darkness and the nightmare was still with her as she lay there, her body damp with perspiration. She wished there was a moon to soften the impenetrable night, for all was uncannily quiet because the wind had dropped away to nothing again. She could hear the rushing of her heart as the nightmare tried to keep its hold on her senses, and she turned on her side, closing her eyes, determined to defeat it. But a small sound in the room made her open her eyes again immediately.

Something was in the room with her, she knew as plainly as if it had brushed against her. Fear of a different kind now spread rigidly through her, and she was motionless, unable to move and unable to cry out. A stealthy, tearing sound crept through the curtains, and then there was silence again.

Amy screamed as the terror sharpened and every nerve quivered. She hardly heard the door closing, and as she tugged the curtains aside to stumble from the bed she didn't know that she was alone in the room now. She almost fell over a forgotten stool as she felt frantically for the door, her hands sliding over the wood as she sought the handle. The empty, chilling darkness moved all around her and tears filled her eyes as she shook the handle, trying to move the resistant door. She began to scream again, thumping her fist on the solid wood, and then suddenly it burst open and she was out in the dim passageway where the candles smoked on the walls. A tall shadow blotted out the light and someone caught her arms.

The blood seemed to freeze in her veins as

she cried out again, struggling against her captor. A sharp pain stung her cheek, and she was jerked into an abrupt, numbed silence.

'God above, Miss van Allen, what's wrong?'

Jonathan was standing there. He was still wearing his heavy gray greatcoat and was removing his tall silk hat, into which he dropped his gloves. 'Well?'

She stared at him, a wave of weakening relief surging over her. 'It's you,' she whispered faintly, leaning back against the wall, her eyes closing.

He put out a hand and made her look at him, and he could see the fear which still darkened her eyes. 'What's happened?' he asked, a little more gently this time.

'Some — something was in my room.'

'It was probably just a dream — ' he began.

'No!' she cried, 'no, it *wasn't* a dream, something was in my room with me, I could hear it!'

She swayed a little, glancing back into the shadowy room, and he caught her, pulling her close for a moment and smoothing her tousled red hair. 'All right,' he murmured. 'It's all right now.' He could feel the wild thundering of her heart and the trembling which shook her whole body.

Her voice was muffled. 'Something was in there, I could hear a strange sound, like something being torn slowly . . . '

'I doubt if some*thing* was in there, Miss van Allen,' he said, releasing her. 'It was much more likely to have been some*one*, someone intent upon stealing. Come, we'll see if anything's missing.' He lifted a candle down from one of the brackets and, with his arm still lightly around her shoulder, they went back into the room.

The light spread through the shadows, making them shrink away as the flames grew stronger when he lit a candlestick. The pale blue damask walls were tinged with rose in the warm light, and the royal curtains were turned to the deepest purple.

'Does it look as if anything's missing?'

Slowly she went to her box of jewelry, but a cursory glance inside told her that nothing had been taken: A search of everything valuable revealed the same — nothing had been taken and indeed, nothing seemed even to have been touched. And yet . . . Slowly she moved around the room again, opening drawers and lifting the lid from her jewelry box. Something was wrong somehow, although she couldn't see exactly what. At last she shook her head. 'I can't see anything.'

He went to the fire, poking a little life back into the dying embers and then pressing a small log on with his boot. 'Describe again exactly what happened.'

'I woke up suddenly, and I heard a sort of tearing sound. It sounds so feeble now — '

'Tearing material? Paper?'

'I don't know — just tearing, that's all I can say.'

'Maybe you should spend the rest of the night in another room — Olivia's maybe, for that is aired.'

'No, I'll be all right here.' She was beginning to feel a little foolish now, and she sensed that he was still of the opinion that she had been dreaming. She *had* had a nightmare, but it was no dream after she had woken.

'Well, would you like Mary Danthorpe to keep you company for the rest of tonight?'

'No!' she said quickly. 'No, I don't want her here!'

He gave a faint smile. 'No, well maybe you're right. She is hardly the light-hearted company you need right now. Very well, if you wish to remain here, then by all means do so, but tomorrow I will see to it that you are moved elsewhere. This room is somewhat isolated, but tradition has always had it that this is the room to which guests are shown. Maybe now is as good a time as any to break with that tradition.'

'There's no need, truly there isn't.'

'You may not think so, but I do. There are rooms nearer my own, and I will sleep easier if I know that I can hear you if you call.'

'As you wish.'

'I would have preferred you to move tonight, but at this late hour and after all my journeyings today, I'm in no state to argue the point.'

She remembered Olivia suddenly, and was ashamed that her own fears had put all his problems out of her mind. 'I should have asked . . . Had she been to Oxford at all?'

'No, it was the wild goose chase she intended it to be. No doubt they're well on their way in the opposite direction by now.'

'I'm sorry.'

'So am I.' He spoke drily, crossing the room to the large window by the escritoire and looking out over the park where the first gray touches of the winter dawn were staining the eastern sky. 'It's dawn and I've spent two nights fruitlessly searching for her. I'm damned tired — and no longer in a mood to view her actions with brotherly sympathy.'

'I don't think you really mean that.'

'No? No, well maybe it's merely my customary irritability showing through yet again.' He turned, and his glance fell on the sealed letter she had written to Winfield. It lay on the escritoire next to his hand, and he picked it up. 'So, the inestimable Mr Kenney is to receive the news for which he has been waiting.'

She looked away. 'I've written, yes.'

'Accepting him?'

'Yes.'

For a moment it was as if his gray eyes could see right into her soul. 'Then,' he murmured, 'congratulations are surely in order, Miss van Allen. I wish you, and Mr Kenney, all the very best for the future.'

'Thank you.' His words were like a dull pain inside her. 'What — what will you do about Livvy now?'

'Do?' His voice was sharper somehow. 'There's nothing I *can* do! I can't protect her good name for an indefinite period, nor can I search the whole of Britain county by county in the hope of finding her. So, I'll just have to pray that your judgment proves to be more sound than mine, won't I?'

His tone was clipped and suddenly bitter, and that same bitterness was in his eyes as he looked across the room at her.

'My judgment?' she asked uncertainly, disturbed by the change in him.

'About friend Pemberton. If *you* are right, then at the very least he will eventually make an honest woman of her. If *I'm* right, then she may say farewell forever to any hope she may have had of respectability or future happiness, for he'll use her until he tires of her, and then he'll desert her. And, no doubt, by then she'll have a squawling memory of his undying love to cradle in her foolish arms!'

She stared at him. 'Don't — don't say that, please!'

'Why not? Doesn't it fit the rosy picture you have of him? How very sad for you! But you see, he is sufficiently implicated in the theft of the sapphires for *me* to know he is guilty, for the *world* to know he is guilty. Further, his name has been linked in a very unsavory manner with that of my late wife, and now, on top of all that, he has run away with my sister, thus showing that he has a complete disregard for her safety, well-being, or character! *I* know he is guilty, mankind knows he is, guilty, but you, Miss van Allen, *you* believe he is the most of an angel you've ever known! Forgive me, madam, but I find your apparently unshakeable loyalty to him incredible, to say the least. God above, what more will it take to convince you of his worthlessness? Must he pen a confession in his own blood? Obviously the fellow has an exceedingly winning way with him, for he can cast his will over women whenever it so pleases him — first Alice, then Olivia, and now you. The others I can maybe find excuse for, but not you, Amy Magnolia van Allen, for you are by far too perceptive, too intelligent, and too practical to be fooled by mere words, no matter how silvered and magical those words may be. So — I am led to the inevitable and distasteful conclusion that he used far more than mere words to convince you that night at Oakleigh Hall!'

She continued to stare at him, a bewildering blend of white-hot anger and deep, painful hurt rendering her silent for a long while. Slowly she turned away from him. 'I think you've said enough to convey to me exactly what your opinion of me is, sir, so I will wish you good night.'

'Miss van Allen . . . '

'Please go, Lord Chalbourne.'

She kept her back toward him as he walked from the room, and only when the door closed behind him did she bow her head as the tears fell hotly down her cheeks. She went to the bed, climbing slowly into it and pulling the clothes over her face as she wept, but it wasn't the savageness of his last words to her that lingered, it was the perfume of southern-wood on his coat when he'd held her.

9

Her eyes felt sore the next morning when she awoke at last. She lay there staring up at the bed's royal blue tester, and a thin shaft of sunlight pierced the curtains to fall brightly across her tired face. The whole of the previous night seemed like a monstrous nightmare now, except that she knew it had all really happened, all really been said. How could she go down to breakfast now to face him this morning? How could she say anything, maintain any sort of pretense, when she knew now exactly what he really thought of her?

An echo of the night's awful fear returned quite suddenly when she heard a small sound in the room beyond the curtains. Silently she knelt up, peeping out through a crack in the curtains to see Mary Danthorpe standing by the dressing table, Alice's book in her hands. She was so intent upon the book that she didn't hear Amy stirring.

'Mary?'

The woman put the book down quickly. 'Ma'am?'

Amy slipped from the bed and stood

looking at the maid. 'What are you doing?'

'I . . . Well, ma'am, I came to waken you, and I saw that the book was damaged.' The bright little eyes met Amy's gaze without flinching, and the voice was level and toneless in spite of the woman's obvious discomfort at being discovered.

'Damaged?' Amy picked the book up. The spine, which yesterday had been in perfect condition, was now hanging half off the rest of the book. Amy stared at it, and suddenly the sounds of the night became crystal clear. She had heard the spine of the book being torn — and why would anyone tear it? Only if they knew that the piece of paper was hidden there! Amy put the book down again. 'I don't know how that's happened, but maybe it can be sent to a book binder.'

'His Lordship always uses a firm in Cirencester, ma'am.'

'Very well, see that it's sent there when I have finished reading it.'

'Yes, ma'am.'

The maid's eyes slid away and she went to bring Amy's wrap which had been warming by the fire, and Amy put it on and then sat in front of the dressing table for the woman to dress her hair. The brush crackled through the long red tresses, and Amy gazed at the book's damaged binding. Her mind was racing. The fragment of letter was important enough for someone to risk coming to her room in the middle of the night to get it. But who? Who knew that she even had the book? She went over those she had seen the previous day after leaving Alice's room, and she knew there were any number who definitely saw her or who could have seen her, ranging from Jeffreys, through the maids by the drawing room door, right through to Mary Danthorpe, who had attended her the previous evening.

Mary pinned the hair up, and Amy washed in the warm water the maid had already brought for her. She went constantly over the puzzle of the book and the paper, but the only conclusion she could come to was that it was indeed a clue to the whereabouts of the sapphires. But how much of that conclusion was born of her own wish that it should be so? And how much was bafflement as to what else it could possibly be? When she was dressed, she waited as Mary brought the grenadine shawl, and then the reticule, and all the time there was silence.

Thoughts of the mystery of the book vanished, however, as she went down the stairs on her way to face Jonathan. Her heart was heavy as she nodded to the footman who waited by the breakfast room door, but as she went into the cheerful blue and white room, she saw that he wasn't alone, for a small, untidy boy was standing before the table, cap in hand and clumped boots leaving faintly dirty marks on the clean blue carpet.

Jonathan stood, holding his hand out to her. 'Ah, Miss van Allen, you are just in time to hear what Ben here has to say.'

His hand was warm around hers as he led her to her place, but she noticed how he avoided her eyes. The boy shuffled awkwardly, sniffing loudly and obviously resisting the temptation to wipe his nose on his scruffy sleeve. He was thin and pinched looking, with spiky brown hair and wide eyes which rested nervously on her as she sat down.

Jonathan returned to his own place. 'Miss van Allen, this is Ben Turner. His father is one of my best keepers. Ben usually helps on the estate, specializing in a sixth sense which tells him exactly where the poachers have set their latest snares, but he's been away from Great Chalbourne for two weeks now, helping to look after an aging relative. He didn't return to the village, until late last night, and so hadn't heard anything of what had been going on here. However, the moment he heard, he realized that he had some important information which I should hear. It is important, and I want you to hear it, Miss van Allen. Very well, Ben, repeat what you've told me.'

'Yes, m'lord. Well, it was the day before the Hunt Ball, and I was out at midnight with Dad over by the old huntin' lodge in Chalbourne Woods. We was reckoning to sniff out some of old Poky Ferguson's snares. The old feller'd been out the night before and we knew as he'd been up to no good. It were proper dark, but a good moon was up and I was gettin' on well — old Poky'd bin proper busy, I can tell you. Reckon he was after providing for the whole of Dursley market! Any road, I heard hooves over by the lodge, so I hid — well, folks don't go out in the dark lessen they'm up to sommat, not in the heart of the woods anyway, and I didn't want to get caught snooping or owt like that. Well, I sawed Mr Pemberton first off. I knowed it was him on account of that big dun horse he always rides, and then when he took off his hat I sawed his fair hair. He wore a scarf round his mouth and that, but I knowed it was him all right. He waited a while, and I was gettin' proper cold and stiff, and then this other horse come from Chalbourne Park way, a gray horse it were, ridden by a woman. When she got that bit closer I saw as it was Her Ladyship. They both dismounted and — and . . .'

'Go on, Ben,' said Jonathan gently, 'tell her exactly what you saw.'

The boy's tongue passed over his lips. 'And they hugged each other and all that, proper close and loving. After a while they got to just talkin', and he got a bit angered up about sommat, I don't know what for I couldn't catch their words as the wind were wrong for that, but she were proper upset, wringing her hands like and shaking her head. Any road, in the end she calmed down a bit and he took a little drawstring bag from his saddle — blue it were I think, any road it looked blue in the moonlight. He opened it and took out — well, he took out the sapphires, ma'am. I sawed them sparkling in the moonlight and I could see the shape of the necklace as plain as plain, even to the one big stone what hangs down the center.'

Amy stared at the boy in dismay. 'Oh, no. No — '

'There weren't no mistake, ma'am, for I've seen the necklace and Her Ladyship wore it when she drove through the village when His Lordship brought her back here after they married.' The boy glanced uncertainly at Jonathan, as if unsure if he'd done the right thing by mentioning the past like that.

Jonathan nodded. 'Go on, Ben.'

'Then — then he put the necklace back in the bag and gave it to her. He k-kissed her then and she held him right tightly before she got back on her horse. She rode off back toward this house, and I waited until Mr Pemberton rode off too, then I finished breaking Poky's snares and came back to join my dad. I didn't say anything on account of it weren't my business and my dad've always lammed me proper hard if I talked little-tattle, he reckons as that's old biddies' work, not the work of men.'

Amy swallowed miserably. She'd been wrong, all along she'd been so very wrong. 'Ben, you are absolutely certain that it was Mr Pemberton?'

'Yes, ma'am. Like I said, there ent no one else round these parts as looks like him, or rides a dun horse, like that. Pale dun it is, with a white face and four white legs, and a proper high stepper. Reckon there's hot blood in that animal. I like horses, ma'am, and so I'm pretty sure as that was Mr Pemberton's dun. I'd swear on a stack of Bibles.'

Jonathan tossed a silver coin to the boy, who caught it deftly. 'You've done well, Ben. Now you must just repeat to the parish constable exactly what you've told me and Miss van Allen.'

'*All* of it, my lord? I mean, about the kissin'

and all that? It'll get clear all the way to Bristol if I does!'

'It will do more than merely reach Bristol anyway, Ben, so just tell the truth to the constable.'

'All right, my lord, if that's the way you wants it.'

'It is. Now go with Jeffreys and wait for the constable to arrive. He should not be long.'

'Yes, m'lord. Good-bye sir — ma'am . . . '

Amy nodded. 'Good-bye, Ben.'

When they were alone again, Jonathan leaned forward to pour her a cup of coffee. 'Tell me, Miss van Allen, are you convinced at last, or must there be more?'

'I cannot but be convinced, sir.'

'You believe the boy, then?'

'Why should I not?'

'Oh, it merely crossed my mind that you would probably think his tale was of my concoction, that I am at last bending the law to suit my own ends.'

'A great deal of wild thoughts apparently cross your mind, sir. This would merely appear to be yet another in a long line.'

He studied her pale face for a moment, and she knew he could not fail to notice the redness around her eyes. 'You do realize, don't you, Miss van Allen, that if Pemberton is caught now, the boy's evidence is enough to hang him?'

'Yes. But do you realize how this is going to affect Olivia?'

'I do, I realize only too well. None of this is of my choosing, I have to live with it as surely as my sister does.'

'No doubt you will more than manage to rise above it, sir, but I am not so sure of Livvy's ability to sustain the same brave face. She is going to need all the help it is possible to give, for she loves Mr Pemberton with all her heart, and to discover that he is, after all, a charlatan of the worst kind, is going to break her heart far more than it has already been broken!'

He was hesitant, choosing his next words with care. 'I know, and that is why she is going to so need your presence here — indeed, why *I* am going to need your help too.'

'Are you afraid that your insulting behavior last night has decided me to leave after all, sir? Then let me assure you that I still intend to remain, and that you and your needs do not enter my head for even the most brief of seconds. My sole reason for remaining anywhere in your immediate vicinity is that I wish to do all I can to help poor Livvy.'

'I do realize that my gross conduct is fully

deserving of your attitude this morning, Miss van Allen, but — '

'There can be no buts, sir, for you were insufferably rude. Your accusation was a base and unwarranted attack upon my honor. You've uttered such noble words concerning the saving and protecting of your sister's character, but that did not prevent you from so swiftly and falsely damning mine. No doubt you justify yourself because I made the sad mistake of traveling without a chaperone — there can be no smoke without fire, and all that.' She mimicked his English accent with cruel caricature. 'I find you and everything about you totally abhorrent, Lord Chal-bourne, for you are contemptible, shallow, vain, and pompous, and certainly no gentleman. With those disastrous qualities, you should make an excellent match of it with Christabel, for *she* is no lady! Good day to you!'

She threw her unused napkin to the table and got up, but as she turned to leave the room, she looked straight out through the window and she saw a column of scarlet-uniformed soldiers riding toward the house. At the sight of those uniforms, the years peeled back in a moment and suddenly it was a hot August day in Washington again and the British fifes and drums were sounding triumphantly as the city burned. She could feel again the numb pain when they'd brought the news of her brother's death, and she could smell the thick, choking smoke as the flames licked through her home. Then she had known only a bitter and consuming hatred for the British . . .

She looked down at his still face again, her eyes bright with unshed tears. 'Soldiers?'

'A detachment from Cirencester spent last night in the village, and I sent word to them immediately I heard Ben Turner's story this morning. I don't intend to allow Pemberton any small chance of remaining free, Miss van Allen, and if that means alerting the whole of the British army, then so be it.' He got up, slowly picking up her shawl which had fallen, draping it gently around her shoulders. 'I was going to tell you they were coming as I realized full well that the sight of them would not fill you with pleasure.'

'The British are coming?' She gave a short, mirthless laugh as she watched how blood-red the uniforms were against the snow. But then something made her look beyond the column of soldiers, back along the drive toward the wrought-iron gates. A dark red barouche was moving slowly toward the house, the tired horses with their heads low. She stared in disbelief for a moment. 'Look,' she whispered, 'look!'

'Pemberton's barouche!' He ran toward the door.

★ ★ ★

The servants and soldiers crowded the hall as Charles Pemberton carried Olivia into the house, putting her gently down on the sofa by the fire. She was barely conscious, lying motionless where he put her. Her face was ashen and there was a clean bandage around her forehead, but already fresh blood was seeping through to stain it. Her clothes were dirty and torn, and there was another bandage around her right arm, the sleeve of her riding habit having been cut away entirely.

Amy hurried to kneel beside her, catching her limp hand. 'Livvy?'

'She cannot hear you, Miss van Allen, for the doctor in Gloucester gave her some laudanum that she could make the journey back here.' Charles's voice sounded tired and resigned.

'Gloucester?' Jonathan was cold. 'So that was the destination you chose!'

'I chose nothing, Chalbourne. You surely do not imagine that I countenance a foolish scheme like this, do you? Running away with

216

her and thereby *ruining* her, and also virtually shouting to the world that I was guilty of everything of which I stand accused? Allow me a little more feeling for Olivia, and a little more intelligence where my own affairs are concerned!' Charles ran his hand through his fair hair, turning to look around the silent hall where all eyes were upon him, accusing and hostile.

Amy stared at him. It was so very hard to believe in his guilt . . . 'Mr Pemberton,' she asked quietly, 'what happened to her?'

'Her horse threw her. When I returned from Dursley the other night, I found a note from her waiting for me, and in it she had written that she had run away to Gloucester, where she would be waiting for me at the Three Feathers Inn. I gained the impression from the note that she had already left some two hours before, and so I took my barouche and went after her, intending one thing only, and that was to bring her back here to Chalbourne Park before the escapade could be discovered. I had reached the steep descent from the Cotswolds down to the vale before I found her. She was lying at the roadside and there was no sign of her horse. I took her on the short distance to Gloucester, lodged her at the Three Feathers, and sent for a doctor. He dressed her wounds and advised me to wait a full day before attempting the journey back here. I took his advice, and he prescribed laudanum to dull the pain for her while she traveled — we've been on the way back here since first light this morning.'

Jonathan laughed shortly. 'Well, you would have been better advised to drive on away from here, Pemberton, for by God you've stepped right back into my hands.'

Charles's eyes flickered disdainfully. 'It is obvious from your face that you do not believe I have told you the truth.' He glanced at Amy. 'But I would have expected a little more understanding from you, Miss van Allen.'

She flushed and lowered her eyes to Olivia's white, drawn face.

Jonathan was relentless. 'It does not matter at all whether what you've just said is the truth or not, sir, for it's your *past* activities which have come back to point their bony fingers at you now.'

Charles removed his heavy cloak, dropping it casually over a chair before he swung to look at Jonathan again. 'And what is it you've dreamed up against me this time?' he asked wryly, 'Murder? Arson? Maybe you've decided that nothing less than high treason will suffice in your blood feud against me! Or may I take solace in the thought that you are just miffed again that I've trespassed upon hallowed Chalbourne land? Do enlighten us all, Chalbourne, for I've no doubt that these good people here are just as agog as I am to know what's in your mind!' He waved his hand to encompass the precisely drawn up line of soldiers and the silent crowd of waiting servants.

Amy could have wept at the futile, defiant bravery in his words, for how could he know the weight of the evidence against him now? But even now — even now she could not believe she had been wrong about him. There was something so honest, so courageous, and so infinitely believable about him as he stood there looking scornfully at Jonathan.

Jonathan smiled coolly. 'You stole those sapphires, Pemberton, and by God, by the time I've finished with you you'll wish you had never even *heard* the name Chalbourne! What have you done with them?'

'Nothing, for I haven't touched them. And I warn you, Chalbourne, you've gone too far now. I've endured your persecution for long enough, and you've now openly accused me in front of a great many witnesses. No man's honor can bow beneath that!'

'I accuse you, Pemberton, because I can now prove that you are guilty.'

'*Prove* it? Are you then some wizard that

you can prove the impossible?'

'I have a witness who saw you handing what I believe to be the fake necklace to my wife in Chalbourne Woods the night before the Hunt Ball.'

Charles's face was visibly paler as he stared at Jonathan. 'A witness? How well did you grease your man's palm, Chalbourne? I trust he squeezed you tightly for his damnable services!'

A nerve flickered at Jonathan's temple, but that was the only sign he gave of the depth of his anger. He nodded at the waiting sergeant, and two of the soldiers came to bind Charles's hands tightly behind his back.

Charles looked helplessly at Amy then. 'You surely do not believe this cock and bull story, do you?' he cried.

'The boy saw you,' she whispered miserably. 'He saw you . . . '

'Do *you* believe it?' he cried again, wincing as they tightened the ropes.

She shook her head almost, imperceptibly, not daring to glance at Jonathan although she could feel his incredulous gaze on her. 'No,' she said softly, 'no, I don't believe it. I *can't* believe it of you.'

Charles smiled faintly. 'Then I thank you, Miss van Allen.'

'Get him out of here!' snapped Jonathan,

his barely controlled anger making his voice shake.

Amy remained where she was as the soldiers dragged the protesting Charles out, and the servants were whispering together while the sound of the hooves on the wet gravel gradually became fainter and fainter as the soldiers rode away with their prisoner. Jeffreys hurried to clear the hall, ushering the maids and footmen out, and all the time Amy was conscious of Jonathan as he stood nearby.

At last she looked up at him. 'I'm sorry . . . ' she began.

He turned and walked away without a word, and she lowered her eyes. For a few moments she struggled against the tears which seemed to have been so close all the time since the night before, and then slowly she began to chafe Olivia's limp fingers. 'Livvy? Livvy, can you hear me at all?'

Maybe it was imagination, but she thought the cold little fingers moved slightly in hers, but there was no stirring of the girl's pale lips, no fluttering of the long, dark lashes. The laudanum kept Olivia in the deep sleep the Gloucester doctor had intended, and her breathing was light and rhythmic, for all the world as if she was merely resting; only the blood-stained bandage around her forehead gave any hint that it was anything else.

Jeffreys returned to the sofa. 'Shall I have some of the men carry Miss Olivia to her room, madam? I have already instructed Sally to see that the bed is warmed.'

'Yes, I think that is best, Jeffreys.' Amy got up. 'Has the doctor been sent for? I don't think we should just rely on our own nursing abilities.'

'Yes, I sent a man to the village the moment I saw Miss Olivia's condition, madam.'

She smiled at him. 'You are very efficient and very thoughtful, Jeffreys. I know a great many Washington hostesses who would give their last dollar to be able to boast a butler as fine as you.'

'Thank you, madam, but I do what I do because I care about His Lordship, and about Miss Olivia.'

'I know,' she said softly, 'I know.' She glanced at the door through which Jonathan had gone. 'So do I.'

★ ★ ★

Olivia's face looked a little flushed in the candlelight, and she turned her head slowly on the lace-edged pillow. 'Amy?'

'I'm here, sweeting.'

'How have you found me? How did you know I was here?'

Amy held the weak hands. 'Charles brought you back to Chalbourne Park, Livvy. You're back home now, not in Gloucester.'

'Home?' The gray eyes were dull, and the speech slurred with the laudanum. 'Jonathan . . . '

'Would you like to speak with him?'

'No. No, he'll be angry with me.' Tears shone in Olivia's eyes then. 'I fibbed, Amy, I fibbed to you and to Jonathan . . . '

'Don't worry about that now, sweeting, just concentrate on getting better.'

'My head aches so.'

Amy smiled fondly. 'That will teach you to fib about headaches, won't it, mm? There's many a true word . . . '

'Is Jonathan very cross with me?'

'No, of course he isn't,' said Amy reassuringly. 'Now then, is there anything you want?'

Olivia shook her head. 'Just to sleep.'

'That's the laudanum.'

'My horse slipped on the ice. I remember falling, but that's all.'

'Charles found you.'

'Can I see him?' Brightness entered the dull eyes for a moment.

'He — he's not here at the moment, sweeting, so you just try to sleep and then you'll feel better in the morning.'

'You do forgive me, don't you, Amy? Please tell me that you do, because I'm so utterly miserable for having deceived you.' The words ran together muzzily, but the fingers tightened in Amy's as Olivia looked pleadingly at her.

'Of course I do, Livvy.'

'Thank you,' came the drowsy whisper. Olivia's eyes were closing, and her lips moved silently as she thanked Amy yet again, but then her fingers became still again and her head slipped sideways as she fell back into the same deep sleep.

Sally tucked the bedclothes gently around her and then looked across the bed at Amy. 'I've not had a chance to thank you, ma'am.'

'Thank me?' asked Amy absently, still looking at Olivia and wondering how she was ever going to be able to break the news about Charles's arrest.

'For not telling His Lordship 'bout my part in taking the note.'

'Oh. Oh, that's all right, Sally.'

'But you took the blame for me, ma'am. There ent many ladies as would do that for a maid, and I don't rightly know how to thank you so's you'll know exactly how grateful I am.'

Amy smiled. 'You've thanked me enough, Sally.'

'If there's ever anything I can do for you . . .'

'I will remember.'

'Yes, ma'am, you be sure to do that, for I'd do anything for a lady as fine and sweet as you.'

Amy went down the stairs past the griffins, and each step she took was slow and heavy. Jonathan must be informed that Olivia had regained consciousness for a while, but she had no wish to be the one to tell him. With a deep breath, she decided that she would ask Jeffreys to convey the news to him, and as she reached the foot of the stairs, she saw that Jeffreys was standing near the fire with Jonathan, helping him to put on his heavy greatcoat. The main door had been opened and she could hear the sound of a carriage and horses drawing up by the porch. Jeffreys picked up Jonathan's hat and gloves.

'You will be staying at the Falcon, sir?'

'Yes, Jeffreys, I can be reached there if absolutely necessary.'

'Yes, my lord.'

Jonathan pulled on his gloves, flexing his fingers as he did so, and then he saw Amy. He said nothing.

Slowly she walked toward him. 'My lord?'

'Madam.'

'Livvy came around for a while . . .'

'She's all right?'

'I think so, yes. I haven't told her about Mr Pemberton though.'

His gray eyes were steady. 'No doubt you'll find just the words, madam.'

'You — you are going out?'

'Full marks for observation, madam. Yes, I am going out. I have legal matters to attend to in Bristol and shall not be back for a day or so.' He inclined his head coldly. 'Good night, Miss van Allen.'

'Good night, sir,' she replied stiffly, her manner every bit as off-hand and abrupt as his. She turned to walk away from him, and she did not look back, even though she was longing to do so. There were no tears stinging her eyes now, she just felt hollow. She was resigned to the hopelessness of the situation, and in that single moment when he'd said good-bye so coldly, she had determined that from now on she would make herself immune to him, she would *make* herself immune . . .

10

Olivia slept for most of the next day, the drowsy remains of the laudanum keeping her quiet and relaxed while her injuries mended. The cut on her forehead was no longer bleeding and only a light bandage was needed now, and the bad graze on her arm needed only a gently yellow salve to soothe it. She had woken once or twice, but still as yet she was too muzzy to think clearly, and she had not asked about Charles Pemberton, much to Amy's relief.

Amy sat in her own rooms. She did not know how she would eventually tell Olivia the truth about Charles, and it was a moment she knew she would willingly put off. She gazed across the sunlit room toward the window, and outside all was bright and clear, with the snow dazzling in the morning light. Wisps of smoke rose from unseen houses in the distance, and the woods were a dark, dark line, a glossy green in places where holly trees grew. Holly. Holly meant Christmas. Amy got up and went to bring the case of Christmas souvenirs she had brought with her from Washington. She took them out one by one and laid them gently on the bed. For Olivia she had chosen a brooch fashioned to look like a sprig of mistletoe. Its leaves were studded with small emeralds and the berries were large, faultless pearls. It was a beautiful piece of jewelry, and Amy had known the first moment she saw it in the fashionable Washington jeweler's that it was just the perfect thing for Olivia. Alice had been a little more difficult, for after all, Amy didn't know her at all, but in the end she had chosen a heavy silver hairbrush, chased in an intricate design and set with diamonds in the form of the letter A. Amy ran her fingers over the soft bristles. Alice would never receive her gift now, and Amy would never know if her choice had been right — but as she looked at it, she felt that Alice would have liked the pretty hairbrush. The final present in the small case was also the largest, and she carefully lifted out the shelf clock she had at long length chosen for Jonathan Chalbourne. It had been made by the Connecticut clockmaker who was all the rage in America at the moment, Eli Terry. She, studied the elegant wooden case with its flanking pillars and scrollwork crest, and quite suddenly it seemed quite the wrong gift for Jonathan Chalbourne. But would anything be the *right* choice for him? With a doubtful sigh she began to carefully wrap the clock in its protective cloth again, and then she was cross with herself for even bothering to wonder if he'd like her gift or not. Just let him show his indifference to her clock and she'd be praying that it dropped on his foot, for *that* would surely evoke a more positive reaction from His Lordship! She smiled at her own thoughts, for she knew in her heart that if he allowed her to realize that he did not like her gift, then she would be deeply hurt. She could tell herself till she was blue that she wasn't going to care, but all the time she would.

She ate a lonely luncheon in her room, and afterward she read a little more of *Sense and Sensibility*. But handling the book again inevitably brought her thoughts to the mysterious piece of paper she had found. She unfolded the handkerchief and studied it again, sipping the glass of dry white wine which had been put on the tray with her meal. *3 4L Cupbd*. What did it mean? Were the sapphires in a cupboard somewhere? But where? And what did *3 4L* mean? Exasperated at her inability to decipher anything more, she replaced the paper in its hiding place. When Jonathan returned she would brave his dislike and ask him about the writing, for it could be that he recognised the hand. Then she began to wonder about the intruder, who had come to her room. Who had it been? Who *could* it have been? The answer to that last question was that it could have been just about anyone at Chalbourne Park, for she had no way of knowing who knew she had found the book. She stared at the reticule after she had put the folded handkerchief away again. Instinct, intuition, call it what you would, she was *sure* that what she had found pointed the way to the sapphires — if *only* she could understand the clue!

After luncheon she walked through the silent house, still deep in thought about the discovery in the book. But the thoughts merely went round and round in her head until it began to ache with the frustration. She determined then to put all thoughts of the paper out of her mind for the time being, and instead she would enjoy her stroll through the long, low passageways and exquisite old rooms.

There were small, uneven steps meandering up and down in the passages, for no reason other than that it seemed that over the centuries the house had settled on different levels. Sometimes the floorboards creaked alarmingly as she walked over them.

There was a quaint, timeless charm about everything at Chalbourne Park, and as on her first day there she thought again that those who had lived here in centuries gone by could quite easily come back now and continue their lives as they had before. Nothing seemed to have changed, and all she saw was quite right for the nineteenth century, just as it had been for the sixteenth or the eighteenth. The music room was a light, airy chamber where a harp stood in one corner and a beautifully decorated harpsichord in the other. She sat for a while at the harpsichord, playing a minuet. She half expected to see a lady in the full satin or silk fashions of the previous century moving lightly to the music in the sunlit center of the room where the leaded windowpanes made lozenge-shaped patterns on the worn carpet.

At the end of her idle afternoon, she walked slowly back through the hall, and as she reached the marble table in the center, she halted, looking around at the Christmas greenery on the walls. The holly leaves had that dull, dry look now, and the berries seemed about to pass into that wrinkled stage which she always associated with the dismal aftermath of the Christmas season. There was something so depressing about the poor decorations, and she stood where she was, sighing heavily.

'Is something wrong, madam?' asked Jeffreys, and she turned with a start.

'I didn't know you were there.'

'I did not mean to startle you, Miss van Allen, but I heard you sigh so . . . '

'I was looking at those dreadful bunches of dismal greenery.'

'Dreadful, madam? Dismal?'

'Well look at them! Surely something a little more joyous and fitting could be managed than those!'

'I . . . '

'I think,' said Amy firmly, 'that we should do something about them, don't you? Back home I take a great pride in seeing to it that my house is decorated to perfection, and this displeases me immensely.'

'But, madam, with Her Ladyship so recently . . . I mean, I do not know if Lord Chalbourne would approve!'

She eyed the butler. 'The *hell* with Lord Chalbourne,' she said shortly.

'Miss van Allen!'

'I have decided, Jeffreys, that we shall make this house look a little more Christmassy.'

'But . . . '

'And from my knowledge of His Lordship, I doubt that he'd even notice if we placed a large painting of a nude lady above the fireplace!'

The butler blinked.

'So,' Amy went on, 'will you have the servants come here to the hall, please?'

'Miss van Allen . . . '

'Jeffreys!'

'Yes, madam, I will instruct them immediately.'

She remained by the table, her fingers drumming in anticipation on the cold white marble of the table. Yes, she thought as she looked around, she would make Chalbourne Park look as if Christmas was just around the corner, and if it didn't *ooze* with festivity by the time she'd finished, it wouldn't be for lack of trying on her part.

Jeffreys assembled the curious servants in the hall, but he still felt he must make one last attempt to make Amy change her mind. 'Miss van Allen, what if His Lordship is really angry about this. I mean — it may not look well with Lady Chalbourne not long in her grave, and then his wrath may fall upon me.'

'Don't concern yourself about that, Jeffreys, for if His Lordship is about to be angry with anyone, it will be with me. And anyway, he has already allowed these other decorations to remain up, so I cannot see that he is really going to have any objection.'

The butler nodded reluctantly. 'Very well, madam.'

Amy dispatched a group of maids to the woods to bring back all the evergreens they could find, and she sent a boy with a pony and sledge to help them. Another maid was sent to pick the dead flower heads in the walled garden, while a kitchen boy mixed up a bucket of whitewash with which he and the maid then proceeded to paint the flower heads. Bunches of mistletoe were brought from the orchards and the Christmas roses were picked in the garden. The hall was soon piled with bunches of holly, myrtle, box, ivy, and mistletoe and the sweet perfume of rosemary from the small bunch which had been placed on the marble table.

After tea, Amy set the maids to making wreaths and posies, and the cook remembered some metal hoops she had seen in an outhouse, and soon these were being twined with ribbons and greenery, pearly mistletoe berries, shining crimson holly berries, and the pale clear green of the ivy berries. The decorations were draped around the edge of the tables, around the numerous portraits, and up the sides of the fireplace, and the footmen balanced on rickety ladders as they suspended wreaths from the chandeliers, and the ribbons moved gently in the rising heat from the fire.

Amy took great delight in arranging large bowls of the leaves and putting the whitewashed flower heads among the dark greens and browns. She sent a footman to bring several boxes of candles from the cellars, for, as she pointed out, all this greenery would make everything dark, so many, many more lights were needed. Jeffreys submitted to her instructions without a murmur, and the footman obediently opened the first box, handing the candles to the maids as they brought the spare candlesticks from all the unused rooms in the house.

Amy made the traditional kissing bunch herself, choosing only the most choice leaves and berries, and the widest, brightest of the scarlet and white ribbons. She suspended the oranges and apples amid the leaves and then two footmen carried it out to the porch where with great difficulty they at last fixed it above the highest step. There it swayed to and fro in the gentle breeze, the ribbons fluttering and flapping gaily. Amy stood back, pleased, as she admired it.

'There, Jeffreys, is that not a great improvement?'

'I — er — yes, madam.'

'You don't sound convinced.'

'There's just so much of it.'

'That is the idea,' she said with satisfaction, for as she looked around now she could feel quite definitely that it was not long to Christmas. She also noticed the new excitement on the maids' faces, and the different air which seemed to permeate the gathering in the hall as everyone collected the unused twigs and leaves and put them in a large sack which had been brought from the stables.

There was only one sour face there, and that belonged inevitably to Mary Danthorpe. The woman had hardly done anything to help, and no one had bothered to gripe with her about it. Amy had left her alone too, but only because she respected the maid's undoubted loyalty to Alice Chalbourne, and therefore equally undoubted disapproval of the afternoon's jollifications — for jollifications they had been, with everyone delighting in the break from the dull routine of everyday tasks.

Now Amy caught Mary's eye, and she beckoned. 'Mary?'

'Yes, ma'am.' The disapproval was there in every fiber of the woman's stiff body as she stood before Amy.

'After all this work, I would like a bath when I go to my room. Would you attend to it for me?'

'Yes, madam.'

'And I will take my dinner in my room again, as I am alone, so you may inform whoever it is that the dining room need not be set out for me.'

The bright eyes flickered coldly. 'Yes, madam.'

'That is all.'

Amy watched the woman as she made her way through the thronged hallway, and she was conscious that in spite of everything, Mary had managed to take a sliver of the pleasure from the day. For a while Amy had forgotten Jonathan Chalbourne and she had enjoyed herself, but now the sadder mood of before hovered on the edge of things again.

★ ★ ★

Amy turned crossly in her sleep. 'No . . . '

'Madam!' Jeffreys' voice was urgent. 'Miss van Allen, please wake up!'

With a start she was awake. 'What's wrong?' she cried quickly, her thoughts going immediately to Olivia. 'Is it Miss Olivia?'

'No, madam, Miss Olivia is asleep and as well as can be expected.'

Rubbing the sleep from her eyes, she struggled up in the bed. He had drawn the curtains slightly and the room was lit by the single night candle, and by that light she could see that it was two o'clock in the morning. 'Jeffreys, do you know what time it is?'

'Yes, madam, but I am in something of a quandary, and I am forced to disturb you.'

'Quandary? What quandary?'

'It's a little embarrassing, madam . . . '

'*Will* you get to the point?' she asked exasperatedly.

'Yes, madam. Captain Brooking has arrived, madam, and he says that he has been invited here by Miss Olivia for Her Ladyship's funeral.'

Amy stared at him. 'Captain Brooking?'

'I do not know what to do, for he and Lord Chalbourne are most definitely not on speaking terms, and yet if Miss Olivia has invited him . . . '

'She has, Jeffreys, she has.' Amy slipped from the bed.

'What am I to do, madam? Lord Chalbourne would most *definitely* not wish Captain Brooking to gain entry to Chalbourne Park!'

'The Captain has been invited, Jeffreys, and therefore he has every right to expect a modicum of hospitality! And *etiquette* demands that he be treated with courtesy and consideration.'

'Yes, madam.' The butler looked uncomfortable.

Amy eyed him for a moment. 'And, I suppose, because Miss Olivia is indisposed and His Lordship has taken himself elsewhere for the time being, then the poker buck falls in my lap.'

'I beg your pardon, madam??'

'The responsibility is mine.'

'Oh, I sincerely hope so, madam,' he said with disarming candor.

She smiled then. 'Well, you're honest about it, I'll say that for you.' She sought her wrap. 'Will you see to it that a room is prepared for the Captain, Jeffreys, and then I will receive him in the drawing room directly I've been made a little more respectable.'

'Very well, madam. Shall I send Mary Danthorpe to you?'

'No, I can manage without her — I don't intend dressing.'

'But *madam!*' The butler was scandalized. 'You cannot receive a gentleman in your undress!'

'Jeffreys, my nightgown and wrap more than amply conceal every portion of my person, and I do *not* intend going through the rigmarole of getting dressed in all my day toggery simply to spend a few minutes explaining things to the Captain — who, no doubt, is as tired as I am.'

'Yes, madam.'

She sat by the dressing table and picked up her hairbrush, and then she turned. 'Well, get on with it, Jeffreys, or we will none of us get any more sleep tonight!'

When he'd gone she finished brushing her hair and then looked at herself in the mirror. Was Jeffreys maybe right? *Should* she send for Mary Danthorpe after all? No. No, she wouldn't, she was right about her nightgown and wrap, beneath them she could have been possessed of four cloven hooves for all the Captain would be able to see! She re-arranged the folds of her wrap, patting her hair into place for a final time, and then went down to receive Alice Chalbourne's brother.

She saw his reflection in a mirror on the drawing room wall long before she reached the room. He was of medium height and slender build and his hair was thick and fair and it curled slightly at the back of his neck. Like all hussars he sported a Hungarian moustache, and his face bore a pensive expression as he waited for her. He wore a dark blue hussar uniform with a dolman jacket which had rich silver braiding and buff facings. His spotless white breeches were revealingly tight, and his black hessian boots were so highly polished that she knew she would be able to see her face in them. His pelisse was edged with black fur and was thrown casually over his left shoulder, and his shako was draped with golden festoons and flounders.

He turned, his expression wary as she entered, and his sabretache swung dashingly as he bowed to her. 'Captain Michael Brooking of the Eleventh Hussars. Your servant, ma'am.' His eyes she saw were the same startling brown as his sister's had been.

'Captain Brooking.'

'I realize of course that I am too late to attend my sister's funeral, Miss Chalbourne, but your letter took some time to find my regiment in Belgium and when I received it I was about to leave for England anyway to visit your fiancé at Oakleigh Hall.'

'I'm not Miss Chalbourne, sir, my name is Miss van Allen, and I too am a guest here. Miss Chalbourne, I fear, is indisposed, and Lord Chalbourne has some business to attend to in Bristol, so I'm afraid that I'm the only one here to receive you.'

He relaxed visibly, smiling at her then. 'Do I detect an American accent, Miss van Allen?'

'You do indeed, sir, I am from Washington.'

'A fair city.'

'You know it?'

He nodded. 'A little. It was my privilege to

241

be aboard the sloop *Favourite* when she brought the peace treaty to New York, and I traveled with the British peace commission when they went to Washington.' He took her hand and raised it to his lips. 'But I surely missed that city's greatest asset when I missed you, Miss van Allen.'

She flushed, withdrawing her hand. 'May I offer you some refreshment, sir?'

'You are most kind, but I ate a very fine dinner at Cirencester before completing my journey here.'

She smiled uneasily. 'Won't you sit down, Captain Brooking, for you must be tired after such a long journey. Has your regiment been in Belgium for long?'

'Since Waterloo. We're at Hazebrouck now, as part of the occupying force.'

'I understand you were wounded at Waterloo.'

'Yes, I was with Vandeleur's Fourth Cavalry Brigade on Wellington's left flank during the battle, and I was wounded in the final cavalry charge.'

Nervously she fidgeted with the belt of her wrap. There was something unreal and unsettling about passing the time in polite conversation when all the time she knew she had to tell him so much that he would find unpleasant. 'I — I'm so sorry that your visit here is because of such a tragic circumstance, sir.'

He nodded slowly. 'I still can't believe she's dead. During the journey here I kept hoping that it was all just a dream and that I'd wake up, or that I'd arrive here and she'd be waiting to greet me . . . Did you know my sister, Miss van Allen?'

'No, I did not arrive here until after she — after her death. I met Miss Chalbourne in Washington and I came here to attend her wedding.'

He gave a heavy sigh. 'No doubt Alice's death has seriously interfered with their marriage plans.'

She couldn't go on any more without telling him everything. 'Captain Brooking, I think that there is a very great deal of which you are not aware, and it has fallen to me to have to tell you what has been happening here recently.'

'Happening?' he asked quickly.

'It's complicated and unpleasant, sir, and I do not think you will like it in the slightest.' Her fingers coiled and uncoiled the ends of her belt.

He gave a wry laugh. 'Indeed? Then I can only assume that Jonathan Chalbourne is more than a little involved in whatever it is!'

'He is.' Reluctantly she began to tell him

about the theft of the sapphires, about his sister's obvious involvement, and about Charles Pemberton's apparent part in it. The only thing she left out was her discovery of the piece of paper in Alice's book — apart from that, she spared him nothing.

He stared at her without speaking for a moment when she had finished. 'Ch-Charles has been arrested, you say?' he murmured absently.

'I fear so.'

Slowly he got up, his face darkening as if quite suddenly the full import of it all was borne in on him. 'Slanderous lies!' he cried. 'How *dare* Chalbourne allow such infamy to attach to my sister's name! To *my* name!'

'Please sir . . . '

'I cannot believe it, not even of Chalbourne!'

She stood, timidly putting a hand on his arm. 'Please, sir, for I find all this most difficult and embarrassing, and most distressing.'

Briefly his hand was over hers. 'Forgive me, Miss van Allen, I realize that it is not your fault and I should not allow my feelings to show so obviously!' He turned away. 'If you are a guest here, then it cannot have escaped your notice that there is a great deal of animosity between Chalbourne and myself.'

'I am aware of it.'

'Maybe that is why I see his hand in all this.'

'Captain Brooking, I truly don't think Lord Chalbourne . . . '

'Tell me, Miss van Allen, do *you* think my sister stole the sapphires?'

'I would find it very hard *not* to think it.'

He nodded slowly. 'But if you had only known her, Miss van Allen, then you would find this story as incredible as I do. Just as I find it incredible that after all these years it was Charles Pemberton she loved.'

'She kept his letters.' Amy glanced at him. 'Captain Brooking, I cannot find it in my heart to exculpate your sister, but I do find it difficult to believe in Mr Pemberton's guilt.'

He gave a short laugh. 'And to think I intended driving on to Oakleigh Hall tomorrow morning to stay there with him over the Christmas season . . . Now I shall just stay here long enough to attend to any of my sister's affairs which are outstanding, and then I shall be forced to return to my regiment.' The dark brown eyes rested thoughtfully on her face for a long moment. 'If Alice stole the sapphires, then what reason did she have? Whatever else I may say of Chalbourne, he did not stint on her allowance, she lacked for nothing. So *why* did she do it?'

'I don't know.'

'Unless, of course, she and Pemberton *were* lovers, and he had debts.'

She stared at him. 'I don't think . . . '

'As I recall from our days at Oxford, he always had a sad propensity for losing at cards.'

'I don't think he had anything to do with any of this,' she said shortly.

'What a dragon he has to defend him.' He smiled at her.

'I happen to believe him, sir. And I *want* him to be innocent, for Olivia Chalbourne's sake.'

He sat down again, leaning back to look up at her. 'What of this witness, Miss van Allen, this boy who says he saw Charles with the necklace in the woods. Can there by any doubt?'

'No. The boy recognized the horse.'

'The *horse?*' He began to laugh suddenly. 'The damned, damned horse . . . '

'Sir?'

'Again you must forgive me, Miss van Allen, it just strikes me as sad that the color of a horse should maybe cause a man to hang. Still, he is apparently guilty — so your faith in him is as misplaced as is mine in my sister.'

She bit her lip. 'I feel so sorry for Olivia, Captain Brooking. She loves him so very much and the shock of everything has proved too much for her.'

'I do not know Miss Chalbourne at all, but your great tenderness and friendship toward her convey to me the irrefutable fact that she cannot in *any* way be as unpleasant or ill-mannered as her singularly boorish brother.'

'She isn't.'

'Which curt reply further conveys to me that your opinion of Chalbourne rather matches my own, Miss van Allen.'

'We are his guests, sir,' she reminded him quickly.

'Correction. *You* are his guest. I am an unwelcome, unwanted intruder and will no doubt be sent on my way with the aid of his boot behind me the moment he sets eyes on me.'

'Captain Brooking, you have been invited here by his sister, and I'm sure Lord Chalbourne is not a man to deny that.'

'Then you don't know him at all, Miss van Allen. He loathes the very sight of me, which is why I was so damned surprised to find myself actually invited to these hallowed Gloucestershire acres.' He smiled. 'I should have guessed that Miss Chalbourne was writing without his knowledge. However, if I can rest my head here until tomorrow morning, then I can be on my way back to Belgium without Chalbourne's even knowing.'

'I'm sure there is no need for you to leave so hastily, sir, for you have come a very long way and you need a little rest before setting off again.'

'How kind and thoughtful you are, Miss van Allen.' His smile was warm and his eyes moved slowly over her figure before coming to rest on her face again. 'But I do not for one moment imagine that Chalbourne will experience the same gentle concern for my well-being.'

The door opened and Jeffreys came in. He hovered by the door for a moment, glancing back over his shoulder into the hall, and then he looked at Amy, clearing his throat several times before at last speaking. 'Er — forgive me for interrupting, but there is a slight problem . . . '

'*Another* quandary, Jeffreys?'

'I fear so, madam.' He was avoiding her eyes.

'Oh, very well. If you will excuse me, Captain Brooking?'

He stood, bowing quickly. 'By all means, Miss van Allen.'

She followed the butler into the hall, and there she halted abruptly, for Jonathan was standing by the fireplace. His hands were clasped behind his back, and he was looking around disapprovingly at the fresh greenery which hung from every corner and wound around every edge. Then he saw her and his glance was withering as he saw that she was in her undress.

He wasted no time on pleasantries. 'By what right did you allow that fellow into this house, madam?'

'Would you expect me to ignore the fact that Olivia had invited him?'

'Is *that* the story he told you?'

'No, sir, it is the story *she* told me. She wrote to him as you instructed, but she also invited him here.'

'Olivia would not defy — '

'Olivia would and did, sir. She told me that she considered your attitude toward your wife's only living relative to be extremely wrong under the circumstances, and that she had deliberately gone against your wishes. I neither know nor care why you and Captain Brooking are at odds, sir, but the fact remains that he came here because he was invited, and I did the only thing I possibly could by receiving him.'

'In your undress.'

'Top marks for observation,' she said coldly.

'So, between you, you and Olivia have obviously decided that my wishes and reasons are to be questioned in my own house!' he snapped.

'There are so many orders emanating from you, sir, that it is inevitable that sooner or later lesser beings such as myself realize we have to decide which must be adhered to and which may be safely passed by.'

'As far as *you* are concerned, madam, they are obviously all in the latter category! And pray do not apply levity to things you do not understand. You know nothing of all this, *nothing!*'

'Nor have I any wish to, sir,' she said quietly, her eyes flashing angrily.

'If, as you say, my sister has invited him, then you did indeed take the only course open to you by inviting him in.'

'Thank you.'

'But do not expect the exceedingly short duration of his stay to be a pleasant experience, Miss van Allen, for there is far too much between Michael Brooking and myself — by far too much.'

'Tell me, sir, could it really be that the rest of the world is out of step and you are the only one marching in time?'

250

His eyes darkened, and Jeffreys, who had been waiting nearby, stepped forward quickly, and spoke to Amy. 'Madam, I have informed the Captain that the room prepared for him is now ready.'

'Thank you, Jeffreys.'

Jonathan dismissed the butler and then looked at Amy again. 'Did Brooking intimate what his plans are now?'

'He only intends staying to see to any of his sister's affairs which need his attention, and then he is returning to Belgium. He was expecting to spend Christmas at Oakleigh Hall, but has obviously discarded that plan now.'

'There are none of Alice's affairs which even remotely require his attention, and I will inform him of that right now.'

Her heart sank as he strode toward the drawing room door, and then gathering her skirts she hurried after him.

Michael Brooking stood slowly when Jonathan walked in.

'Chalbourne,' he said stiffly.

'I will not waste words, Brooking. You have been invited here without my permission, and I therefore expect you to understand that nothing has changed between us. There is no one on this earth less welcome beneath my roof than you. That being understood, I further expect you to have the common decency to leave Chalbourne Park again tomorrow, and not to make an already embarrassing situation more embarrassing.'

Amy stared at him, horrified at such out and out rudeness.

Michael gave a cool smile. 'The Chalbourne leopard has not changed his spots after all, it seems. I told Miss van Allen here that I should have realized that the invitation had been sent unknown to you.'

'You should indeed.'

'Very well, I have little choice but to leave again tomorrow. If there are any of my sister's affairs which — '

'Alice had no affairs which could in any way have required your attention.'

'Then maybe you wish me to take any of her unwanted belongings . . . ?'

'You may take everything, sir, for I have no wish to keep anything which was hers.'

There was a momentary silence during which Amy could hear her own pulse throbbing in her ears. Then Michael nodded. 'I will take whatever you wish, Chalbourne. If it can be packed ready to be taken to Wildmoor?'

'It will be attended to.'

'I will visit her grave tomorrow morning, and will leave directly everything is ready.'

'I trust you are not expecting a valuable hoard of jewelry to fall into your outstretched hands, Brooking, for if you are, then you will be disappointed. The only things you may take with you are those things which she brought with her at the time of the marriage.'

'I don't want anything else,' said Michael curtly, a dull red warming his face at Jonathan's continued insulting tone.

'Alice wanted a great deal which was *not* hers, sir.'

'I have been made fully aware of what my sister is supposed to have done!'

'There is no 'supposed' about it, Brooking, she damned well did it! Tainted blood will out.'

Amy held her breath as Michael's hand went to his saber. The muscles of his face worked with fury, but then he gradually conquered it, and his hand moved away from the saber again. 'So,' he said softly, 'all blame for everything is to be placed upon my sister's poor shoulders, is it? That is why you are so eager to show such a sad lack of grief at her death? Poor little Alice is to bear the brunt of your mistakes, your thwarted dreams, and your vicious revenge-seeking!'

Jonathan's eyes glittered unpleasantly. 'Take a little more care, Brooking, and do not attempt to play games, for you above all others know why I behave as I do. Any more of your pathetic attempts to convey an air of righteous indignation — which I suspect to be simply and solely for Miss van Allen's benefit — and I will do again what I did before. Only this time, I warn you, I shall not content myself with merely aiming for your shoulder.'

Amy's hands twisted together nervously. 'My lord, I hardly think — '

'Miss van Allen, please keep out of this.' Jonathan glanced briefly at her, and she saw the hard determination in his eyes. Nothing she could say this time would deter him, and she knew it. She fell silent.

Michael drew himself up stiffly. 'It could be, Chalbourne, that you would not find me so easy a target this time.'

'Captain Brooking!' cried Amy, afraid quite suddenly that a challenge was about to be issued. If she could not sway Jonathan, then maybe Michael would see a little sense.

He hesitated, looking at her for a moment, and then he smiled. 'Have no fear, Miss van Allen, my temper may be hasty, but it is not rash. I will terminate this confrontation right now and spare you any more of this. I thank you for the most gentle way you broke such bad news to me, and I thank you too for the pleasant conversation I had with you.

Good night, Miss van Allen.' But his eyes were cold again as he nodded at Jonathan. His pelisse swung angrily as he turned to walk away, and his spurs jingled loudly as he left them.

Amy looked accusingly at Jonathan. 'How *could* you?'

'With creatures as base as Brooking, it comes exceedingly easy, I promise you.'

'He was not the one who behaved basely here tonight, sir, *you* were! He came to this house because his only sister has died, and you went out of your way to be more insulting, more unpleasantly arrogant, and infinitely more rude than ever I have witnessed before!'

He took a long breath. 'Miss van Allen, his presence here at Chalbourne Park is by far more of an insult to me than anything I have said or done here tonight. Pray, do not try to defend him to me.'

She stared at him. 'But you were trying to provoke him into a duel!'

'I was not.' He smiled a little. 'I have no need to provoke him, Miss van Allen, for I have sufficient cause to call him out whenever I choose, and he knows it. I may be as rude as I wish and he will not throw down any gauntlet. Oh, I grant that his study of barely controlled anger was a masterpiece of theatrical guile, but he is ever and was ever, a mere actor. He had no intention of calling me out because he does not dare to do so.'

'But you called him out before?'

'I did.'

'Why?'

'Because — ' His lips pressed angrily together then. 'I have no need to give you my reasons, Miss van Allen. I know my Brooking, you do not. Tell me why it is that you are so busy being shocked at my despicable attack upon the poor, grief-stricken fellow that you have not stopped for even one moment to consider his dubious reactions? You are so eager to leap to his defense in the face of my aggression, but did you not wonder at his cowed acceptance? Any man worth his salt would have taken me by the throat for what I said — but not Brooking. *He* has bowed to my behavior, and he has further elected to *remain* beneath this roof for the rest of tonight! I trust you can make something admirable of his behavior, Miss van Allen, I know that I cannot.'

'I've tried very hard to make something admirable out of you, sir, but truly I think the task is beyond me, for you *have* no good points!'

'You labor at a considerable disadvantage with only a few meager facts at your disposal.'

'Then *tell* me the facts! Give me a sporting chance!'

He studied her for a moment. 'Am I right in assuming that you find Brooking's company every bit as congenial as he obviously finds yours?'

'I do not dislike his company, if that is what you mean.'

'It will do, madam, it will do. So I'm led to suppose that you will be no more disposed to hear ill of *him* than you are to hear ill of Pemberton. On the other hand, you have shown yourself throughout to be more than prepared to believe the very worst of me. If anyone here requires a sporting chance, Miss van Allen, I think it is me. I bid you good night.' He inclined his head and left her standing alone in the drawing room.

The moments passed and she did not move. Every meeting she had with him became a confrontation, every word exchanged a bitter recrimination . . .

Jeffreys came quietly in. 'Excuse me, Miss van Allen.'

'Yes? What is it?'

'I realize that it's very late, and that the fault is entirely mine that I have not spoken to you earlier . . . '

'What *is* it, Jeffreys?' she asked again, in no

mood for the man's tortuous mode of explanation.

'Before His Lordship left for Bristol, madam, he left instructions that I was to consult with you about changing your room. Forgive me, Miss van Allen, but the charge completely slipped my mind until this moment.'

'Change my room?' She'd forgotten all about it. 'I'll leave it up to you, Jeffreys.'

'Well, madam, there are two rooms which I think you may find to your liking.'

'I don't think I am in any state to discuss the finer points of bedchambers right now, Jeffreys.'

'Quite so, madam. Maybe if I tell you which rooms, then maybe you can look at them yourself when you are ready, and then inform me which one you have decided upon.'

'Very well.'

'They are in the same corridor as Miss Olivia's room, madam. One is the second on the right and the other is third.'

'The second and third on the right in Miss Olivia's corridor,' she repeated mechanically. 'Thank you, Jeffreys, I will look at them tomorrow.'

'Thank you, madam. And again, forgive me for forgetting my duties.'

'That's quite all right, Jeffreys,' she, said, walking across the room, her wrap billowing behind her. 'And now, I think I'll go back to my bed for what remains of this odious night. Good night, Jeffreys.'

'Good night, madam.'

11

Amy's sleep was restless and disturbing, and she tossed in the bed as she dreamed. She was walking down a dark, misty passageway with Jeffreys, and the butler was holding a tall candle which smoked and flared as he walked. The mist writhed around them, cold and clammy as it touched her face, and their footsteps echoed on the wooden floor and around the paneled walls. By a door the butler halted, and when he spoke his voice was horribly distorted. 'This is the cupboard, madam, I thought it would be just to your liking.' She stared into the dark space which was revealed as the creaking door swung open, and by the light of the candle she could see the necklace glittering and sparkling. She stepped forward, reaching out toward it, but Alice's laughter was all around her. Still she reached out toward the necklace, but then there was nothing beneath her feet, no floor, no support, and she was falling into the bowels of the earth, falling and falling through air which was cold and dank and which stank of the grave . . .

With a sharp cry Amy woke from the grip

of sleep. Her heart was thundering and her forehead was damp, and her hands trembled as she reached out to the bedpost for support. She leaned her head weakly against the cold wood, listening to the pounding of her own heart. For a moment it was as it had been the night the intruder had come, but outside in the corridor the first maids were going about their early morning tasks, and occasionally she could hear more moving in the attic rooms above. The very normality of the sounds made her laugh at herself then. It was only a dream, a silly, foolish dream.

She lay back again, sighing. She seemed destined to have broken, complicated nights, for she had had nothing but interrupted or very late nights since her arrival in England. If this continued, she could look a little disreputable, to say the least.

Suddenly, though, her thoughts returned to the dream. How strange that sleep should intermingle the matter of her new room and the mystery of the necklace. She smiled to think of Jeffreys carefully showing her, not to the second room on the right, but to a cupboard! *This is the cupboard, madam, I thought it would be just to your liking.* And yet — was it so strange? Slowly she sat up again, reaching out to take her reticule from the table beside the bed. She unfolded the handkerchief and took out the piece of paper. *3 4L Cupd.* Was *that* what her dream had been all about? If the second room on the right was written as *2R*, then would not the fourth room on the left be written as *4L?* She stared at the paper, her mind racing as she went over the thought time and time again. Was that what it meant? A cupboard in the fourth room on the left? But what did the *3* mean? She glanced at the golden tassels of the bed hangings for a moment. The third floor? The third passage? The third wing?

Chalbourne Park did not have three wings, and the third floor was the attic story above her own room. As to the third passage, well, that all depended upon the point from which you began to count. She hid the paper away again. The third floor, that seemed the most likely. The third floor, fourth room on the left, in the cupboard.

She slipped from the bed and put on her wrap again, pausing only to slip her feet into some stockings and slippers, for it was very cold. After a perfunctory brush of the hair, she left the room.

The staircase the servants used to reach their room was at the far end of her own passageway, and she listened for a moment at the foot of it, but there was no sound from the floor above. The air was bitterly cold as she went up, and as she reached the top her heart began to rush with excitement again. What if — what if she was about to find the necklace? She counted the doors swiftly, and at the fourth on the left she halted. Maybe someone was still in the room? She tapped on the door, but there was silence. Slowly she opened it, and the slanting light from the small roof window made the little room seem uneven, and there was condensation on the ice-cold glass which made the clear blue of the sky outside virtually impossible to discern. Amy's breath froze as she went into the room, and the door begun to slowly squeak to a close behind her. It was a storeroom containing heavy wooden chests which when she opened them proved to contain new clothing and livery for the army of servants at Chalbourne Park. But there was no cupboard. She turned slowly back toward the door, and then she saw the small cupboard immediately behind it. It was a tall, narrow cupboard with one single door which had a knob handle. The handle turned easily as she opened it.

The musty smell of damp wood touched her nostrils as she looked inside. Brooms and feather dusters rested inside, and above them a single shelf containing one small box. Eagerly she lifted the box down, but a keen disappointment swept through her when she opened it to find nothing inside. She replaced the box and closed the cupboard. Nothing. A sudden thought about secret hiding places made her pull the cupboard away from the wall, but behind it there were only spiders' webs and still more dust. There were no tiny openings in the wall, no hidden places where the necklace might still lie. Then she wondered about the top of the cupboard itself, and she dragged a stool from a corner and stepped onto it to look on the top of the cupboard. She ran her finger through the thick dust, and she was still standing there when she heard footsteps outside the door, steps which halted.

'Who's in there?' demanded an authoritative voice.

Jeffreys! Slowly she stepped down from the stool, and as she did so the butler came in, and the frown died on his face as he saw Amy. 'Miss van Allen?'

'Good morning, Jeffreys,' she said awkwardly.

'But madam, these are the servants' quarters!'

'I know. I — er — was looking for something.'

'Looking for something?' he repeated. 'May I ask what for?'

'No, Jeffreys, you may not!' she said firmly, taking cowardly refuge in her superiority. 'And I have not found it, so I will go back downstairs now.'

Embarrassment colored her face. What must he be thinking? He had come across a house guest snooping around in the servants' quarters. But to her relief her answer put him at a loss for words, and he mutely stood aside as she gathered her skirts to briskly walk out and along the passageway toward the steep staircase down to the floor below.

But as she descended the stairs, she forgot the butler and thought instead of her fruitless search. A mocking line from a children's rhyme went through her head. ' . . . *and when she got there, the cupboard was bare . . . .*' 'Aye,' she said aloud to herself, her skirts swishing richly on the rickety wooden steps, 'and this poor doggy surely had none!'

She halted at the foot of the stairs. She had been so certain that she had solved the code on the piece of paper, and yet there had been nothing at all in that cupboard in the loft. A bitter disappointment filled her as she walked on toward her own room. But what if she had only been partly right? She was certain that the *4L* referred to the fourth room on the left, but maybe she was wrong about the *3*. There were only three floors altogether at

Chalbourne Park . . . No. No, if you included the cellars, then there were four. And if you counted the storys from the cellars, then the third one was the one on which she was walking right now! She halted outside her own door, looking along the passage toward the staircase. Mentally she walked up the stairs past the griffins, and at the top she halted, turning left. The doors moved past her mind's eyes, and came to a halt at the fourth. The music room.

Gathering her skirts again, she ran along the passageway and into the main corridor. The music room was warm already, for a fire had been lit in the hearth and a wire guard placed around it to protect the fine Persian rugs from flying sparks. The morning sunlight did not enter this room, and the worn carpet in the center of the floor was without its spangling of patterns from the leaded windows. The harpischord did not look as inviting in this light, and the gold on the harp was dull and flat. She glanced around for a cupboard, and she soon saw that there was only one. It stood in a far corner, a white and gold piece after the French style, with curved legs and intricate handles. Eagerly she hurried across the room toward it, and when she opened it her gaze fell on pile after pile of manuscripts and sheets of music. She took a long breath, glancing at the clock which stood on the mantlepiece. Did she have time before the breakfast gong sounded? Even as she thought it, the gong echoed dully through the house. Undecided, she hesitated, but then the desire to prove her theory grew too much, and she knelt down before the cupboard to drag out the heavy bundles of paper.

Spiders scattered into the shadows and their webs clung stickily to her fingers, but she persevered in spite of her aversion to such things. The paper was piled all around her on the carpet and she gazed at the empty cupboard. Again there was nothing.

She stood, running her hands all over the interior, but there was no knob, no tiny lever which would expose a hiding place. She dragged a small chair over and stood on it to look on the top, but again there was just dust and some more spiders, and it was obvious that the cupboard hadn't been moved for months. Getting down again, she knelt on the floor to push her hands timidly beneath the cupboard, shuddering as something scuttered swiftly over her fingers. She felt around, but again the amount of dust revealed not only that Lord Chalbourne's housekeeper should have a strict word with some of the housemaids, but also that there was nothing there.

With a heavy sigh she got up after she had painstakingly replaced all the papers, and she barely resisted the temptation to slam the cupboard doors crossly. She dusted her wrap a little and left the room. Maybe she was wrong after all . . . Still dusting her skirts and picking fronds of spiders' webs from the soft fabric, she returned to her own room, but all the time she was thinking about her theory. She was right, she was sure of it — but she wasn't entirely right, and there was the rub. She had solved only part of the mystery, and until she could discover which part, then there was little more she could do. She took a deep breath; she would have to talk to Jonathan about it, and *that* was something she did not view with pleasant anticipation.

Mary was waiting for her. 'Good morning, ma'am. I came to dress you for breakfast but the gong went so long ago now . . .'

'Yes, Mary, I know. Could you perhaps see that a tray is brought up here?'

'Yes, ma'am. Oh, Miss Olivia's maid Sally was here not long back. She said as Miss Olivia was a lot better this morning and had been asking particularly to see you.'

'I'll go after breakfast.'

'Yes, ma'am.' The woman bobbed a brief curtsey and left the room, and Amy watched her curiously, for there was an almost light note in her voice, and there was certainly a lightness in her walk this morning.

After she'd eaten, Mary dressed her again in the black chenille day dress. Amy looked at herself in the cheval mirror. How she *loathed* wearing the same dress every single day, it was not at all good for the morale, and the Lord alone knew her morale needed lifting at the moment, not depressing! She stared at herself. Was it possible to tell from her face how very unhappy she was? She was trying so hard to show a brave face to the world, but inside the pain was keen. Unrequited love was the stuff of ladies' novels, and she herself had smiled a little at reading of it; but to endure it herself put such a different light upon the subject. Never again would she find it even vaguely amusing.

She sat before the dressing table and Mary began to brush and pin her hair. Amy glanced at the woman in the mirror. There was a lightness about her today — it was almost as if she were humming silently to herself . . .

The last pin had been put in place when there was a light knock at the door, and when Mary opened it Michael Brooking was standing there, his hussar uniform so handsome as he bowed to Amy. 'Good morning, Miss van Allen.'

'Good morning, Captain Brooking. Please come in.'

'I was hoping to speak with you at breakfast, but when you did not come . . . '

'You wished to speak with me about something in particular?' She smiled at him, but quite unbidden Jonathan's condemning words of the night before came into her head. Just why had a man like Michael Brooking meekly endured all those insults and then allowed himself to be further humiliated by remaining at Chalbourne Park for the night?

He smiled a little sheepishly. 'This morning I have been to my sister's room, Miss van Allen, and I confess I found it a very upsetting experience on my own. I was wondering . . . '

'If I would help you?' she finished for him.

'Yes. Miss van Allen, I would be most grateful if you would.'

'Of course, Captain.'

'And a little later, maybe we could ride to the churchyard together?'

She nodded. 'Yes. But first, however, I have to see Miss Chalbourne. The moment I have done that, then I will be at your disposal.'

His dark brown eyes were appreciative as be smiled at her. 'Forgive me, Miss van Allen, but I find you one of the most captivating women I have ever seen. I thought so last

270

night, and now this morning, with the sunlight on your hair — '

'Captain Brooking . . . ' she began, a little embarrassed by his outspoken praise — embarrassed, but not displeased.

He smiled. 'Allow that inside every man there is a veritable poetic genius striving to be recognized.' He looked at Mary then. 'Good morning, Mary, I trust that you are keeping well.'

'Good morning, master.'

'I am not your master now, Mary,' he reminded her.

'There ent but one master, sir, and that's the master of Wildmoor.'

He did not correct the woman again, and it seemed to Amy that he gave an almost imperceptible nod of his head, but then he returned his attention to her and seemed to forget the maid. 'I understand, Miss van Allen, that you have been reading my sister's book.'

'*Sense and Sensibility?* Why yes, it should be over there beside the bed. Mary, would you bring it here, please?'

Mary brought the book, but instead of giving it to Amy as she should have done, she gave it to Michael.

He looked at the broken spine, but said nothing. 'If you have finished with it, Miss van Allen, then I would like to put it with the rest of my sister's belongings to be taken to Wildmoor.'

'Of course.'

'She was very fond of Miss Austen's novels, and when I knew this one had been published — '

'*You* gave it to her?'

He nodded. 'Yes, for her birthday in September. It's only a book, but as it was the last thing I gave her, then I would like to take it with me as a memento, a keepsake.'

She smiled sadly. 'I'm so sorry about everything, Captain Brooking,' she said gently, 'for I do understand about losing someone so dearly loved.'

'Well, maybe she is better off as she is now, Miss van Allen, for she was unhappy. So young still, but so very unhappy . . . ' His voice died away for a moment. 'I should not have allowed her to marry Chalbourne, but at the time — well, it seemed the right thing.'

Amy got up, picking up her shawl and reticule. She did not want to enter into any conversation which criticized Jonathan — she had criticisms of her own, but she would not allow herself to be drawn into such things by another. 'I will go to Miss Chalbourne now, Captain Brooking, and then I will help you afterward. Where shall I be able to find you?'

'I will wait in the drawing room, Miss van Allen.' He took her hand and raised it to his lips. She felt the light brush of his moustache against her skin and it was not an unpleasant sensation. She drew her hand away slowly, and then inclined her head and left the room.

★　★　★

She walked slowly, wondering how best to break the news about Charles Pemberton to Olivia, but before she reached Olivia's room, she saw the maid Sally hurrying along toward her.

'Oh, Miss van Allen, Miss Olivia's just sent me to look for you again.'

'Again? Is something the matter?'

The maid swallowed. 'Well, ma'am, she asked me about Mr Pemberton, and I didn't rightly know what to tell her. She's still not well enough really . . . '

'Yes?'

'She guessed as something was wrong and she got it out of me in the end.'

'Oh, dear. How is she?'

'Proper upset, ma'am, proper upset. She made me tell her over and over what Ben Turner said, and then she said as I was to fetch you quickly 'cos there was something very important she had to tell and she had to tell it to you first.'

'Important? About what Ben said, you mean?'

'Reckon so, ma'am. She wouldn't tell me, said that there was only you she could tell first off.'

Amy sighed. What could it be? 'I'll go to her right now, Sally.'

'Yes, ma'am. Thank you.'

The maid hurried along behind her, but she remained outside the door when Amy opened it.

Olivia was propped up comfortably on some pillows. Her face was still very pale, but she had more color now. There was no bandage around her forehead so that Amy could see the ugly gash and the bruise which marred the perfect skin.

Amy smiled at her. 'And how are you feeling now?'

'The headache is tolerable.' Olivia toyed with the hem of the sheet, her fingers moving agitatedly. 'Amy, about Ben Turner . . . '

'What about him?'

'He is absolutely certain that he saw Charles?'

'I believe so.'

'He recognized him?'

'Well — he said it looked like him, and he was sure about the horse.'

Olivia bit her lip. 'Amy, Sally says that Ben saw Charles on the night before the Hunt Ball at about midnight.'

'Then it could not have been Charles.'

Amy stared at her. 'But . . . '

'I know it could not because I was with Charles at Oakleigh Hall on that night.' A dull flush bloomed on Olivia's cheeks as she looked at Amy. 'I spent the entire night with him.'

Amy continued to stare. 'Olivia!'

'I'm saying that whoever it was that Ben Turner saw with Alice that night, it was not Charles Pemberton.' Olivia lowered her eyes, biting her lip for a moment. 'We have been lovers for some time now, Amy. I knew that Jonathan would be away that night and I also knew that it is quite a simple matter to slip away without Alice being any the wiser. I — I needed to talk to you about it first, before I told Jonathan . . . ' Olivia's eyes filled with tears. 'Amy,' she whispered in a breaking voice, 'Charles is defending me by saying nothing, but I can't let him do that.'

Amy took the other's shaking hands. 'All right, sweeting, don't cry now . . . '

'I'm so afraid of telling Jonathan, of telling him that I've been — been . . . He'll be so angry.'

Amy squeezed the fingers. 'He'll be even

more angry if you say nothing and Charles is sent to the gallows for something he did not do,' she said firmly. She took a deep breath. 'Would — would you prefer it if *I* told him?'

Olivia's eyes went hopefully to hers. 'Would you, Amy?' she asked softly, her fingernails digging into Amy's flesh. 'Would you do that for me?'

Amy nodded. 'Yes, sweeting, of course I will.' I'm in his bad books so much already, she thought, that one more thing will make hardly any difference to his loathing for me.

'You see, Amy, I know that Captain Brooking has arrived, so Jonathan will already be furiously angry with me. That's why he hasn't come to my room at all.'

'Your brother was away until very late last night, Livvy, and I'm sure *that's* why he hasn't been to see you, and it's not because he's so angry with you,' soothed Amy, none too sure in her heart that she had judged Jonathan Chalbourne correctly at all on this particular point.

'Do you think so?' Olivia's voice was pathetically hopeful.

'Yes, sweeting, I'm sure.' Amy stood. 'I'll go and see him now.'

'You must be wishing you'd never sailed from America, Amy.'

Amy smiled. 'Life *was* less complicated

over there, I'll admit.'

'Have you written to Mr Kenney yet?'

Amy stared at her. The letter. She'd forgotten all about it. 'I've written, but I haven't posted it yet.'

'You've missed the letter carrier again now, too.'

'Well, there's time enough.'

Olivia studied her face for a moment. 'Amy van Allen,' she said softly, 'those aren't the words of a woman in love.'

'I know. Well, I'll go and face your brother now.'

Outside the door, Sally was still waiting. Amy smiled at her. 'Has Miss Olivia had her breakfast yet, Sally?'

'She said as she wasn't hungry, Miss van Allen.'

'Well, you go down to the cook and see to it that a fine tray of breakfast is brought up to her, and then you tell her that *I* said she was to eat it because everything will be all right now.'

The maid smiled, her eyes brightening. 'Oh, yes, ma'am, yes — I'll see to it right now!'

Amy watched the maid hurrying away, but her own heart felt heavy in spite of her encouraging and optimistic words. Jonathan was not going to like what she had to tell him one little bit — but if he was a bear to Olivia now, then he'd have Amy Magnolia van Allen to contend with! But how to engineer the conversation, that was the problem . . .

12

Jonathan was in the stables when at last she found him. He was standing with his head groom watching the paces of a chestnut hunter as a boy led it around the cobbled yard.

Amy shivered in her shawl, but it was not so much from the cold as from nervousness. There was warmth in the sun, and the snow on the stable roofs was melting slowly, the drip-dripping plainly audible all around.

Jonathan and the groom were discussing the hunter. 'What do you think then, Harry?'

'Sand crack can sometimes be got over right well, m'lord.'

'Sunfire's a good horse, I don't want to lose him. Take him to the smith then and see that everything possible is done to cure him.'

'Yes, m'lord. Reckon he'll not be right enough for the Derby, though.'

'Well, I can survive without another Derby winner.' Jonathan smiled at him.

'We're all right sorry about everything what's happened, m'lord — and we want you to know we're all behind you, whatever happens.'

'Thank you, Harry.' Jonathan seemed to sense Amy's presence suddenly, for he turned. 'Good morning, Miss van Allen.'

'May I speak with you, my lord?' she asked.

'Go ahead.'

'In private, if you please.'

He nodded at Harry, who touched his hat and left them. 'Well?'

'Why have you not seen Olivia yet?'

His eyes darkened. 'That is none of your business, madam.'

Her chin came up. 'Oh, yes it is, sir, it's my business because you have made it so.'

'*I* have?'

'You have requested me to remain here to help look after Olivia, and that is precisely what I am doing. And right now, I happen to think that she would benefit from a *kindly* visit from you, sir.'

His riding crop tapped his shining boot slowly. 'A kindly visit is something I might find a little difficult at the moment, Miss van Allen.'

'Because she had the audacity to defy you?'

His eyes moved over her face for a moment. 'Because of the manner she chose to do it in. Anything else I could forgive, but not the inviting of Michael Brooking to my house. So, if that is all, I have things to attend to — '

'No, it is *not* all.'

'Madam, when it comes to intractable, difficult women, you must surely take the crown! When I say that I have other things to attend to, then that is the end of the conversation, madam!'

'And when *I* say that that is not all, then it is *not!*'

He stared angrily into her blue eyes, his hands on his hips, and she looked back with matching anger and determination. Suddenly his eyes lightened a little and to her surprise he smiled. 'Very well, Miss van Allen, you perceive a white flag waving above my vanquished head. What else is there that you wish to talk to me about?'

'Sir, it is very difficult to tell you, but I must, and I want your promise in advance that you will not be unbearably angry again.'

'Is this in connection with being a heavy host or a heavy brother?'

'A heavy brother.'

'And the American woman-o'-war is sailing in to the attack on my sister's behalf, I take it?'

'Yes.'

He smiled again. 'I am beginning to be a coward where you are concerned, Miss van Allen, for it is easier to capitulate than it is to cross swords.'

'I trust you will still feel the same way when I have finished.'

'If I find it humanly possible to remain tranquil, then I promise to be so, Miss van Allen.'

'Well, it concerns Mr Pemberton.'

His smile faded. 'Pemberton?'

'Don't look at me like that, sir, for this is important and not idle time-wasting on my part.'

'Very well.'

'Lord Chalbourne, the man Ben Turner saw with your wife that night in the woods could not possibly have been Charles Pemberton, because Olivia can prove Charles to have been elsewhere at the time.'

His eyes narrowed a little. 'And how can she do that?'

Amy swallowed. 'Because Olivia spent that entire night with him at Oakleigh Hall.'

'Am I to understand that Olivia and Pemberton have been lovers, Miss van Allen?' he asked in a falsely light voice. 'Yes.'

The riding crop tapped again. 'Miss van Allen, if I find this to be some — '

'Some feeble attempt on my part to save Mr Pemberton at all costs?' she finished for him. 'No, sir, it is not. Olivia told me herself that she had spent that night with him, that she was in his bed throughout the hours when Ben Turner claims to have seen him in the woods. She is speaking the truth, sir, for she had no reason to lie.'

'Except that she may wish to save her lover's neck!'

'She's telling the truth,' repeated Amy. 'She knows how the loss of the sapphires has affected you, and she cares a great deal about it. She also cares that she has offended you by her invitation to Captain Brooking. She loves you a great deal and has no wish to hurt you at all, but she loves Charles Pemberton with all her heart, and she will not stand aside and allow him to go to the gallows for something he did not do. It has taken a great deal of courage for her to defy you by running away as she did, and it has taken even more to admit now that her behavior in private has been far less than the perfection you would wish.'

'I could have wished for more perfection on Pemberton's part, too!'

'They are in love.'

'And that releases him from responsibility?'

'No. No, sir, but it goes a long way to explaining why he allowed it to happen. He loves her, and she is very much in love with him — I do not find it at all surprising that — '

'Aye, well the ways of the flesh *are* known

to me, Miss van Allen.'

'I have little doubt of that, sir.'

He smiled faintly. 'I am a man of the world, madam, not the dissolute, rampant rake your tone would seem to suggest. So, Olivia is prepared to stand up in court and tell the world that she and Pemberton have been lovers and that she can provide him with an alibi for the night in question?'

'Yes.'

'And no doubt, when questions are asked of servants, it will soon become apparent that there has been *something* going on between her and Pemberton.'

'Undoubtedly.'

'Am I doing well for tranquility, Miss van Allen?' he asked suddenly.

'A-admirably.'

'And surprisingly, she thought,' he said drily.

Her face reddened a little, for that had been exactly what her thoughts had been. 'What will you do now?'

'There is only one thing I can do, Miss van Allen, and that is to get my sister's sworn and written statement providing Pemberton's alibi, and then to take myself post-haste to Cirencester and secure the fellow's immediate release.'

'I'm sorry, sir,' she said.

'Sorry? Madam, you have had your way and now you're sorry?'

'Yes, because Mr Pemberton's innocence means someone else's guilt. Someone somewhere is going free when he should be in jail. Ben Turner saw a man meeting your wife in the woods, and he also saw the necklace — either the fake or the genuine sapphires — and if it was not Mr Pemberton, then who was it?'

'That, Miss van Allen, is something I would dearly like to know. Dearly. However, even with Pemberton in gaol, I could not have attempted to wring a confession from him about the sapphires' whereabouts — alas for my cause, the torture chamber is a thing of the past.'

She remembered the fragment of letter then. 'There is something else I would like to talk to you about, something which I think is connected with the sapphires . . . ' she began.

He smiled, putting a finger to her lips. 'You have provided me with sufficient work for this morning, Miss van Allen, so please, may this other thing wait until tonight?'

'But — '

'I must see Olivia and then go with all speed to Cirencester, and already it is mid-morning.'

'Tonight?'

He nodded. 'If it concerns the sapphires, then it merits my complete and undivided attention, Miss van Allen. I swear upon my honor that I shall listen very closely to you tonight.'

She smiled reluctantly. 'I will hold you to that, sir.'

'Miss van Allen, if I'm not mistaken you would hold Beelzebub himself to his promise. By the way . . . '

'Yes?'

'Jeffreys was most anxious about the Christmas greenery.'

'Oh.'

'I find no fault with it, no fault at all, not even with that — that *thing* hanging in the porch.'

'That *thing*, sir, is a kissing bunch!'

'Really?' He raised an eyebrow. 'Could you not have thought of a less bleak and less draughty situation for such an interesting device? I much prefer to do *my* kissing in the warmth, Miss van Allen — but of course, you Americans may have other notions entirely.'

She flushed. 'I had not considered *your* requirements at all, my lord,' she said.

He smiled, inclining his head to her and tapping on his silk hat. He walked toward the gate into the walled garden, and as he went he called for the head groom. 'Harry? See that the landau is made ready immediately.'

'Yes, m'lord.'

'And see that Captain Brooking's chaise is harnessed and ready for the very moment he decides to leave.'

'Very well, m'lord.'

The sun went behind one of the small clouds which were scattered over the skies, and the warmth went immediately from the morning air. There was a sudden cold, damp chill which made Amy shiver as she stood there alone in the stableyard. She watched some stableboys running across to lead the landau's team out, and some grooms opened the doors of a coach house. The gleaming lacquerwork of the landau looked proud and excellent, while beside it there stood a somewhat travel-stained chaise.

Michael Brooking! She began to hurry toward the gate in the wall. It seemed like hours ago now that she had promised to help him with Alice's things! He must be still in the drawing room wondering what had happened to delay her!

★　★　★

Mary Danthorpe had lit a fire in her late mistress's room, and the leaping warmth shimmered on the walls and the bed hangings. A pot-pourri jar by the hearth released the perfume of lemons and roses into the air, and as Amy walked in on Michael Brooking's arm, the maid was standing by the bed, her hands clasped neatly before her.

'I thought you'd prefer to have the room warmed, master,' she said, ignoring Amy.

'Thank you, Mary,' he said.

'I've taken the liberty of putting out her things,' went on the maid, indicating the bed. 'There's nothing there that she didn't bring with her from Wildmoor.'

He nodded. 'That will be all for the moment then, Mary.'

'If you want me, I'll be — '

'If I want you, Mary, I will no doubt be able to find you.' He held the woman's gaze firmly. 'That will be all,' he said again.

Her bright little eyes slid to Amy for a moment, and then she bobbed a curtsey and went out.

He smiled at Amy. 'Poor Mary is inclined to forget that I am a grown man now, and not the little boy she once knew at Wildmoor.'

'Mary Danthorpe is inclined to forget a great many things,' she replied shortly.

'I make allowances for her. She was very devoted to my sister and must be feeling her loss very keenly.'

Amy felt somehow that she had been rebuked, and yet there was nothing in his face or manner to give weight to that feeling. He looked around the room, smiling a little. 'This room is furnished exactly as her room at Wildmoor was furnished, down to the last footstool. Alice didn't want to leave Wildmoor, but when she married she had little choice — and so she recreated part of Wildmoor here at Chalbourne Park.'

'I can tell by your voice that you love Wildmoor as much as your sister did, sir.'

'I do. I feel about Wildmoor as Chalbourne feels about this place. It has belonged to my family for hundreds of years, and I'd move heaven and earth to keep it.' His dark brown eyes met hers. 'Heaven and earth,' he said again, more softly.

She smiled a little uncomfortably, for there was such intensity in his voice. 'Maybe — maybe we should begin, Captain.'

He glanced momentarily at Alice's portrait on the wall, and then he nodded. 'Yes, let us begin,' he said quickly, turning to the things on the bed. 'I confess to finding that portrait's gaze a little shaming.'

'Shaming?'

'Because I am her brother and I have accepted those accusations against her.'

'You have accepted them, Captain, because

they are true. I don't think there can be any doubt at all that she took the necklace.'

'For Charles Pemberton.'

Amy looped at him. 'No, sir, not for Mr Pemberton. There is new evidence,' she said slowly, having no intention of telling the exact nature of that evidence, for Olivia's private life was no concern of his. 'Evidence that he could not have been the man seen in the woods with your sister that night.'

He was silent, staring at her. 'What did you say?' he asked at last.

'There is evidence that Mr Pemberton is innocent.'

'Does that mean they have a clue to the identity of the real culprit, then?'

'No, merely that Mr Pemberton has an excellent alibi for the night in question.' She was puzzled by his reaction, for at the very least she had expected him to show pleasure for his old friend, but he had not — he seemed totally taken aback by her news. 'Are you not pleased for Mr Pemberton, Captain Brooking?'

'Pleased? Yes, yes of course I am.' He laughed then. 'It was just the shock, that's all. Why, maybe now I can make my visit to Oakleigh Hall after all, eh? And maybe too I will have an opportunity to spend a little more time in your sweet company before I have to return to Hazebrouck.' His smile was warm.

After her fiery conflicts with Jonathan, his obvious admiration came as a soothing, flattering balm. It was not unpleasing to have a man as good-looking, dashing, rich, and eligible as Michael Brooking looking at her in that way. She smiled back, knowing that she was a little guilty of encouraging him by smiling, but she was enjoying the mild flirtation and the good it was undoubtedly doing her flagging morale.

He picked up the copy of *Sense and Sensibility* from the bed suddenly. 'Miss van Allen, I know that this book has been damaged somehow, but nevertheless I would like to give it to you.'

She had encouraged him too much, she thought, for their acquaintance was too new for her to consider accepting a gift from him. 'That is most kind of you, but the book was your gift to your sister, and should therefore remain with you.'

'But I wish to give it to you.'

'Surely you are betrothed, sir, or at least paying court to someone — should you not give *her* such a gift?'

'I am not courting anyone, Miss van Allen, for until now I have never met anyone I considered even vaguely worthy.' He took her hand, his eyes warmer again as he looked into hers.

She took her hand quickly away. 'Perhaps you should know, sir, that I am about to become betrothed, and I think too that this conversation has already progressed much further than etiquette would find acceptable, don't you?'

'Who is he?'

'I hardly think that you would know him, Captain Brooking, for he is an American.'

'And he has allowed you to sail across the world without him? If you were mine, Miss van Allen, I would not let you out of my sight in such a way.'

'May I remind you, sir, that I am *not* yours, and that I am beginning to find your conduct decidedly unbecoming.'

He was contrite. 'Forgive me, Miss van Allen, for I have been less than considerate, but I have not much time in which to pursue you, have I? I am reminded that in *Sense and Sensibility*, Elinor Dashwood's sensible, conventional, and somewhat reticent approach to love almost cost her her happiness.'

'And *I* am reminded,' she replied tartly, 'that Marianne Dashwood's rash approach to the same subject almost ruined her.'

He smiled then. '*Touché*, Miss van Allen, I stand corrected — and defeated. I should not have rushed my fences so awkwardly, and I trust that my behavior has not insulted you too much so that my cause has been set so far back that it is irretrievably lost for all time.'

'Your cause cannot include me, sir.'

'But I'm forgiven?'

'Yes, you are forgiven. And now — '

'I'm curious about how the book came to be damaged though,' he said, interrupting her without even seeming to notice that he did so. 'It seems to have been deliberately ripped.'

'I fear that I am guilty of causing at least a little of the damage, Captain Brooking.'

'*You?*' He laughed. 'I cannot imagine you ever maltreating someone else's property.'

'I dropped it and the spine was bent a little at the end.'

'That is hardly in the same league as the damage we see now, is it?'

'I . . . no.'

He studied her. 'What happened to the book, do you know?'

She was tempted quite suddenly to tell him everything, from her discovery of the piece of paper to the intruder in her room and her theory about the meaning of the code, but even as she thought of telling him, she discarded the idea. She hardly knew him, and besides, she hadn't told Jonathan yet.

He smiled. 'Well?'

'No, I don't know what happened to the book. I suspect that it met with a mishap at the hands of one of the maids and that she was subsequently too frightened to admit to it.'

'Yes,' he said slowly, 'yes, of course.'

'We have been here a considerable time now, Captain Brooking, and we haven't done any of the things we came to do.'

They began to go through Alice Chalbourne's belongings, but touching her possessions served only to make Amy more and more aware of the portrait's silent presence. Alice seemed to be watching all the time, her eyes following them. Amy looked at Michael. He seemed disturbed too, for he kept glancing at the portrait and his face was much paler than it had been.

He straightened suddenly. 'I think it best if I just have Chalbourne's men take everything to the chaise. Mary would appear to have done most of the work already.'

'Yes. Is the portrait to go to Wildmoor too?'

'No!'

'But surely . . . '

'The portrait remains here.' He smiled quickly then, realizing that he had been a little abrupt. 'I'm sorry, I'm a little overcome at seeing all my sister's belongings. I — I would prefer not to remain in her room any more, I find it by far too distressing.'

She nodded. 'Of course, Captain, I quite understand.'

'Do you?'

She looked at him. 'I think so.'

He said nothing more, going to the door and holding it open for her to go out, and she heard his audible sigh of relief when the door closed behind them and the portrait was shut safely away behind it.

★   ★   ★

They ate a late luncheon, but Michael did not eat well. The change of mood which had overtaken him in Alice's room seemed to have remained, robbing him of appetite. He seemed sunk in his own thoughts, answering Amy's questions absently and sometimes not at all.

'Shall you drive back to Wildmoor now, sir?' she asked.

After a moment his gaze met hers. 'Wildmoor? No. No, if Charles is to be released today, I shall go to Oakleigh Hall as originally planned.' He folded his napkin, smiling suddenly. 'And also as originally planned, I think you and I should ride to the church now, don't you? Maybe the ride will shake off this gloom which overtook me in my sister's room. I have not been good company over luncheon, have I?'

'*I* haven't exactly sparkled, sir.'

'You do not need to, Miss van Allen, your beauty has more eloquence than any words.' He smiled again. 'I shall not give up. When I want something then I persist until I have it. You are the only woman worthy of Wildmoor.'

She stared at him. 'Perhaps I did not make myself clear earlier . . . '

'Oh, you did. You did. I just do not admit defeat — it's a family failing.'

She put her napkin down, nodding to Jeffreys, who came to draw her chair away. 'I will go and change for the ride, Captain.'

'I will await you in the stableyard.' He bowed over her hand and she resisted the temptation to snatch her hand away.

The sun was still shining when she walked through the walled garden, but it was cooler now and the gentle dripping of melting snow had ceased as the temperature fell below freezing again.

They rode slowly out of the stableyard beneath the clock tower, and across the snow-covered park where a small herd of red deer scattered before them. The horses, like all the bloodstock at Chalbourne Park, were of the very highest quality, responding to the lightest command, and Michael smiled as he maneuvered his sorrel gelding alongside her.

'I'd have fared better at Waterloo with a mount like this beneath me! I may curse Chalbourne, but I admire his eye for horseflesh.'

'Have you not equally excellent animals at Wildmoor, Captain Brooking?'

'Come there with me and judge for yourself.'

'You, sir, are incorrigible.'

The churchyard was quiet and deserted when they reined in at last by the lychgate. The sound of the Chalbourne River hissing and splashing on the other side of the road, drowned the sound of the breeze as it whispered through the dark, overhanging yews which shrouded the path to the church. A robin perched on the churchyard wall for a moment, his little eyes bright and his breast a vivid scarlet before he was gone again, dipping low over the graves.

Amy and Michael walked slowly across the snowy grass to Alice's grave. A covering of fresh snow lay on the mound of new earth, and the delicate wreaths of hothouse flowers had shriveled and browned in the freezing air. Amy stood in silence as Michael looked down at his sister's last resting place.

Slowly he removed his shako, running his

gloved hand through his soft, fair hair. 'Poor little Alice,' he said quietly. 'If she had had just that little more strength, that little more sense of purpose, then this would not have happened.'

She stared at him. 'Sir, you cannot be condoning what she did?'

'Condoning it?' He laughed shortly. 'I meant only that had she not panicked as she obviously did, then she would still be alive — I said nothing of condonation. That moment of frightened panic meant that she now lies here in this place, so far away from all that she really loved and cared about.'

'Wildmoor?'

'Yes.' There was anguish on his face in that moment, and he looked away to hide it from her. He gripped his shako so tightly that his kid gloves were stretched until they shone across his knuckles. 'Would to God those damned sapphires could be found and returned to Chalbourne, and then my sister's memory could be left in peace and my family's name cleared of the undoubted stain which it now endures! If I only knew where to begin, then I would find them myself and take great pleasure in giving them into his hands.'

Amy thought of the piece of paper. Miserably she hesitated. Should she tell him?

298

'Captain Brooking — I . . . '

He turned toward her and she saw the unshed tears which softened his eyes. 'Forgive me, Miss van Allen, I should not embarrass you with such a show of unmanly emotion.'

She put her hand on his arm. 'There is no need to apologize, Captain Brooking, for I more than understand, and I do not think it unmanly at all.' She paused. 'Captain, I too would like the sapphires found, and I wondered — thought . . . '

'Yes?'

She opened her reticule and took out the paper. 'When the book fell, as I told you, well, this fell out from the spine. I don't know if it has any significance, but somehow I feel that it has.'

He stared at the paper, and then slowly took it from her. 'It was hidden in the book?'

'Yes. Do you know whose writing it is?'

'No. The — the blue hand is Alice's though.'

Her heart leaped. 'Then those figures and letters could indeed be a clue to where she put the necklace?'

'That's impossible to say.' He looked at her then. 'Why do you think they do?'

'Because someone went to a great deal of trouble to put the paper in the book, and because someone came to my room in the middle of the night to find it and in so doing managed to rip the spine of the book and damage it.' She told him in detail about the intruder. 'So you see, Captain,' she finished, 'I am sure this code, or whatever it should be called, tells where the necklace is. Besides, if you look at the words in black, someone wrote to her asking to be informed about the hiding place. Her accomplice wrote those words in black, Captain Brooking, I'm sure of it.'

'I think you may be right, but I cannot see how we can discover his identity.' He was momentarily silent. 'Have you any thoughts about the precise meaning of the code?'

'Yes, I was convinced that it meant the third floor at Chalbourne Park, the fourth room on the left, in the cupboard.'

'And?'

'It was an attic storeroom and there was nothing in the cupboard there. So I then wondered if the floors had been counted from the cellars, but that brought my search to the music room and there was nothing there, although I emptied the whole cupboard. I'm sure I'm right, but there must be one thing I've got wrong somewhere, although I don't know what.'

He smiled. 'Feminine intuition, Miss van Allen?'

'I suppose so. Don't you think the paper is important then, Captain Brooking?'

'It may be, but the variations which may be drawn from that code are endless and I fail to see how we could hope to solve it.' He returned the paper to her.

She sighed. 'I know, I just feel so *sure* though. Anyway, when Lord Chalbourne returns, I'll show the paper to him. Maybe *he* will recognize the hand in black, or can at least shed a little light on the code.'

'You're showing it to Chalbourne?'

'Yes.'

'I wish you luck, Miss van Allen. But now, I've said my farewells to my sister, and maybe we should return to the house. I wish to be well and truly gone from Chalbourne Park before Chalbourne himself returns.'

A little disconcerted by his virtual dismissal of the paper's importance, she put it back in her reticule. 'You will be going to Oakleigh Hall?'

'Yes — no doubt Charles will need cheering up after his ordeal at Chalbourne's hands.'

'Lord Chalbourne had good reason for what he did.'

At that moment the church bells suddenly rang out joyously as the bellringers began to practice the Christmas peals again. Michael turned at the lychgate, his face bitter as he gazed along the tunnel of yews toward the church door. 'Sounds of festive joy!' he cried savagely, 'and Alice is barely cold in her grave! Tell me, Miss van Allen, does Chalbourne also have good reason for permitting such blatant violations of all reverence and feeling?'

She could say nothing, lowering her eyes before the fury and outrage in his.

A new sound rattled along the road toward them and she turned to see the Bendon britschka bowling swiftly in the direction of Chalbourne Park, the noise of its passing echoing between the cottages along the village street The wheels cracked through the thin ice covering the puddles, sending splashes of dirty water jetting to the sides of the road, and the horses strained and sweated as they dragged the heavy carriage along the valley at a spanking pace which had been maintained since leaving Bendon Place an hour or more earlier. Amy's spirits sank as she watched it. Oh, no — not Christabel!

Michael did not seem to hear the carriage's approach. He put his hand to Amy's face, turning it toward his own. 'I should not have shouted at you, for it is not your fault,' he murmured. 'None of this is your fault, and I wish only that I . . . ' He did not finish.

Instead, before she knew what he was going to do, he bent his head forward and put his lips over hers.

She was immobile with shock for a moment, but then she recovered and drew angrily away, glancing quickly at the britschka as it passed. Christabel's face smiled maliciously out and Amy knew that the kiss had been witnessed.

Without a word to Michael, Amy remounted, kicking her heels angrily and urging the animal away from the lychgate. He mounted his own horse and rode swiftly after her. He was silent as he reached her side, for one glance at her stormy face had told him that he had more than overstepped the mark this time.

His chaise was outside the porch when the house came into sight, and the servants were loading the last of Alice's trunks onto it. The Bendon britschka swept up alongside the chaise, the tired horses stamping to a thankful standstill at last as the coachman jumped down to open the door. As Amy rode on toward the stableyard, she saw Christabel climbing down, a vision of fashionable beauty in a pelisse of bright yellow velvet and a black beaver hat from which streamed her favorite ostrich feathers.

Amy dismounted in the stableyard and

began to walk toward the gateway in the wall, and Michael almost vaulted from his own mount to hurry after her.

Angrily she ignored him as he called her name, and she had reached the hall of the house before he finally caught her arm, but then he froze for he saw Christabel's tall figure by the fireplace. Amy moved away from him, but Christabel's thoughtful gaze had not missed a thing as she slowly removed her gloves and handed them to Jeffreys, who waited beside her. 'Inform Miss Olivia that I have called,' she murmured.

'Yes, my lady.'

Christabel smiled coolly at Amy. 'Why, good afternoon, Miss — er — van Allen,' she drawled huskily.

'Good afternoon. Lady Christabel.'

The pale blue eyes moved speculatively over Michael, and Amy exhaled slowly, knowing she would have to introduce them. 'My lady, allow me to present to you Captain Michael Brooking of the Eleventh Hussars. Captain Brooking, Lady Christabel Bendon.' She spoke lightly, smiling as she did so, for she was determined not to let Christabel see how upset she was about the incident by the lychgate.

'Brooking?' repeated Christabel. 'Alice's brother?'

He bowed over her hand. 'Your servant, my lady.'

'How delightful to make your acquaintance after all this time, sir. But I had no idea you were a close friend of Miss van Allen's.'

Amy's face reddened as she awaited his inevitable response.

'I'm not, my lady. Miss van Allen and I only met last night.'

'Really?' Christabel's voice was smooth and creamy, and her eyebrows arched sleekly. 'You surprise me, sir. But then, maybe not . . . Ah, Olivia *darling!*' She swept away from them as Olivia entered the hall. 'How absolutely marvelous to see you feeling well again!'

Olivia smiled reluctantly, glancing at Amy and Michael before holding out her hands to Christabel. 'Hello, Christabel, how good of you to call.'

'I simply had to know if you were fully recovered from your beastly indisposition.' Christabel linked her arm through Olivia's and they walked toward the two by the fireplace. 'Is it not exciting that Alice's brother has come to Chalbourne Park at last?'

'Er — yes.' Olivia smiled shyly, extending her hand. 'Good day, Captain Brooking, how pleased I am to meet you.'

Christabel was nonplussed. 'You have not

met him yet, Olivia?'

'No. No, I was still unwell last night when he arrived, and Miss van Allen received him for me in Jonathan's absence.'

'Really?' said Christabel again, the familiar sleek arch curving her eyebrows as her glance flickered maliciously toward Amy.

Michael bowed. 'Miss Chalbourne, I must thank you for your most kind and considerate invitation.'

She flushed. 'Not at all, sir, it was only right that I should write to you.' Olivia glanced miserably at Amy.

He continued, 'I fear that our meeting must only be very brief, for I am about to leave for Oakleigh Hall. I trust that you will understand my haste to be gone from here and will not therefore be offended with me.'

'Not at all, sir, I fear I understand quite well.'

'Maybe we shall meet again, for no doubt you will visit Oakleigh Hall yourself during Christmas,'

She smiled. 'I shall indeed, Captain Brooking, and I look forward to speaking with you again then. But please, will you not at least take some tea with us before you leave?'

'I fear not, Miss Chalbourne, for my chaise is ready and waiting, and I have only to say farewell to Mary Danthorpe before leaving.' He smiled charmingly at her.

'Of course, sir.' Olivia warmed visibly to his winning manner.

He offered Amy his arm then. 'Mary will no doubt be waiting in your rooms, Miss van Allen, so please allow me to escort you.'

There was little Amy could do but accept his offer with as good a grace as she could manage. She looked at Olivia. 'I will join you directly, Livvy. I have only to change from this riding habit.'

'Yes, Amy. Christabel and I will have tea in the orangery, so please join us there.'

Amy accepted the arm he offered, but the moment they had left the hall behind them, she moved away from him, hurrying up the staircase as swiftly as she could.

'I realize that I have erred well beyond the bounds of decent behavior, Miss van Allen,' he began, following her.

'You have indeed!'

'Please — '

'If you are about to beg forgiveness yet again, sir, then you may save yourself the effort, for I shall *not* forgive you this time! I went with you to the churchyard because I felt you would be glad of a little company on such a sad occasion, and you repaid my kindness by taking a gross liberty!' She had reached the door of her room. 'Please remain out here, sir, and if Mary is inside then I will send her to you!'

Outside the sun was setting and the red, fiery colors lay across the snow, mingling with the long shadows and the dull gray of the clouds which were beginning to creep across the eastern skyline. He was outlined against a window, and his dark brown eyes were almost black as he smiled faintly. 'Very well, Miss van Allen, if that is the way you wish it to be, then I will abide by it. I wish to God, though, that you were a woman of less high principles.'

She gave him a haughty, angry look and then opened the door, leaving it open as she went into the firelit room. Mary was waiting patiently by the fire, with Amy's day dress draped neatly over a chair to keep it warm. But the woman's eyes went immediately past Amy to Michael as he stood waiting in the passage.

'Oh, master!' she cried, taking a bundle of letters from her pocket. 'I found all the letters you sent to my lady!' She held them out.

Amy stared at the writing on the letters. It was written in black ink, and was familiar and sloping — it was the same writing as that on the slip of paper she had found. With a gasp she turned around to stare at him, but he was already in the room, his hand clamping tightly over her mouth before she could scream!

'Close the door quickly, Mary!' he hissed, one arm around Amy so hard that she was pressed against him.

Startled, Mary obeyed him. 'Master?

'She found Alice's message, as you thought she had! But now that she's recognized my writing, she knows too much!' He glanced around and saw Amy's wrap. 'Bring that belt!'

Amy struggled helplessly as they bound her hands painfully behind her back. *He* was Alice's accomplice, it had been a plot between brother and sister! And she'd been fool enough to show him the very thing he'd come to find! He must have been in England all along! What a fool she'd been, what a *fool!*

He kept his hand over her mouth, speaking to Mary. 'We can't keep her here, she's expected to take tea with Miss Chalbourne shortly, and they could send someone to look for her. Is there somewhere else?'

'There's my lady's room, no one will go there . . . But master, what shall we do now? If she knows everything — '

'Give me time to think, woman!' he snapped.

'But if she knows!'

'Hold your tongue!'

Amy's eyes were huge as she stared from

one to the other, and then he nodded at the door. 'See if the way is clear.' As Mary obeyed him again, he took a handkerchief from his pocket and forced it into Amy's mouth. 'That will silence you for a while, my lovely,' he murmured.

He jerked her toward the door as Mary beckoned, and they moved along the passageway toward the main corridor, where they halted again. There was no sign of anyone, not a maid, not even a coal boy, and Michael gripped Amy's upper arm firmly as he thrust her along the wide corridor toward Alice's room.

The door closed behind them and Mary lit several candles from the fire which still burned in the hearth. Alice's portrait shimmered in the candlelight as Michael removed the handkerchief from Amy's mouth.

'You've been too sharp, my lovely Amy,' he said softly, 'by far too sharp. If you hadn't recognized my writing, then you'd still have been harmless. I could have left you and this house and gone to Oakleigh Hall to collect the sapphires, and no one would have been any the wiser.'

'The sapphires are at *Oakleigh Hall?*' she gasped.

He nodded. 'Yes, sweetheart. You were so nearly right about the code, but you see, you had the wrong house. She hid them there when she accompanied Miss Chalbourne for a portrait sitting on the day before the Hunt Ball. I knew that hiding them here at Chalbourne Park was pointless, for I could never come to get these — but Oakleigh Hall had been bought by my old friend Charles.'

'*You* were the man in the woods!' she cried. 'You were the guilty one and you deliberately implicated Charles Pemberton in your crimes!'

'Implicating him was the last thing I wanted, I assure you. His arrest came as just as great a surprise to me as it did to him.'

'I don't believe you, sir, for you even rode a horse which was exactly like his!'

'It was a frustrating coincidence which made me choose that dun horse, Amy, just as it was coincidence that nature provided me with such similar coloring and figure to his. His arrest did not suit my plans in the slightest, far from it, for I needed him at Oakleigh Hall so that when I went there, as his guest, I could collect the necklace from wherever my sister chose to hide it. It was a very simple plan, Amy, and it would have gone so very well had not Chalbourne decided that he would sell the necklace rather than part with some of his land. Alice panicked, terrified of being discovered, and she tried to get to Oakleigh Hall to retrieve the real necklace, but she was killed and the truth came out.' He gave a dry laugh. 'And suddenly everyone was looking for the sapphires, including me, for although it had been arranged that Alice would hide the clue in that book, she hid the book itself so well that Mary here couldn't find it.'

'But why did you do it?' asked Amy then. 'You had no need to steal, for you are a wealthy man in your own right. So, why?'

'Ill-judged gambling has cost me my family's fortune, Amy.' He glanced at Mary for a brief moment, an almost appreciative look passing through his eyes. 'And Wildmoor is in considerably more difficulty at the moment than Chalbourne Park,' he finished.

Amy stared at him. 'Why did your sister risk ruin herself in order to help you? She had no reason . . . '

'No reason?' He laughed. 'Have you an interest in history, Amy?' He turned to look at Alice's portrait.

'History?'

'The Borgias have always fascinated me, and Césare Borgia in particular. He had such power over his sister, Lucrezia — Alice was my Lucrezia, Amy. She did my bidding in everything, married when I told her to and obeyed me afterward whenever it so pleased me. She may have been Lady Chalbourne, but she was still Alice Brooking. Her loyalty lay with her own flesh and blood, not with the husband who loathed her so. I decided all those years ago that Chalbourne was wealthy enough to be entirely suitable — if ever I stood in need, then his wealth would be at hand. At *Alice's* hand.'

'And now you are in need?'

'Wildmoor is in need.' Again he glanced at Mary. 'Wildmoor stands close to the sea, on land which was once part of the sea, and there are only dikes to keep the sea away. The North Sea's tides and storms rage constantly through the winters, and those dikes have to be maintained if Wildmoor is not to be inundated. The weather, the land itself, the present financial situation throughout the whole of the land — together with my love of gambling — all these things combine to make the running of Wildmoor a vastly expensive exercise. I planned well over those sapphires, Amy, and all would have gone sweetly had not that damned book been hidden so very well. However, all is not lost, thanks solely to you, my sweetheart. Not only did you find Alice's book, you also found the precious secret it held.' He smiled, reaching out to put his hand softly against her cheek. 'But you told me all you knew swiftly enough, did you not? I did not have to work very hard, did I?'

She looked away, sickened by her own gullibility. She had seen only the grief-stricken brother, anxious to make amends for what his sister had done — the truth had been hidden from her behind his charming smile and soft, engaging words.

He was still smiling as he watched the expressions passing over her face. 'Each time I mentioned the book I could see the indecision in your lovely eyes. Mary was right when she guessed that you'd found the paper. She knew it that night she came to find it — '

'It was Mary?'

'Yes. She searched for the paper, and when it wasn't there she knew that somehow you'd found it and either destroyed it as being useless, or you'd kept it because you were curious about it. I had to come here then, for she judged that your constant altercations with Chalbourne would make you easy game for a little gentle persuasion from me.' He laughed shortly. 'How fortuitous indeed that my way had already been made so clear by Miss Chalbourne's action in inviting me. Dame Fortune could not have made an easier path.' He took Amy's face in his hands then. 'But I find you every bit as desirable as I have led you to believe,' he murmured softly. 'And even now you tempt me.' He nodded at

314

Mary. 'Find something to bind her feet with; she must not escape.'

Mary picked up a candlestick and went to the dressing room. 'There may be something left behind in here,' she said.

He looked down into Amy's eyes again. 'Oh, what sweet pleasure there could have been with you — I doubt that ever again will I want a woman as much as I have wanted you in this short time.' He pulled her close then, bending his head to kiss her. He lingered a long, long time over the moment, his lips moving sensuously on hers and his fingers twining in her hair. She could feel the desire in him, feel it in the way he pressed her so close and in the increasing urgency of his kiss. But he drew away, his face a little flushed. 'It would be so easy to allow heart to rule over head,' he said softly. 'Had you been a lesser woman, my Amy, then there would have been a place for you in my plans, but you are too noble and your principles are too high. Besides which, you are in love with Chalbourne, I have seen it in your eyes when you look at him. I cannot have you and it is too late to save Wildmoor, but those sapphires will ensure that I have a good life in some other land — away from the laws of Britain.'

She was staring at him. Too late to save

Wildmoor? What did he mean? But even as she looked at him, he turned suddenly, realizing that his desire for her had made him unwary and that he'd said far more than he'd ever intended Mary Danthorpe to hear.

Mary stood in the doorway of Alice's dressing room, all color draining from her pale face as she looked at. him. 'No!' she cried, 'No, master! It was all done for Wildmoor, for *Wildmoor!*'

'Not even the Chalbourne sapphires can save Wildmoor now, Mary,' he said, his voice reasonable as he tried to pacify her. 'The tides breached the dikes this autumn and the sea came in.'

'The sea's never destroyed Wildmoor before, it hasn't destroyed it now!'

'Damn you, half the land is under water and the other half has never been much better than marsh! The sea has claimed back that which the Brookings stole from it centuries ago! Nothing can be done to save Wildmoor from the water now; the next bad storm will take the house itself! What the economic problems had not managed quite to do, the sea itself has more than completed!'

Dropping the length of string she had found in an empty wardrobe, Mary stumbled across the room toward Alice's portrait, her eyes shining with sudden hatred as she turned to face him. 'You knew this all along,' she whispered. 'You knew it when first you told her she must take the necklace! She believed she was saving Wildmoor, but it was your skin she was saving — '

'My sister always did as I told her!'

'She lies dead, and for nothing! *Nothing!*' Mary's fingers moved lovingly over the portrait's face, lingering on the eyes and mouth. 'My dearest lady, my sweet mistress . . . ' Again she turned on him, her expression savage. 'You wanted that necklace for yourself, to provide for your own comfort, you had no thought for her at all! I won't let you do this, you shall not get away with — '

He took a swift step toward her, striking her face with such a heavy blow that she fell unconscious to the floor at the foot of the portrait.

Amy's eyes were huge with fear then as he turned back toward her. 'I am left with no choice,' he said softly, 'for if I am to live, then there must be no one who knows what I have done. No one, my sweetest Amy, not even you. Mary's life had been forfeit from the outset, but you — I had not thought that I must kill you, Amy.' He caught her arm, and she was too terrified to scream or do anything as he thrust her toward the dressing room door. He picked up the piece of string Mary had dropped and then pushed Amy roughly into the dressing room where she stumbled and fell heavily to the floor. He tied her ankles tightly together and then forced the handkerchief into her mouth again. For a moment he crouched over her, gazing down into her face. 'I could have loved you so, Amy,' he whispered. 'No woman would have been so cherished as you, but if I cannot have you, then no one else shall either.'

He straightened and she struggled on the floor, managing to turn just a little to look through the doorway. He was dragging Mary's limp body into the dressing room too, and he had gone out again and closed the door when, unbelievably, Amy heard Olivia's voice in the room beyond.

'Why, Captain Brooking, there you are. Lady Christabel and I were wondering where Miss van Allen had got to. I've been to her room but there's no sign of her.'

'I believe she went out to the stables again,' he said, and Amy could hear the smile in his voice.

'The stables! I confess we did not think of that.'

'No doubt she will join you presently. I hope you do not mind me taking one last look at my sister's room before leaving, Miss Chalbourne.'

Amy struggled helplessly, the handkerchief muffling her agonized voice. *I'm here, Livvy, I'm just in here . . .*

'Mind? Why of course not, Captain, please carry on.'

'Well, I have almost done all I came to do, and so I will bid you farewell, Miss Chalbourne. Until we meet again at Oakleigh Hall then?'

'Until then, Captain. Good-bye.'

'Good-bye, Miss Chalbourne.'

The door closed and someone was still moving around in the room beyond. It must be Livvy! Amy struggled again, twisting her wrists until the belt cut into her flesh, and her heart almost stopped with joy when the dressing room door opened — but it was not Olivia who stood there, it was Michael. He stood for a long moment, just looking down at her, and then he closed the door again and was gone, the outer door closing softly behind him.

Silence descended over the dressing room. The walls of the room were crimson in the fading rays of the sun, and the minutes ticked slowly by as Amy lay there. Mary made no move, lying where he had left her, crumpled like a child's doll. A low sound caught Amy's attention then, and she looked quickly toward the door. A crackling sound ... As she looked, the first drift of smoke crept beneath the door, stinging her nostrils. He had set fire to the bedroom! They were to be burned alive!

13

Tears ran down her cheeks as she began to struggle again, her bonds drawing blood from her chafed wrists and ankles, and in the bedroom the crackling of the flames was growing louder as the moments passed, and the smoke came more strongly beneath the door, drifting acridly through the cold air in the dressing room. She tried to rouse Mary, but the woman was completely unconscious. *Mary! We'll burn, we'll burn to death — your hands and legs are free! Free! Please wake up!* The utter helplessness and inevitability seemed to destroy her very soul as she lay there, watching the smoke creeping into the little room.

She glanced around then and saw the candle. It stood on the windowsill where Mary had put it earlier, and the brilliance of the sunset outside made the steadily burning flame almost invisible. It smoked a little, swaying from side to side above the wick, and Amy stared at it. If she could only get to her feet somehow, then she could maybe burn away her bonds . . .

Twisting violently from one position to

another, she managed to edge closer and closer to the wall below the window, and by more painful wriggling, which drew blood from her wrists and ankles, she managed to get herself into a sitting position. Weakly she leaned back against the wall, fighting away the agony as she strove to regain her strength. She listened with almost desperate hope for sounds that the fire in Alice's room had been discovered, but all was quiet but for the hiss and roar of the flames. There were no shouts of alarm, no one was beating on the outer door.

With a deep breath and one immense effort, she forced her back against the wall and tried to straighten her legs. Slowly, and with almost unbearable pain, she slid herself up the smooth wall. Her limbs trembled with the exertion when at last she was standing, swaying a little as she tried to keep her balance. She mustn't fall now — not *now!* Her breaths came in shuddering gulps, and the smoke was burning her eyes and throat. The handkerchief made her want to heave as it rubbed against her tongue and teeth. Nausea swept over her for a moment and she closed her eyes, taking huge breaths to quell the weakening sensations. Gradually the sick feeling passed and she turned her head to look out, her eyes watering in the blaze of crimson and gold as the sun sank even lower in the west. The snow was blood-red and the shadows as black as the finest velvet.

She could see the porch and the drive, and as she looked she saw Michael Brooking climb into the waiting chaise. The coachman flicked his whip and the carriage moved away, taking Alice's brother to Oakleigh Hall and the sapphires. She watched it as it drove smartly away down the drive. Somehow the sight of his imminent triumph goaded her, and she edged along the windowsill toward the candle.

He wouldn't succeed! He *wouldn't!* Not while she had life and breath in her body! She could feel the heat of the candle near her hands, and she winced with pain as the flame seared against her flesh. She must endure it, to give in now would be to die! She almost fainted when the pain intensified as she positioned the bonds above it, and she could smell the burning cotton as the string began to smoulder. There wasn't any pain, she told herself, staring at the wafts of smoke streaming under the door now, there wasn't any pain — no pain . . .

The cotton gave quite suddenly — one moment she was bound tightly, and the next her arms were free. With a sob she fell to the floor, taking the handkerchief from her mouth. The smoke was thick now, burning in her throat and lungs as she strove with her burned hands to untie the string which held her ankles. Then she got up, running to the door, but it wouldn't open. She tried again and again, but it had been locked on the other side. She was still trapped in the dressing room. Pressing her ear against the wood she could hear the fire very plainly now. It roared and rushed as it gained strength, and when she knelt to look through the keyhole, she looked at a scene which might have come from hell itself. The flames leaped hungrily around the rich furnishings, and through the dancing light and smoke Alice's portrait stared toward her. The dark brown eyes were so lifelike and the face seemed to be vibrant flesh and blood.

Amy drew sharply away from the keyhole and then went to crouch by Mary, shaking the woman's shoulder. 'Mary? Mary, wake up, please? God *damn* you, wake up!' But there was no movement to the still figure.

Desperately Amy went to the window. She was choking and fighting for her breath now. She must have some air, she must breathe. Maybe someone was out there, maybe they would hear if she called! Someone *must* be there, please God let someone be there . . . She struggled with the window catch, shaking it violently as it resisted, and then it opened and the fresh, ice-cold winter air swept over her. She inhaled deeply, filling her lungs with the clean freshness of it and leaning out as far as she could from the thick, poisonous atmosphere behind her.

A carriage had just halted on the drive below, and she stared at it in disbelief. It was the landau! Jonathan had returned from Cirencester! As she looked, Daniels jumped down from his box and went to open the door. Charles Pemberton climbed down first, pausing at the foot of the house steps to wait as Jonathan followed.

She called but the wind snatched her voice away. She began to sob as she called over and over, repeating his name. 'Jonathan! Jonathan!'

He turned, obviously hearing her but not knowing where she was.

'Jonathan!' she pleaded, her voice distorted by weeping, 'Help me, please help me!'

Then he looked directly up at her window, and she saw the shock change his face as he saw the smoke and flames lighting the windows of his wife's rooms. He caught Charles's arm, pointing up briefly and then turning to run into the house.

As he passed from sight, she sank weakly to her knees, blinded by tears of relief as she leaned her forehead against the wall. It seemed a lifetime before she heard the bedroom door being forced open, and men were shouting.

The dressing room door was rattled and then jerked violently as someone flung his shoulder against it time and time again. It burst open at last and Jonathan stood there for a moment, trying to see her through the dust and smoke. Behind him the bedroom burned, the flames leaping wildly around the furniture and wall hangings. Window panes shattered as the heat split them, and men were shouting as they formed a chain to toss pails of water over the fire. Smoke, fumes, and steam swirled in the hot air and the sound of the eager flames made a roar which seemed to fill the whole of the house.

He crouched beside her. 'Amy?'

She turned to him and he caught her close, holding her for a moment before gently lifting her into his arms and turning to carry her to safety.

'Mary . . . ' she whispered. 'Mary's here too.'

He called to some of the men and as they went in to lift the unconscious maid, he carried Amy out through the blazing room. She saw the portrait. The face was grotesque now, bloated and running as the oil paint bubbled and melted in the intense heat, and as Amy stared at it the flames began to consume the canvas itself.

She closed her eyes to shut the sight out, and as he carried her into the corridor she heard Olivia's anxious voice. The men's shouting died away behind and Amy heard the incongruously soothing sound of a clock chiming in one of the nearby rooms.

He carried her to her own room, laying her gently on the bed and loosening the high collar of her riding habit. He turned to Christabel, who had accompanied Olivia. 'Go and see that someone sends for the doctor!'

She nodded and left. Olivia sat on the other side of the bed. 'Amy? Oh, your poor wrists!'

He bent over Amy. 'Are you in much pain?' He asked gently, holding her fingertips.

'The necklace — you must go . . . '

'Go?'

In a halting, barely audible voice she told him about Michael Brooking. 'You must go to Oakleigh Hall, you may still be in time. The third floor, fourth room on the left. In the cupboard. That's where the necklace is hidden.' She looked up at him but he seemed indistinct, his face dark and featureless. Her lungs hurt her so and she could taste smoke on her lips. Her burned wrists throbbed and everything seemed to be going blacker. She struggled to remain conscious. 'He's gone by the road,' she whispered, her voice growing weaker, 'but if you go across the park . . . '

He nodded. 'I'll go straight away. Olivia, you'll stay with her, won't you?'

'Of course, I will.'

He looked down at Amy again, but she had lost consciousness.

★   ★   ★

Amy opened her eyes. The room was in darkness, but for the firelight which moved in lilac tones on the pale blue walls. The perfume of carnations drifted soothingly all around her, and she looked at the clock on the mantlepiece. Ten o'clock. It must be at night . . . The fire shifted in the hearth, and the shadows moved away, shrinking briefly from the sudden brightness of the shower of sparks, but they soon crept back again. The painting of Wildmoor was lit quite plainly from below. The lonely house in the fens, and beyond it the dikes and the sea — the sea which had come back to seize its own.

Someone moved in the chair by the fire. She saw a woman's skirt. 'Livvy?'

The skirt rustled. It was Christabel. The folds of primrose silk were burnished orange in the firelight as she walked toward the bed.

'So, you're awake at last,' she said, and there was no gentleness, no concern in her voice. Her face was cold as she leaned her hands on the bed, staring down into Amy's eyes. 'You'll not have him, do you hear me? I won't let you take him from me!'

'Have him? I don't understand . . . '

'You don't fool me — you want Jonathan! Don't try denying it, for you've talked in your sleep, and it was all quite plain! Well, you may forget it, forget it entirely! I warned you that you would regret making a fool of me, and so you will! I'll see to it that he knows all about that sweet, loving kiss by the lychgate!'

'No — '

'Oh, yes. And I'll embroider it so much that by the time I've finished he'll believe that the only reason you were left to die was because you and Captain Brooking had a bitter lovers' quarrel! I'll see to it that Jonathan believes you to be a scheming slut, an adventuress with the morals of a she-cat! He'll despise the very sound of your name before another day is out, that I promise you!'

'Send Olivia to me,' whispered Amy, too weak to struggle up. Her head throbbed and she was unable to do anything to stem the other's bitter malice.

'Send Olivia?' asked Christabel lightly. 'Very well. But don't imagine anyone will believe that I am your enemy, sweetheart, for I've been the very soul of concern these past few days.'

'Days?'

'Yes — you've been unconscious for three days.'

Amy stared at her. 'The fire . . . ?'

'Let Olivia tell you all about it.' Christabel straightened, then hesitated and took one of Amy's bandaged wrists tightly in her fingers and squeezed hard.

The pain coursed swiftly through Amy, engulfing her so completely that she could only make a tiny, broken sound. A velvety redness swam before her eyes as the pain washed back and forth through her, diminishing only very slowly and gradually. And when the redness and pain had gone, the room was empty.

Olivia's black crepe skirts rustled as she hurried into the room not long afterward, followed by Christabel. 'Amy? Oh, Amy, I'm so glad you've come around at long last. We've been so worried about you!'

Christabel looked down at the weak figure in the bed too, her light blue eyes showing equal anxiety. 'The moment she opened her eyes I came running for you, Olivia. Oh, *what* a relief, Miss van Allen!'

Amy stared up at the honey-haired woman,

her lips moving but no sound coming out.

Olivia sat on the edge of the bed, gently taking Amy's hand and taking care not to touch the bandaged wrist at all. 'How are you feeling now, Amy? Are your poor wrists hurting very much?'

'I — I feel so tired, and my throat is dry. My wrists are bearable.' Amy's voice was little more than a rasping croak.

'We put some elder ointment on them, and some hypericum balm — that's the dark red color staining the bandage, so don't be afraid that you're still bleeding. Christabel has been so marvelous, Amy. She's taken endless trouble to sit with you.'

Amy's eyes moved slowly to Christabel's face. 'I must remember to thank her properly some time,' she said.

Olivia made herself a little more comfortable. 'You'll be wondering what happened.'

'Did Jonathan reach the necklace first?'

'No, not exactly. He arrived just as Captain Brooking's chaise was leaving Oakleigh Hall again. The Captain saw Jonathan riding across the park and told the coachman to make as much haste as he could. The foolish fellow drove like the very wind, and at the gates he turned right instead of left, and drove as quickly as he could back *toward* Great Chalbourne instead of *away* from it!

The road was slippery by the Devil's Elbow, and the chaise went out of control.' Olivia looked at Amy. 'Captain Brooking was killed when the chaise fell down that steep slope, Amy. The chaise crashed all the way to the river at the bottom, he must have been killed instantly. They found the necklace in his sabretache, carefully hidden away again.'

'It's safe then?'

'Perfectly safe, thanks to you.'

Amy closed her eyes, conscious of Christabel's bitter hatred. The recovery of the necklace was the last thing Christabel had wanted, for it took away so much.

'Amy,' began Olivia, 'I'm afraid Mary Danthorpe died too. When they brought her from the dressing room she was hardly breathing at all, and she didn't recover. She died that night without recovering consciousness.'

'He hit her so very hard,' murmured Amy. 'She was only little, but he struck her as if she was his equal. An officer and a gentleman, was he not?' She paused. 'Did the fire do much damage?'

'Enough. About three rooms on the first floor have been destroyed, but the structure of the building is intact and so it can be rebuilt. It could have been so much worse, Amy. No one had seen the flames and smoke, not even Daniels when he drove the landau along the drive. If you hadn't freed yourself . . . How *did* you free yourself? We know you were bound because of your wrists and ankles, but . . . '

'There was a candle on the windowsill. I managed to get up and burn the bonds away. That's how I burned myself.'

'Oh, my poor Amy,' murmured Olivia, leaning to smooth Amy's hair back from her forehead. 'What a *dreadful* time you've had since coming here, how you must be absolutely hating England!'

'Well, at least the mystery has been solved and the sapphires are back where they belong,' murmured Amy.

Christabel's eyes were hooded as she gazed down.

Olivia sighed. 'If Jonathan hadn't come back when he did . . . Oh, Amy, to think that I was actually in Alice's room when that dreadful man was there, and I spoke so politely to him. He was all charm and perfection, and all the time you were in that little room, your poor wrists and ankles bound so cruelly, waiting to die!' Tears filled the gray eyes. 'I feel so very bad about it — and so does Christabel! We both feel we should have done more to find you.'

Amy's disbelieving eyes slid to Christabel.

Christabel was no doubt cursing the fact that Jonathan had returned in time to save her, and further cursing that he had personally carried Amy from the jaws of death. The fire had killed Mary — a few minutes more and it would probably have disposed of Amy too. But Christabel's lovely pale blue eyes revealed nothing as they unwaveringly met Amy's gaze.

Olivia held up her hand suddenly and Amy saw the ring on her finger. 'You are betrothed again then?'

'Yes, the ring was on my finger again before Charles left here on the night of the fire.'

'And Jonathan agreed?'

'Readily. I think they cleared the air a great deal during their journey back from Cirencester after Charles had been freed.' She flushed then, remembering the nature of the evidence which had freed him. She glanced nervously at Christabel. 'Everything is so wonderful for me again, and would you believe, Jonathan and Charles actually seem to get on now! So, all's well that ends well, mm?'

Amy nodded, but inside her own heart was heavy. For her, all would be well only when at last she left Chalbourne Park and journeyed home where she belonged. Washington.

Olivia squeezed her fingers very gently. 'You must rest well tonight, Amy, because it's

Christmas Eve tomorrow.'

Amy stared, her lips parting in surprise. 'Christmas Eve?'

'You've missed three days, and we've all been so wrapped up in our problems anyway that we haven't noticed just how close it's been creeping all the time. Yes, Amy, tomorrow is Christmas Eve, and you simply *must* be well enough to enjoy it with us. There's to be a celebration and *everyone's* invited. No more mourning, no more black after tonight.' She bit her lip. 'I know it's a little soon and there will be many who will condemn us for it, but it does seem a little hypocritical of us to mourn her after all she did — and what better time to make a fresh beginning than Christmas?'

'Yes, indeed,' murmured Christabel. 'So you simply must be well enough to enjoy tomorrow, Miss van Allen. After all, what would this particular Christmas Eve be without you, the heroine of the hour?' The perfect lips curved into a cool smile. 'You simply must be there to enjoy every moment of it.'

The awful promise was there in the careful words and in the glittering eyes, and Amy looked away without replying.

Olivia got up then, not noticing the atmosphere which existed between the other two. 'You must be so tired after all you've endured, so we'll leave you to rest again now. Is there anything I can get for you? A drink maybe?'

'No, thank you. I'm quite all right.'

Olivia smiled. 'I do so want you to be happy here from now on, Amy. I want you to enjoy your stay, not be made miserable by the Chalbourne family and all its problems. The troubles are over now, and it's nearly Christmas — I just know everything will be splendid from now on. Good night, Amy.'

'Good night, Livvy.'

Christabel smiled sweetly. 'Good night, Miss van Allen.'

Amy remained silent.

She lay there when they had gone. Glancing at the clock she saw that it was gone eleven now. In lest than an hour it would be Christmas Eve. The sapphires had been recovered and the guilt placed where it rightly belonged. Olivia was happy again and the people of Great Chalbourne could look forward to a secure new year. But there were tears on Amy's cheeks as she lay there; everyone else was happy again, but her problems remained to hurt her, her unhappiness had not diminished at all.

'Oh, Jonathan,' she whispered to the firelit room, 'I love you so.'

14

The pale silver light of dawn was filling the room when she awoke the next morning. Fresh logs had been put on the dying fire, and the flames were a bright yellowy-orange as they began to take hold on the tinder-dry wood.

Jonathan stood by the window, his green brocade dressing gown vivid in the gray light. His hair was tousled and unbrushed and when he turned suddenly to look at the bed, she saw that his shirt was partially undone and his cravat hanging loose. He smiled, crossing the room toward her. 'Good morning, Amy.'

How good it was to hear her first name on his lips. 'Good morning.'

'How are you feeling now?'

'I can still taste the fire.'

He nodded. 'It will pass. You had a very unpleasant, very frightening experience.'

'I would not wish to take it up as a hobby,' she smiled.

He sat on the edge of the bed beside her. 'And is Jeffreys' hypericum balm soothing your burned wrists?'

'*Jeffreys*' hypericum balm?'

'Well, to be more precise, *Granny* Jeffreys' hypericum balm. Nothing would suffice as far as he was concerned but that a preparation of her special medication was applied to your burns. If his granny swore by it, he insisted, then it was infallible and your burns could be guaranteed to be cured in the winking of an eye.' He smiled. 'Or maybe it was the winking of several eyes.'

'I think maybe it was. However many eyes it was, something has made my wrists feel better this morning than they were last night.'

'Sally dressed them again last night when you were asleep. You have an adoring admirer in my sister's maid, Amy — but then she has reason to be adoring, hasn't she?'

Amy hesitated. 'Reason?'

'You took the blame for something of which Sally and my sister were guilty — namely the delivery of that note. Olivia informs me that you had refused to take it.'

'I did. You were sufficiently miffed with me already, and had asked me not to interfere any more.'

'Aye, well the manner of my asking was not exactly gentlemanly and I would prefer to forget how much of a bear I was. Especially as I have so much to thank you for now.'

'There is no need.'

'Yes, there is. I don't think anything I can say to you now will convey to you the depth of my gratitude. Without you I would not now have the sapphires.'

'Without me *he* would not have found out where they were! To think that I actually confided in him! I showed him the paper and told him my theory about the meaning of the code!'

'You weren't to know.'

'I believed him, I really believed he was the heartbroken brother anxious to clear his family's name! Was ever there a greater fool than me?'

'We all do foolish things in this life, Amy. No one is excepted from that human failing.' He spoke quietly and he was not looking at her, but across the room as if he was looking into the past.

'What are you thinking about?'

'My one great foolish act, I suppose.'

'And that was?'

'Marrying Alice Brooking. Well, it is to be set completely behind me now, behind us all in fact. Did Olivia tell you there is to be no more mourning?'

'Yes. From today.'

He nodded. 'It is hypocritical to make a show of mourning her, for far from feeling any grief at her death, I think it is best that she has gone.'

She stared at him. 'You cannot mean that.'

'But I do, Amy. I do.' He searched her face for a moment. 'I've never talked to anyone about her before, but I would like to tell you — if you are prepared to listen.'

'I would like to know.'

'You haven't been here long, Amy, but you must have heard about my late wife's strange moods.'

'Yes.'

'Have you wondered about them at all?'

'Many people are subject to moods, some worse than others.'

'Not moods as extreme as Alice's. They were too disconcerting for most of those who came into contact with her, and by far too embarrassing sometimes for her to be allowed to come and go as she pleased. She could not cope with them herself, so how could anyone else be expected to? One day she could wake up feeling light-hearted and frivolous, chattering away about all manner of nonsense until your head rang with the endless rattle. The next day she could wake up sunk in the depths of the blackest of despairs, she'd be rendered incapable of doing anything for herself except cower in a corner with her face hidden from the world. But between these extremes there would be the other Alice, the Alice I fell in love with that day I traveled to Wildmoor to purchase a blood stallion from her brother. That other, delightful Alice could be there for weeks on end without the moods creeping in to change her, and so I had married her before I knew. I was blinded by the rapture of finding a perfect bride. She *was* perfect after the corrupt world I'd been moving among in London, and when after a beginning when she appeared to be indifferent to me, she suddenly accepted my proposal, my joy knew no bounds.' He smiled wryly. 'I later found out that the change of heart had come about because her brother had told her I was entirely suitable as a husband and she was to accept me if I proposed. Alice always did her brother's bidding, no matter what. But at the time that I fell in love with her, I did not know all that. Knowing her was to me like stepping from a hot, crowded room into the cool of a summer evening. It may sound foolish, Amy, but that was how it was. She was intoxicating, and I was more than willing to be trapped by her. You know that Charles Pemberton experienced the same thing, don't you?'

'Yes, he told me.'

'I don't know what it was about her which could turn a man's head, but whatever it was

341

it was very potent; there was something fey about Alice Brooking, and it drew men like pins to a magnet. Well, Charles was luckier than I was, he escaped — no doubt only because he wasn't wealthy enough for her brother's purposes. For those few weeks before I married her, Alice was at her very best, and I doubt if there had ever been a happier man on God's earth than myself. The first time I began to wonder a little was on our wedding night. Alice had come to Chalbourne Park with her old nurse, Mary Danthorpe — she wouldn't do anything without Mary's permission — and when I went to her room that first night . . . ' He looked at Amy. 'I hope I do not embarrass you.'

'No.'

'The first thing I saw on her bed was a doll. A child's doll. Carolinda, the damned thing was called. I wonder how many bridegrooms have found themselves expected to share a bed with their bride and her doll.' He smiled then. 'In my short but full life, I had come across many a thing, but this was not one of them. I was in love with her, and with the usual arrogance of my sex, I thought that all would be all right after that first night. However, marriage for Alice was a matter of holding hands and whispering sweet words;

she was not prepared at all for anything which went beyond that. To say that our wedding night was a disaster would be to put it mildly. She made me feel that I was a fiend, a monster, a devil incarnate — dear God, I don't know which of us was the more shaken by that night, for never in all my experience had I been made to feel as she made me feel. And yet, the very next morning, she came down to breakfast all smiles and happiness, giggling about a gardener's boy she'd seen chasing his hat when the wind blew it away. No one normal could have behaved as she did, Amy. It was as if the previous night had not happened, as if it just had not happened! I found it unnerving. That same day she had the first of the many black despairs I was to witness, and it lasted for a whole week, after which she emerged in that same happy, frivolous mood she'd displayed on the morning after our wedding night. By then I knew for certain that she was unstable, and too damned late I began to make inquiries about her background — if only I had done so before, then I would have known that her father had died insane, confined to his room for the last five years of his life, and that her great-grandfather had been the same, living in a world infested with demons and hobgoblins. One of her aunts had died in an asylum, and Alice was showing the symptoms of exactly the same mental illness. I learned all that, and I learned that our disastrous wedding night had resulted in Alice's expecting my child.'

'Oh, Jonathan . . . '

'Can you imagine how I felt when I received that news? I went to her room and she was huddled on the floor in a corner, her knees drawn up tightly and her face hidden in her arms. I called her name and she looked up at me. There was such bewilderment in her poor eyes, such emptiness — and I knew that one day I could maybe find myself seeing that same madness looking at me from my own child's eyes. I was so angry then, Amy, so bitter and angry.'

'Was that when you challenged Michael Brooking?'

'Yes. He'd known about the family history, and he knew that for the illness to be halted, then neither he nor Alice should have married — that with them the Brooking line should have ended. But far from discouraging the marriage between Alice and myself, he had positively encouraged it, and all for his own ends. Already I had noticed that pieces of jewelry which had been given to her had vanished — if he had gambling debts, then she would send him some valuable in order that he could survive that little longer. Heirlooms which had been in my family for years simply disappeared without trace. She went to Wildmoor to stay for a while about three months after the wedding, and she returned without a single piece of jewelry to her name. She'd given everything to him. I forbade her to see him any more after that; he seemed to have some evil sway over her and I was determined to put an end to it. But I did not forbid her to write to him, and that was my mistake — though I can only say that with the knowledge of hindsight.' He smiled at Amy. 'Hindsight too tells me that I was a fool to merely aim for his damned shoulder, I should have put an end to him there and then, God knows, I had provocation enough.'

'I'm so sorry that everything was so very dreadful for you, Jonathan,' she said softly, longing to reach out and touch his hand which lay so close to hers on the bed. 'What did you do after that?'

'Well, none of it was Alice's fault, she couldn't help the way she was. She was my wife and she was expecting my child, she had the right to my protection. And so I protected her, I kept the outside world away from her because when she was ill it frightened her, and I made her poor life as comfortable as possible. But all love had died, it had withered away the moment I realized the truth, and I felt toward her after that as I felt for any creature which depended on me, whether it was a horse, a foxhound, or even a kitten. Lady Chalbourne's strange absence from all social functions and so on was explained at first by her delicate condition and then by her continued poor health.'

'And the child?'

'She lost the child, Amy. I admit to you what I've never admitted to anyone before, Amy — that when she fell down the stairs I could have wept with relief. The child, my son or daughter, was spared now, spared the awful consequence of Brooking blood. Of course, there was no question at all of there being any more children.'

She was silent for a moment. 'How did you expect to continue keeping it all secret when Olivia came here?'

'I didn't. Life continued as it had done before. For four years Alice led a very isolated life here, and I earned the condemnation of many of my neighbors for what they saw as my unduly harsh and selfish treatment. I allowed her out to drive with me when she was in one of her good moods, and that was how the neighbors saw her — happy, delightfully pretty, and so pleased to be allowed out. They saw *me* as some sort of ogre, forcing her to live like that while I kept mistresses and lived my life to the full.'

'And did you?'

'I assure you I have not been a monk.'

She smiled faintly. 'I did not think you had been, sir. But four years is a long time to keep up such a secret as your wife's illness.'

'It was, but gradually it became accepted that invitations sent here should not include Lady Chalbourne, and that any function held here would not have her to hostess it. Her moods on the whole were easy enough to gauge, and any change could be sensed before it happened. Mary Danthorpe attended Alice when the bad times were there, and I doubt if anyone else even guessed the truth about her. Poor health can explain away so much. Alice was ill, but she was harmless, she did no one any wrong when she was unwell, and the last thing I wanted was to put her in an asylum — she did not deserve that. So, I was prepared to continue; she was my responsibility and I accepted it.'

'And then you knew that Olivia must come here.'

'Yes, my aunt died and I had my sister on my hands. I decided to tell her the truth about Alice.'

'The truth? But Olivia didn't know.'

'No, something happened when I went to

London to drive Olivia back here, and I changed my mind about telling her.'

'What happened?'

'Olivia happened to mention hearing of a man who'd recently had his wife committed to an asylum because he said she was quite mad and therefore a menace to the public. Apparently the woman had done no more than danced in her undress in the garden at night on more than one occasion. Olivia was vehement that the man had been quite right, that a woman who did anything as decidedly odd as that should be locked away. After that I found that I just could not tell her about Alice. I knew that Alice was merely becoming more and more incapable of coping with a normal life, she was retreating into herself and hiding away from everything which frightened her — and there were more and more frightening things all the time.' He smiled a little. 'Olivia can be very condemnatory about things of which she knows nothing, but then maybe you have not discovered that side of her yet.'

'No, I haven't.'

'She takes a very firm stance sometimes; she always did as a child and she does not seem to have changed, and on matters such as this, she did not seem open to persuasion — at least, I may have done her an injustice, but I did not feel that I could tell her about Alice.'

'I think that you did misjudge her,' said Amy softly. 'Olivia could have helped you so much if you had only told her the truth.'

He nodded. 'More evidence of my sad lack of judgment, Amy?'

'Yes.'

'Thank you.'

'You did ask.'

'So I did. Anyway, the result of my misjudgment meant that I continued to conduct Alice's affairs as I had done for the previous four years, nothing had really changed. Olivia was told the same story as others, that Alice was unwell for the most part, very shy and nervous, and unsure of herself in company, and that sometimes she spent a great deal of time in her rooms. Olivia accepted it — our aunt had been an invalid before her death, and so Olivia was used to that sort of thing. Besides, it did not take Olivia long to decide that she and Alice would never get along. Alice had no sense of humor, which in Olivia's eyes was the most heinous of crimes.'

'I know, she told me.'

He glanced at her. 'Does *everyone* confide their thoughts in you, Amy?' he asked.

She smiled. 'I find that many do.'

'But do *you* ever confide *your* thoughts in them?'

Her smile died away slowly. 'No, hardly ever.'

'Keeping one's own counsel may be very admirable, but it is not always the best thing, is it?'

She felt hot, as if at any moment he would be able to read her innermost thoughts about him, and he must not see those thoughts . . . 'So, Olivia did not notice about Alice then?' she asked quickly, changing the subject.

'Not particularly. Not long after her arrival here she met Charles Pemberton, anyway, and after that her head remained in the clouds. Occasionally Alice would go out with her — I chose the times carefully — and they'd drive to Bristol to Madame Secherell's, or maybe to Cirencester to go shopping. But Alice found meeting strangers to be a frightening experience on the whole, although she tried very hard sometimes, when she was feeling brave.' He smiled as he remembered. 'But she was not brave very often.'

'She was brave when she agreed to attend the Hunt Ball.'

'Yes. But an occasion like that was simply beyond her, no matter how brave she thought she was. There were too many new faces, too many eyes watching, and too many voices talking, and from the outset it was impossible that she could remain calm. That was why I was so angry when I arrived home and saw her greeting the guests. Even that early in proceedings I could see the terror mounting as each new name was announced. I could hardly remove her in front of everyone, that would have been impossible and would have caused a furor of condemnation all around, and so I prayed that all would be well — instead, everything bubbled over into the dreadful scene of which you undoubtedly know.' He was silent for a moment. 'Well, it's all over now, a chapter of my life which I want to forget entirely. Do you understand now why I think it is maybe best that she has gone? She could only have got worse, suffered more, descended further and further into the hell which waited for her all her life. It would have happened suddenly, she would enter a final despair from which she would never emerge — as her father, great-grandfather and aunt had done before her.'

'I do understand,' she said softly. 'But are you sure that discarding mourning so swiftly is the right way to forget?'

'Yes. The day after you arrived here, I ordered that the curtains were to be drawn back during the day. I'd walked in Alice's darkness for long enough, Amy, and seeing you — a stranger, a woman who'd never even met my wife, wearing deepest mourning for her . . . It was wrong and I knew it. And your stay here made me see more and more that it was hypocritical to make a show of grief which I did not feel.'

'*I* influenced you?' She was taken aback. 'I did nothing.'

He smiled, putting his hand over hers. 'It was the Christmas greenery which decided me finally — that kissing bunch or whatever it's called, its ribbons so bright and gay, a happy device for a happy season. I don't care now if I flout convention by throwing the doors of Chalbourne Park open to all this Christmas, I feel reborn and I intend that the world shall know it.'

'Brave words.'

'You think I am not capable of doing as I say?'

'Oh, I did not say that, for I think you quite capable.'

'Do you disapprove, Amy?'

'Does it matter what I think?'

'Yes.'

'I don't disapprove, I think you are right if that is how you feel. To do anything else would be pointless.'

He smiled. 'My feelings exactly — so Christmas shall be enjoyed to the full, and

352

after that there will be Olivia's wedding to look forward to.'

'So, I shall be able to accomplish my purpose in coming here after all, I shall throw rice at Livvy's wedding.'

'And then no doubt rush away to make plans for your own.'

'Yes,' she replied after a slight hesitation, 'I suppose I shall.'

'At the risk of sounding facetious and of showing an unkind levity, I will offer you a sterling piece of advice before you take your marriage vows with Mr Winfield Kenney.'

'Advice?'

'Yes, make damned sure you know his family background before you utter one word of promise at the altar.' He smiled ironically.

'I know his family background.'

'No doubt you do — Washington's political circles are renowned for knowing everything of import, and you are truly a daughter of Washington. Maybe it's your very different-ness which makes me want to confide in you. I've taken refuge in the fact that you will soon return to America and I will not see you again. My secret is safe because I doubt if there is anyone more discreet and reliable than you, Amy van Allen, and the fact that the Atlantic will separate us merely sets the seal on my secret's safety.'

'Discreet, reliable, and safe? Is that how you see me?'

He hesitated. 'Partly. You are also very lovely, very provocative, and no man could ever hope to ignore your presence — and I mean that in the most flattering way imaginable. With you beside him, your Mr Kenney cannot fail to succeed in whatever he undertakes. I shall watch his career with great interest, I promise you, even if it will be from afar.'

'Washington does seem a very long way away, doesn't it?'

'The District of Columbia could as well be the District of Jupiter when discussed from the wilds of Gloucestershire.' He smiled.

She spoke with unnatural brightness, forcing herself to return the smile. 'And what of your career? Shall I read of your return to the British political scene?'

'Rejoin *the most corrupt and corrupting mass of rottenness which ever usurped the name of Government*?' he asked, grinning as he used Jefferson's words.

'With the right men there is hope even for British politics,' she said drily.

'No doubt — miracles are said to happen still, I believe — but a return to government is not my intention.'

'What are your plans?'

'The running of Chalbourne Park is my first duty, and I shall be well content with that.'

'So, you will marry again, have a vast family, and preside over your estate until the end of your days, growing bald and fat.'

'What a pleasing picture you paint, but I am assured that my family has a reputation for wiry, hirsute males.'

She smiled. 'I am relieved to hear it, for I cannot imagine you ever being anything other than elegant and perfect, the epitome of the English aristocrat.'

He grinned at that. 'I've had many a moment which would shatter your illusions — as my extreme irritability at times has no doubt already proved.' He got up then. 'I think maybe I should leave now, before the maids arrive and put entirely the wrong conclusion on my presence here at this hour in my *deshabille*. Do you think you will be well enough to get up today?'

'Yes.' *Yes, I'll be up, I shall look Christabel Bendon in the eye when she drips her poison about me . . . Always look the enemy in the eye, never turn your back.*

'I trust you will not find Christabel's presence too irksome,' he said suddenly, as if again he had read her thoughts.

'She is staying for Christmas?'

'I — do not know. She will be here today, that much I do know. I'm taking a ride with her after luncheon, for I have things I must speak of with her.'

She stared at him. Things to speak of? He was still thinking of marrying Christabel?

He smiled. 'We will no doubt not see each other again until later this afternoon or early this evening, but I look forward to then, Amy.' He raised her hand gently to his lips and then was gone.

In the loneliness of the room when he'd gone, she blinked back the tears. Dear God, how she loved him, how she longed to hold him and be held by him. But although the animosity had gone, things had not really changed at all. There was a distance between them — and there always would be, for he did not love her. He intended marrying Christabel and he would not grieve when Amy van Allen left Chalbourne Park to return forever to America . . .

15

From her window she could see Christabel and Jonathan in the stableyard. Christabel looked very lovely in a purple riding habit trimmed with gray fur, and there was a perky black beaver hat perched on her honey-colored hair. Her face was flushed with happiness and she laughed and chattered as she waited with Jonathan for the horses to be brought. Amy's heart felt heavy as she watched how attentive he was.

The sound of church bells drifted along the valley, carried clearly on the cold, still air, and the snow looked very bright in the sunlight as the sun shone down from high in a clear blue sky. Some men were dragging a huge yule log from the woods, and it left a long, straggling trail in the snow.

Hooves clattered on the cobblestoned yard, and she looked down again to see Christabel and Jonathan riding out beneath the clock tower. She watched them as they rode across the park, the red deer scattering before them as they urged their mounts more swiftly through the snow.

Amy turned away from the window. Her

letter to Winfield still lay on the escritoire, and she picked it up. What was Winfield doing now? Was he enjoying the endless whirl of social events which peppered Washington's calendar at this time of year? Was he thinking of her at all? She put the letter down again. She did not really care what Winfield was doing, not any more.

'Oh, you're up at last!' Olivia entered in a flurry of dainty white muslin and a brightly-colored Cashmere shawl. She whirled around, smiling. 'A welcome change from sober black, is it not?'

'Very welcome.'

'Jonathan told me that he'd kept you talking until all hours this morning, so I'm not surprised that you went to sleep again for so long!'

'You should have woken me *before* luncheon, not after.'

'Christabel said that we should allow you to get as much sleep and rest as possible after your dreadful ordeal.'

I'll warrant she did, thought Amy, anything to keep me away while she basks in Jonathan's attention. But she only said, 'How thoughtful of her.'

'Christabel is in a positive fluster of delight,' went on Olivia more glumly. 'She's talked of nothing else all morning but the fact that Jonathan has asked her to go riding with him this afternoon. Oh, I do hope that he isn't going to ask her for her hand. I still do not think I could bear to have her here all the time.'

Amy went to sit in one of the chairs by the fire, sitting carefully so that she did not touch her bandaged wrists, which still stung painfully if anything brushed against them. 'I thought you had changed your mind about Grisly Belle.'

Olivia grinned at the name. 'Changed my mind? Goodness, no! She was so concerned when you were ill though, and I was glad to have her help, I admit, but I couldn't bear to have her around me all the time, every day and every month!'

'You'll be marrying Charles soon and will not then be concerned with how many days she spends here.'

'I *will* be concerned, Amy van Allen, for I'd hate Jonathan to make a second mistake — and Christabel would most definitely be a mistake! Besides, now that the sapphires are safe, he has no urgent need to marry. I'm sure that that's what he intends, though, he's so very solicitous toward her.' Olivia smiled then, sitting on the other chair. 'Still, if that's what he wants, there's nothing I can do about it. I shall not think of it, for it will spoil my

Christmas Eve, and after all that's happened of late, I am absolutely *set* that my Christmas shall be the very best ever! But first things first — how are you feeling now?'

'Much better. That delicious breakfast — or was it luncheon — that Sally brought for me has filled me up completely and has taken away the taste of smoke.'

'I don't know exactly what that meal could be called. Brunch, maybe, or lunchfast. Anyway, I'm glad that you ate it all up.'

'Many more banquets in bed like that and I shall be exceedingly fat and docile.'

'Docile? You? That I would like to see! How are your wrists?'

'Sore, but improving.'

'Granny Jeffreys' patent salve, no less.'

'Jonathan told me.'

'Granny Jeffreys was something of a celebrity when it came to healing.'

'A witch?'

'The next best thing — a wise woman. She told fortunes too.'

'I can't imagine Jeffreys with a grandmother as interesting as that.'

Olivia smiled. 'You'd be surprised at the real Jeffreys — he's not always the perfect butler, you know.'

'Don't tell me he performs magic rites when the moon is full!'

'Not quite — he makes a very good Spirit of Christmas though. You'll see tonight. You *are* joining us all tonight, aren't you?'

'Yes.'

'It won't be the grand occasion it usually is, there wasn't time to arrange very much, but there are quite a number of people coming. I'll warrant the shock waves are still rippling throughout the county after the invitations were delivered. They'll *all* come if they possibly can, if only to gossip about it afterward. Jonathan's casting off mourning in this way can only cause a stir, you know.'

'It would cause a stir anywhere,' said Amy.

'I think he's right, though, don't you?'

'Yes. A cloak of hypocrisy does not sit easily on his shoulders.'

'It's almost as if Alice had never existed now,' said Olivia pensively. 'I don't find myself expecting to see her walk into a room now, not since the fire. I don't even think about her very much. It's funny, but even *now* I can't think why he ever married her. I've tried to see what it was he saw in her, but I can't.'

Amy said nothing.

'Anyway, Amy, I have an ulterior motive in coming to see you now.'

'That sounds serious.'

'It is. *Very.* I've come to snoop and see

what you intend wearing tonight. I'm determined that I shall not be outshone.'

Amy smiled. 'Oh, Livvy, I don't think I will be able to outshine you at the moment, you are positively glowing from one end to the other. Such happiness is disgusting.'

But Olivia was stern. 'I'm glowing, yes, but then so should you be, Amy. Yet you aren't. No, don't try to fob me off, for I have come here to snoop about more than clothes. You have decided to accept Mr Kenney, and you were always so pleased to be with him that I could only think you loved him, and yet you do not look as happy as you should under the circumstances, Amy Magnolia van Allen. I want to know why.'

'Of course, I'm happy, we can't *all* light up like chandeliers!'

'Yes, we can, if we're really happy,' said Olivia firmly. She pointed at the letter on the escritoire. 'It's still there, isn't it? You could have sent it down ready for the letter carrier — who, incidentally, called again today — but you haven't and there it remains. That letter is a complete and utter waste of time and effort if you have no intention of posting it.'

'Of course I mean to post it,' protested Amy, avoiding Olivia's eyes.

'Do you want to marry him, Amy? Look at me and be truthful.'

Slowly Amy looked at her. 'No, I don't want to marry him,' she said.

'But, Amy . . .'

'Leave it, Livvy, please.'

'I'm your friend, Amy, and God knows after all you've done for me recently, I want to help if I can. Why won't you confide in me? The number of times I've turned to you, trusted you, and known I could rely on you — but you've never paid me that compliment. How can I show how much I love you if you will not let me help when you need me?'

Amy stared at her, remembering Jonathan's words about keeping only her own counsel. She was not one to turn to others, but maybe this time she should — maybe it would ease the pain a little to share her unhappy secret. 'I want to tell you, Livvy, but . . .'

'I don't listen to *buts!* What's wrong, Amy? Tell me, please. You'll find that I'm every bit as good as you at listening to problems, and you'll find out how the Chalbourne family earned its motto.'

'Motto?'

'*Perseverance.*' Olivia smiled. 'I shall dig in my heels in a way every bit as stubborn as anything a van Allen can manage, I promise you.'

Amy smiled then. 'All right, I'll tell you.'

She sought the right words, but when she spoke everything came out in a rush. 'I wish to God I'd never come here to England, Livvy, because then I would have been spared so much. I'd never have met your brother, never have been set at sixes and sevens merely by looking at him, hearing his voice . . . He would still be just a name and I'd be happy.'

Olivia's eyes widened. 'You're in love with Jonathan?'

'Yes, fool that I am.'

'Oh, Amy . . . '

'Well, now you know. I love him, but he doesn't love me, he's going to marry Christabel — and I shall go back home and marry Winfield and be a good and obedient wife. I shall help him in his career and be all that a wife should be, and he'll never know that all the time I love someone else. End of story.'

'Does — does Jonathan have any idea?'

'I sincerely hope not!' said Amy with a short, unhappy laugh. 'And you are not to say a word to him, you must promise me that.'

'You know that I won't say anything, and I'm a little miffed that you think I would.'

Amy forced a bright smile. 'So,' she said, determined to change the subject, 'you've come to poke about and find out what I'm wearing tonight.'

'I beg your pardon? Oh, yes — yes, I have.'

'I've almost forgotten what I've brought with me, to be perfectly honest, and I haven't really given any thought to what to wear tonight. Shall we look at my extensive and brilliant wardrobe?'

Amy got up and went to the dressing room, throwing open the wardrobe doors and standing back to look at the array of gowns which hung neatly where Mary Danthorpe had put them when Amy had first arrived at Chalbourne Park.

Olivia came to stand beside her. 'Oh, Amy, what beautiful gowns! Whoever decided that Paris should dictate fashion had not met your American dressmaker, that's for sure. Look at this orris lace, how fine and beautiful it is against the oyster satin. I can see I shall have to make a supreme effort tonight if I'm to be noticed at all!'

'Your inner glow will more than do all that's necessary — and you only want to shine for Charles, don't you?'

'No, I want to queen it over all rivals, including you. And definitely including Grisly Belle — oh, dear, you've got me calling her that now. I shall have to be careful I don't say it to her face!'

Amy smiled. 'I shall ply you with punch and pray that it loosens your tongue just enough.'

'You beast, I believe you would. Anyway, which of these wondrous creations are you going to dazzle us with?'

'I don't know.' Amy looked along the line of gowns and then took down one which was made of gray pompadour. She ran her fingers over the rich, satin-striped taffeta and the embroidered sprigs of tiny white flowers. 'I think this one. Winfield particularly likes me in it.'

Olivia shook her head, lifting down another gown of a pale blue silk. 'Wear this one.'

'Why?'

'Because pale blue is Jonathan's favorite color — and it will go well with your eyes. Yes, take my advice and wear this one.' She winked. 'Besides, it will not take away from my gold satin tunic dress.'

Amy smiled. 'All right, I will wear the pale blue silk, although much good it will do me.'

'You never know.'

'Oh, yes I do, I know only too well.' *I'm discreet, reliable, and above all, safe, Amy, and soon I'll be even safer on the other side of the Atlantic!*

★ ★ ★

There was no moon that Christmas Eve. The daylight faded and the night descended, and high above the stars shimmered in the clear, black sky. Lanterns had been strung in the trees of the park, and their colorful lights shone in the darkness, soft, jewel hues which swayed a little in the slight breeze. Inside the house the lamps were lit and the fires crackled as more logs were tossed on them. In the hall, the huge yule log had been put on the fire there, and already it glowed red-hot as it settled in to burn slowly for several days. There was a smell of mince pies which seemed to have spread through the whole house, warm and appetizing, and so very Christmassy and seasonal.

Sally put the hairbrush down and beamed at Amy in the mirror. 'There, ma'am, do you like it?'

Amy looked at herself. Her hair was piled up into a knot of curls on the top of her head, and long ringlets hung down the back. The knot was held in place by a silver comb which was studded with diamonds, and the stones flashed brightly in the candlelight as she turned her head from side to side.

'It's called — it's called à la Egyptienne,' said Sally, smiling proudly as she managed the correct pronunciation.

'I like it very much, Sally.'

'I saw it in one of Miss Olivia's journals. Her hair is too short to dress like this, and I've been so longing to try it out! Your hair is so long and it curls just right, and it's such a lovely color, just like chestnuts.'

'It's red,' said Amy. 'More like carrots than chestnuts.'

'No, it isn't,' insisted the maid, 'it's lovely! Now then, shall I bring the gown?'

'Yes, Sally, if you please.' Amy got up.

A little later she was looking in the mirror again, but in the cheval glass this time. The pale blue gown had long, full sleeves of diaphanous gauze which helped to hide the bandages at her wrists, and the low, crossover bodice was trimmed with shining silver braiding. Her shoulders rose naked above the gown, her skin pale and clear, and there was no necklace to adorn her throat. The gown's skirt fell fully away from immediately below her breasts, ending in a tiny silver fringe which trembled when she moved. Lifting the hem a little, she looked at her neat white silk stockings and the pale blue-silk slippers which matched the gown exactly.

Sally sighed. 'It looks so beautiful, ma'am,' she said. 'I've never seen a finer gown than that.'

'Don't let Miss Olivia hear you say that,'

smiled Amy, pleased. She looked very good and she knew it.

Sally put the white shawl around her shoulders, touching the pattern of apple blossom which had been stitched all over it. The shawl's long fringe poured over Amy's arms as she arranged it carefully, tweaking and patting until the shawl hung exactly in the way she wanted.

'Are you sure you don't want to wear any jewels, ma'am?' asked the maid, stepping back to survey her.

'Positive — if my guess is right, Lady Christabel will wear more than enough for both of us.'

'Yes, ma'am,' agreed the maid. 'She does like a lot of jewelry.'

'Now then, where's my reticule?'

'Here, ma'am.' The maid gave her the circular, silver drawstring bag. 'It's a shame you can't wear gloves — you don't look finished off, somehow.'

'I can only just about bear the gown against my wrists, I could not possibly endure the tightness of gloves as well.' Amy glanced at the clock on the mantelpiece. 'It's seven o'clock, should you not go to Miss Olivia now? She'll be dithering around if she thinks you're going to be too late to dress her before the first guests arrive.

369

'Oh, yes, ma'am, I'll go straight away. But she isn't having her hair dressed tonight, she's hiding it under one of those turban things.'

Amy smiled at the description of what was undoubtedly an example of the very latest rage. 'Thank you for the trouble you've taken with me, Sally, I do appreciate it.'

'That's all right, ma'am, I enjoyed it.'

Amy fluffed out her gown again when the maid had gone, and then something made her look suddenly at the painting of Wildmoor above the fireplace. She stared at it for a long time, thinking of all that Jonathan had told her, and then suddenly she picked up one of the candles and left the room, hurrying through the house toward Alice's chamber.

She didn't know why she wanted to look at the room again, but she did. She opened the door, and the cold, acrid air swept out over her, making her shiver. The candle's feeble light picked out the devastation left by the fire. The windows had been boarded up to keep the elements out, and everything was blackened and ruined. Smoke stained the cracked mirror of the dressing table and in it she could just make out what was left of the portrait's frame. Alice's face had gone forever. Amy stared around the room, not going inside because the floor was unsafe, and then slowly she closed the door again and turned to walk away. It was as Olivia had said — as if Alice had never been.

Christabel stood in the passage watching her. 'Well now, how good it is to see you looking so well, Miss van Allen.'

'Really.' Amy's eyes swept over the tall figure, taking in the overgown of pink gauze which covered the extreme low, square-necked white slip, the hem of which was a mass of fashionable *rouleaux*. Huge pendent earrings of pink rubies and pearls hung from her ears, and around her neck there were numerous golden chains from which were suspended scent cases, lockets, and an elaborate cross. Her cheeks had been rouged a great deal, giving her an almost feverish color, and she carried a spangled reticule which flashed and glittered as she toyed with her lacy shawl.

'One presumes that you intend honoring us with your presence tonight.'

'I'm not dressed like this to go for a walk,' said Amy drily.

'I would advise you not to come down, Miss van Allen, I would advise you most strongly.'

'I think I can withstand anything you try throwing at me, Grisly Belle.' Amy began to walk past the figure in pink and white.

Christabel caught her arm, forcing her to turn. 'Don't you walk away from me like that!'

'I'll walk wherever I please. Take your hand off me or you'll discover that I can kick very accurately.'

Slowly Christabel released her. 'You may as well know that Jonathan and I are to be married.'

Amy stared at her, striving to keep the dismay from her face. 'Congratulations.'

'Obviously the engagement cannot be made public just yet.'

'Obviously.'

'But don't think I shall allow my triumph to stand in my way, madam. I shall ruin your good name tonight — the whole world shall soon know how warmly you embraced that villain Brooking outside the churchyard.'

'And a Merry Christmas to you, too,' said Amy, turning and walking away again. Tears burned her eyes and she wanted to run away from the mocking glitter in Christabel's eyes, but she made herself walk slowly, her head high. She had sounded so brave, so cool and calm, but inside she knew only the pain of heartbreak.

★   ★   ★

A line of carriages blocked the driveway, and the hall was noisy with conversation and laughter. The yule log burned brightly in the

372

hearth, and the atmosphere was cheerful. Amy detected no hint of disapproval beneath the surface, nothing to suggest that anyone was shocked at the way Chalbourne Park had cast off the shackles of mourning so very quickly. Candles were burning everywhere among the greenery, making everything festive and gay. Tables had been arranged around the edge of the hall, and a magnificent array of seasonal dishes had been set upon their white-clothed tops.

Olivia looked almost ridiculously happy as she circulated on Charles Pemberton's arm. Her gold tunic dress looked elegant, and the long train of the white gown beneath hissed richly on the floor as she walked. Jeweled pins flashed in her golden turban and she wafted her fan backward and forward, her eyes shining and a continual smile curving her lips. Such happiness exuded from her that she had never looked more lovely, and it was obvious from Charles's constant glances, that he was more in love with her than ever. They seemed to walk on air, thought Amy, smiling a little as she watched them.

She was unobserved as yet, having shaken her head when the footman made to announce her. No, she did not want Jonathan to know she was there just yet, she wanted to see him first.

He was with Christabel near the fireplace. He wore a dark green velvet coat and his white breeches fitted so well that they looked as if they had been molded to his figure. His shirt was frilled and ruffled, and there was a jeweled pin in his cravat. Amy's heart ached with love for him, and she had to look away as Christabel saw her suddenly.

Christabel immediately linked her arm through his, leaning against him adoringly. She gazed up into his eyes, bending forward so much that there was hardly any portion of her ample bosom which remained hidden from view.

He looked across the hall then and saw Amy, and excusing himself from Christabel, he threaded his way through the crowd toward the figure in pale blue silk. Christabel's eyes were hooded with anger as she watched.

He took Amy's hand. 'Hello, Amy.'

'Hello.'

'You look very lovely.'

'Thank you.'

'You were not announced.'

'No. No, I thought I would slide in very quietly.'

'You succeeded.' He smiled.

At that moment there was a stir in the room, and everyone began to move toward the opened front doors.

'The wassailers have come,' he said, drawing her hand gently through his arm, taking care not to hurt her wrists. His hand was warm over hers as he led her toward the porch.

The kissing bunch swayed a little in the slight breeze, the ribbons streaming gaily. The wassailers stood in the drive, their faces rosy with the cold as they sang the carols, and their lanterns fluttering a little.

Christabel moved close to Jonathan, linking her arm through his. Slowly Amy drew her own hand away and he looked quickly at her. 'Are you cold out here?' he asked suddenly, ignoring Christabel.

'I . . . a little.'

'Then come inside. Excuse me, Christabel.' He bowed to Christabel, taking her hand away.

Christabel's face was stony and there was pure venom in the glance she threw at Amy.

Their steps echoed on the hall floor as he walked with Amy toward the fire. 'Is something wrong, Amy?' he asked. 'You seem a little — '

'I'm quite all right.'

'If you're sure.'

'I am.' She avoided his eyes. 'Should you not be looking after your guests.'

'There is no need, they are quite capable of looking after themselves. Besides, the wassailers are coming in now.'

The crowd moved back into the warm hall, and the little group of singers came in, their boots leaving snowy footprints on the red and gray tiles. Servants brought a large bowl of punch and a great silver platter of hot mince pies, and as the wassailers enjoyed their well-earned payment, there was a burst of delightful laughter from the far end of the hall.

Amy stared as a shaggy-bearded figure in a brown habit shuffled into the center of the hall. It was Jeffreys, but the butler was almost unrecognizable as the Spirit of Christmas. He wore a flowing white beard, and there was a wreath of holly on his head. He carried an empty glass in one hand and a wassail bowl in the other, and there was a small yule log strapped to his back as he cavorted in a most unbutler-like manner around the hall, exhorting everyone to eat, drink, and be merry.

Jonathan smiled at Amy. 'He is most versatile, is he not?'

'I would not have believed it,' she replied, laughing as the butler took a lady's glass and drank it contents. He shook the tip of his long beard in the lady's face and she squealed with laughter.

Amy looked at Jonathan. 'Only St Nicholas in his sleigh is missing.'

'Sleigh? St Nicholas in a *sleigh*?'

'But of course — all American children know that he drives in a sleigh drawn by eight reindeer.'

'Poppycock.'

'Are you being offensive about my country's customs, sir?'

'St Nick rides on a gray horse in this country, so I fail to see why he should adopt so outrageous a mode of transport as a reindeer-drawn sleigh merely because he's crossed the Atlantic!'

'He does so because he realizes that Americans have more imagination and appreciation than the staid British.'

'Come on now,' he teased, 'you'll tell me next that the eight reindeer have names.'

'Dasher and Dancer, Prancer and Vixen, Comet and Cupid, Donner and Blitzen,' she said, meeting his gaze squarely. 'Of *course* they have names, sir.'

He laughed again. 'All right, I surrender — I vow your version of the good saint sounds more interesting anyway.'

Christabel appeared beside them again, once more stating her claim to him by slipping her hand familiarly through his arm and leaning close. 'Why Jonathan, do tell me what it is you and Miss van Allen are laughing about.'

He frowned a little at her manner. 'We were merely discussing St Nicholas, Christabel,' he said, with a definite shortness in his voice.

'Really? How very interesting.' She leaned even closer.

'Christabel, I thought we understood each other earlier today,' he said coldly, removing her hand.

She stared at him then. 'You can't mean . . .'

'I do, madam.'

Amy looked from one to the other in puzzlement.

Christabel's face flushed a dull red then and the spiteful glitter returned to her eyes as she turned to look at Amy. 'Very well, Jonathan,' she murmured, her fan clacking open angrily, 'then maybe it's time for a few things to be made a little more public.'

'Christabel, I warn you, I am in no mood to make allowances any more!' he snapped.

'No? Then you will not wish to know about the charming scene at the lychgate the other day, when Captain Brooking and Miss van Allen thought themselves unobserved.'

Amy took a long breath, lowering her eyes as she waited for the next thrust. Her heart was pounding in her breast, but she gave no hint on her face of the misery which spread through her as she looked up again into Jonathan's face.

Christabel's fan swept back and forth busily. 'Such a sweet kiss, Jonathan, one could only assume that they were known to each other a great deal more than would at first have appeared.'

He looked at Amy, but she said nothing. She could not deny that Michael Brooking had kissed her, and it was written in her eyes as she met his gaze.

Christabel smiled then. 'She does not deny it, Jonathan.' The fan snapped closed again. 'Now we shall see, Jonathan dearest, how many allowances you are capable of making, shall we not?'

Amy gave her a cold smile. Christabel had carried out her threat, but she would not have the last word, not while Amy had breath! 'Well now, Lady Christabel,' she said softly, 'I understood that it was at midnight on Christmas Eve that the animals spoke, but I am looking at one *chienne* who does not know the time. And now, if you will excuse me, Jonathan, I think I will go to my room. Oh, and congratulations, I wish you both every happiness for the future.' She inclined her head and turned, walking away from them without looking back.

Jeffreys continued his antics and the festivities went on unabated as she gathered her skirts to run up the staircase past the griffins. Tears blinded her as she ran, pushing past a startled maid, and not stopping until she had reached the sanctuary of her room.

She flung herself on the bed, her face hidden. She wept, but in silence, the tears hot and miserable, and her shoulders shaking, but she made no sound. The heartbreak was too much, too full of pain. He was marrying Christabel, and as if that was not bad enough, he would not now even think kindly of Amy van Allen after she had gone . . .

She did not hear him come into the room, and it wasn't until he sat on the edge of the bed beside her, his hand on her shoulder, that she knew he was there. With a start she sat up. 'Go away,' she whispered. 'Please go away.'

'Christabel has gone, Amy. I've told her that she is no longer welcome at Chalbourne Park.'

She stared at him. 'But, how can that be if you are to marry her?'

'*Marry* her? Good God, I don't intend marrying her!'

'She told me . . . '

'A pox on what she told you. She has more claws than an army of cats. She told you that because the opposite was true.' He put his hand gently to Amy's tear-stained cheek. 'You've been wrong all along about my intentions where Christabel is concerned. You once accused me of allowing my empty coffers to show, but my coffers had absolutely nothing to do with why I was being so very pleasant to her. I wished to be as gentle as I could when I informed her that I was not intending, and never would intend to ask her to marry me.'

'I thought . . . '

He smiled. 'I know perfectly well what you thought, you left me in no doubt. I'd been enduring her attentions for a long time, but I could no longer put up with it when Alice died and Christabel's obvious hopes were encouraged all the more. I told her, politely, that I was not interested, but she chose to ignore it. So, today, I went riding with her to tell her once and for all that I had no plans to include her in my life. Ever. I was blunt and verging on the rude, and I fully believed she had accepted the position once and for all, but her conduct tonight gave the lie to that. She had good reason to tell you that she and I were to become betrothed, Amy, just as she had good reason for telling me about the incident by the lychgate.'

'It was true,' whispered Amy, 'he did kiss me.'

'I know.'

'You know?'

'Ben Turner saw everything — including the fact that you rode off in obvious anger afterward. I don't for one moment believe that you welcomed Brooking's attentions, Amy.'

She stared at him. 'What was Christabel's 'good reason'?' she asked slowly.

He got up, going to the escritoire and picked up the letter. 'Do you ever intend posting this?'

'I don't understand.'

'It's perfectly simple — are you going to accept Kenney or aren't you?'

'No, I'm not.'

He smiled. 'Why?'

'Does it matter?'

'It matters very much.'

She hesitated. 'If I accepted him, then I would be being less than honest with him. Winfield is a good man, a fine man, and he deserves more than I can give him now.'

'What has changed your mind?'

'Oh, Jonathan . . . '

'Tell me — I *must* know!' He came back to her, taking her face in his hands. 'Tell me that it is because you love me as much as I love you.'

She stared incredulously into his eyes. 'You love me?'

He nodded. 'Tell me that you love me, Amy.'

'I love you, I've loved you since that very first night,' she said softly. 'I did not think it possible to fall in love so swiftly, but it happened. I thought you loathed me . . . '

'Oh, Amy, I could not loathe you, I could only want you.' He smiled. 'I thought *you* loathed *me*.' He pulled her up into his arms then, his lips very soft as he kissed her.

She clung to him, a wild, disbelieving joy bursting through her. He loved her — he loved her . . .

He drew gently away, looking down into her flushed face. 'I told Christabel today that you were the only woman I'd ever want as my wife, and I told her that I intended asking you to marry me.' He touched her soft red hair. 'I know it's wrong, with Alice so recently dead, I know it's wrong to even *think* of asking you to be my wife at a time like this, but if I do not then I could lose you forever. America is so very far away. Being merely Lady Chalbourne cannot have half the glory of maybe one day being America's First Lady, but it is all I have to offer you. You came here and you conquered me with one glance, Amy, and your victory is complete. Could you ever consider leaving Washington and America to live here with me? Could you marry one of the hated British? Could you, my love?'

'Oh, Jonathan, I could not be happy anywhere without you.'

He kissed her again, holding her tightly, and she closed her eyes, weak with happiness.

He took a small drawstring bag from his pocket and opened it. The sapphires and diamonds of the fabulous necklace flashed brilliantly in the candlelit room, the lights leaping like blue fire, and Amy's breath caught as she saw at last how truly magnificent the Chalbourne sapphires were. Because of these precious stones, three people lay dead . . .

The gold felt cold against her skin as he fastened the clasp, turning her so that she could see her reflection in the cheval glass. One huge, pear-shaped sapphire stood out from its fellows, a deep, almost purple shade which caught the candlelight so that a shaft of royal blue lay across her pale skin.

Jonathan bent his head to kiss her bare shoulder. 'Not even these jewels are worthy of your beauty,' he murmured.

Outside the church bells were pealing across the snow-covered hills and valleys. Christmas Day itself was only an hour or so away now. Amy turned suddenly to look at the Christmas gifts she'd brought with her from Washington, and she smiled at him as an incongruous thought entered her head. The necklace glittered as she slipped her arms around his neck to kiss him.

'I do so hope you like clocks, Jonathan Chalbourne,' she whispered.

We do hope that you have enjoyed reading this large print book.

Did you know that all of our titles are available for purchase?

We publish a wide range of high quality large print books including:
Romances, Mysteries, Classics
General Fiction
Non Fiction and Westerns

Special interest titles available in large print are:
The Little Oxford Dictionary
Music Book
Song Book
Hymn Book
Service Book

Also available from us courtesy of Oxford University Press:
Young Readers' Dictionary
(large print edition)
Young Readers' Thesaurus
(large print edition)

For further information or a free brochure, please contact us at:
Ulverscroft Large Print Books Ltd.,
The Green, Bradgate Road, Anstey,
Leicester, LE7 7FU, England.
Tel: (00 44) **0116 236 4325**
Fax: (00 44) **0116 234 0205**